The Case of the Werewolf Puppy

By Juli Monroe

Cover Art by The Graphic Issue

Dedicated to

My husband who puts up with a lot of crazy
writer shit. You know what I mean, love.
Thanks!

Special thanks to

Stephanie Pile, for her awesome cameo

Pat Eyler for winning the "be a character in my next book" trivia contest on Facebook. I hope you like being a priest.

Casi McFarland for agreeing to be a werewolf. I may owe you for the high-heeled shoe you lost in the fight scene. Bill me. ;)

Chapter 1

Friday morning, September 4, 2009: few hours before dawn

I'M JUST NOT a tentacle kind of guy.

However, when a friend calls and asks for help, what else can you do?

Paul screeched to a halt in front of my house, just long enough for me to jump into his red Prius. Not exactly the Batmobile, but it was better than the alternative: me hoofing it to the fight. I don't own a car. With the excellent Washington D.C. Metro system, it hasn't been a problem. I might have to rethink it someday, but for now I'm happy to let Paul drive.

"What do we know?" I asked him as we raced through the quiet, early morning streets. The moon, heavy and almost full, hung low on the horizon in a sky that was still dark, with not even a hint of the dawn to come. I stifled a yawn. It was way too early for me to be out fighting weird stuff.

"Not much. Apparently something is menacing people at the Washington Monument."

In this town, that could mean a lot, from terrorists to Republicans.

"Any chance you could be a bit more specific?" I eyed him. "And how'd you hear about it?"

He shrugged and completed a sharp turn onto 14th Street, tires squealing. I grabbed the armrest and delivered a quick prayer to whatever deity might be listening. Paul's reflexes are inhumanly quick, but his driving still made me nervous.

"I've got a source."

I snorted. "A source? Since when did you become Nick Knight, vampire cop?"

Yes, Paul's a vampire. Not the sexy, evil, "kill anything in a short skirt" kind of vampire, but the "only kill 'em if they're really evil" kind. Sort of Dexter meets Angel. Not that TV has much right about vampires. In fact, TV gets vampires wrong almost as often as they do my kind.

Oh, I'm human enough, but I'm also a warlock (as in "male witch," not "deals with the devil" kind of spell caster). No, I don't throw around lightning bolts or anything like that, but I brew a mean potion, get weird dreams about stuff that might happen in the future and can cast spells to help me find stuff. It works for me.

Paul glanced away from the road (making me even more nervous) just long enough to give me a wry grin. "Still watching that series? Didn't I tell you I'm not like Nick? I like being a vampire. You'll never catch me angsting about my lost humanity."

My racing heart slowed a bit when he turned his attention back to the road, shooting through a light barely ahead of its change from yellow to red.

"Okay. It's not my fault I think the vampires on the show are hot."

Wisely, he ignored that comment and answered my earlier question. "I've got a ghoul friend who hangs around that part of town."

I started to respond but then realized what he'd really said. Not girlfriend. *Ghoul friend.* I dredged my memory. Just because I'm a part of the supernatural world doesn't automatically make me an expert on everything. "A ghoul? Um, don't they, like, eat dead people?"

He shook his head, smoothly shifting into a lower gear to make a tight turn. "Not exactly. Ghouls have a particularly bad rap, and it's only partly accurate. What they need is raw meat, of any kind. Some of them do prefer human flesh, but not all of them. Benny is actually a connoisseur of sushi. He knows all the best places in town."

I remembered Paul mentioning Benny a while back, but he hadn't mentioned the sushi part. Ghouls easing sushi? Really? Another myth semi–shot down. "What's a sushi–eating ghoul doing by the Washington Monument in the middle of the night?"

Paul shrugged. "He thinks it's pretty. Why?"

I was feeling stubborn. "I just think it's kind of suspicious that a ghoul is calling in a weird occurrence."

Paul braked to a halt and parked. (The spot was all kinds of illegal, but, hey, it's his car, and he's the one who'll have to pay the parking ticket.) Pointing towards the Washington Monument, all lit up for the night, he said. "Suspicious or not, he's right. Something is eating people."

I followed where he was pointing. "Something" pretty well described what was slithering across the grass. It looked maybe eight feet tall, with lots of tentacles, all waving in a myriad of directions. The constant motion made it hard to count, and I gave up at ten. As we watched, one slimy feeler groped around blindly, finally grabbing a nearby man, who had apparently been too stunned by the stygian horror to do the sensible thing and run. He started screaming, and, as we watched, another tentacle rose, slid around his waist and turned him upside down. To my horror, the two tentacles started to pull. A moment later, I heard a wet squelching sound, and the screaming stopped.

Mastering my horror at what I'd just seen, I said. "Come on. Let's do this." True, this was dangerous and dreadful, but it was also something Paul and I could handle. And we'd better get to it before the police showed up. I didn't want to give the Thing any more victims. I opened the door and jumped out of the car, the vampire right behind me.

I scanned the area, looking for other innocents. Several people were huddled on the other side of the Washington Monument, frantically waving and shouting for help. I couldn't help wondering what they were thinking. Were they chalking it up to a drug– or alcohol–induced hallucination?

I glanced from the bystanders to the demon. I didn't know what kind of demon it was, but I knew a nether–region creature when it was looming over my people.

I looked at Paul. "I'd feel a lot better if they were out of the way. How do you want to play this?"

Paul was also surveying the scene. The Washington Monument had a large grassy area in front of it, plenty of room to maneuver, *if* we could get it away from the spectators. The lights from the Monument twinkled in the early morning darkness. It would have been a pretty scene, if not for the tentacles. As we watched, the demon's tentacles started questing about again, and it undulated closer to the people, who were shrieking as they ran.

The demon moved with surprising speed to close the distance.

"Paul, we've got no time to stand around and think. We need to do something. *Fast.*" I measured the distance between the demon and the other people. It didn't look good.

The vampire finally spoke. "You feel up to being bait?"

I nodded. That's where I'd been going too. "Yeah. I'll draw its attention, and you can come up from behind it. Don't take too long." I mentally ran down the potions I had with me and made my plan. "I think I can keep it distracted for about 30 seconds. Enough?"

He nodded. "Then I move in and take it down."

I had a sudden thought. "You *can* take it down, can't you?"

"I should be able to. I've dealt with one of these before." He flashed me a grin. On some level, it always bothered me how much he seemed to enjoy this. Guess it's a vampire thing. "But, if you've got anything in your bag of tricks that will help, though—"

I was already reaching into my back pack for a potion. I tossed it to him. "This should help."

He eyed the tattered Deer Park label. "What does it do?"

"Makes you wicked fast for about 30 seconds."

He frowned. "That's not very long."

I shrugged. "Then you'd better make the most of it." I palmed another potion for myself. "This one will make me really strong for a couple of minutes. Hopefully strong enough to get away if the demon grabs me."

Paul growled low in his throat. His fangs dropped, and his eyes glowed amber. "I'd rather you didn't get grabbed."

"Yeah, me too." The tentacles were moving closer to the bystanders, who suddenly seemed paralyzed by fear, awe or wonder. It was hard to tell, but they were moments away from becoming human sushi. "But we've got to do this now."

I started to jog in the direction of the demon. Paul moved away at an angle, deftly maneuvering to get behind it.

Did I have a rock–solid plan for this? Not really. I knew what I wanted to happen. Or more accurately, what I didn't want to happen.

To that end, I did what seemed to make sense. I ran toward the demon, waving my arms and yelling, "Hey, you! With the tentacles. How about picking on something that can fight back?"

Apparently my shouting broke some sort of spell because the bystanders suddenly scattered in all directions. Okay, part one of the plan was working, which was good because as soon as I got close, I almost doubled over in nausea from the smell. Think dead fish meets sewer, and you'll be close.

I argued with my stomach for a moment, then quickly got it under control just as the demon "turned" my way. (Turn doesn't have much meaning when a creature doesn't have an obvious body.)

Okay, Dafydd. This is what you wanted. I downed my potion and dashed between two waving tentacles. As I got closer, I saw suckers, just like on an octopus. I hoped my potion would be enough to get me free if they latched on.

Physical stuff isn't usually my thing, but I can't help myself. It does my male ego no good to hang on the sidelines while Paul takes all the risks. No comments. Even gay guys have an ego.

So thanks to my "bravado," I found myself hanging from a tentacle. Mom would not have approved. She did not raise a son who would get himself in such a stupid position.

I grabbed the first bit of slime that waved my way and pulled. Even potion–enhanced strength wasn't enough. It had me. Suddenly I noticed another tentacle headed toward me. The guy being torn apart earlier flashed through my head. My survival instincts kicked in and I managed to grab the approaching tentacle. It's hard to get leverage when you're hanging mid–air, but I held it off, for now.

Years ago, when I had a delusion of becoming a

stage magician, I'd studied books detailing escape techniques. What had I learned that could help me now? Hard as I tried, nothing came to mind. The books had been about getting out of ropes, not tentacles. Besides, I'd quit practicing escape routines because I sucked at them. Perhaps if I hadn't given up—

Suddenly the tentacle I struggled with began thrashing about harder. I started to lose my grip. My potion was fading. Then something moved really fast beneath me.

The cavalry, in the form of Paul, had finally arrived.

Was he using his potion? It was hard to tell; he's fast on his own. And strong. He grabbed the tentacle wrapped around my waist and pulled hard. "Now, Dafydd! Get a grip on it and yank as hard as you can."

I discovered a reserve of strength, squirmed out from the tentacle he was holding and yanked hard on the other. I was free! Just as my potion gave out. I hit the ground hard as the demon dropped me, but I still managed a clumsy roll that barely cleared another tentacle. I scrambled away, on my hands and ass, not caring just then about my male ego.

"Get back. I'll take it from here."

Paul didn't need to tell me twice. I stumbled to my feet and ran about 100 feet away, just out of easy reach. Then I turned to watch.

Paul danced around the demon, just ahead of the tentacles. No matter what the creature did, the vampire was always a second ahead. The tentacles moved faster as they tried and failed to grab him. First it used just two tentacles, but before long all ten were in play.

Paul's movements were deliberate and almost like a dance. Dodge. Glide in. Slash with claws. (Yes, vampires have claws in addition to fangs. I'm not sure where they hide when he isn't fighting.)

None of the individual wounds were major, but the cumulative effect was telling. It was slowing down. I relaxed. Paul had this one in the bag.

Which was when the demon pulled out its last trick. It stopped grabbing and sucked in its body. Paul darted in for two quick and deep slices. As my friend danced clear, the demon drew in even more on itself and convulsed. Yes! It was dying.

Wrong. With a screaming squelch, the demon belched forth a spew of black goo. Paul was moving to the right. The thing was either really good or lucky because it sprayed the viscous stuff all over the vampire.

Paul screamed and stumbled back, clawing at his eyes. Even in the dim light, I could see flesh bubbling and oozing on his face.

I started forward, not sure what to do, but wanting to help in some way. I'd only moved a couple of steps before Paul grabbed something from his jacket pocket and swallowed it down.

My potion! Brilliant! He hadn't used it earlier!

If I thought Paul was fast earlier, it was nothing compared to now. Like a whirlwind, he spun off the goo and blurred into action.

One. Two. Three. In as few seconds, he pulled off two tentacles and ripped a huge swath in what served as the demon's body.

Paul staggered back, and the demon screamed. That's the best description I can come up with for the screeching, yowling, otherworldly exclamation. My vampire friend paused a moment, regrouping, and then dashed in again, slicing and biting.

Yuck! I didn't even want to imagine what "tentacled horror" tasted like.

Paul stumbled back, panting, with flesh dripping down his shirt. Hands on knees, he stood watching as the demon shuddered its last breath, then died.

Immediately, I ran to Paul, skidding to a stop in front of him. Calling out his name, I frantically looked for signs he was okay.

He looked horrible. The goo ran down his face and shirt. Black mixed with red like the cover of a cheap horror novel. And the smell! Not quite sure how to describe a mix of acid, rotting fish and some other mysterious tang, but take my word for it. Awful.

I gently but insistently pushed him down on the grass. Then I reached in my backpack for something to clean his wounds.

Though in pain, he hadn't lost his sense of humor. "Baby wipes?"

I scowled at him. "They're cheap and they work. Sit still. I don't want to get any of that stuff on me." I noticed with some alarm that the goo was burning through his white blazer and black t–shirt. (Yes, Paul dresses stylishly to fight demons.)

"Off with that shirt."

He started to speak, but I cut him off. "And no smart–ass comments."

Paul tried to grin, but the motion pulled at his bleeding face, and he winced. Quickly but carefully, we pulled off his shirt, making sure not to get more stuff on his chest. Then I gently but thoroughly wiped his face. I had to double over the wipes to keep the caustic stuff from burning through faster than I could clean.

I knew I hurt him, but I managed to clean faster than it could burn, and finally his face and hands were free of goo.

"Thanks," he said when I was done.

"All in a day's work." I crumpled up his shirt, being careful to keep all the goop inside.

"Speaking of which…" he began.

I thought I knew what was coming. "I know. It's not my job to get physical with the bad guys."

He nodded, his expression stern. "Right. That was the deal. I handle the fighting. You do the mojo."

I started to protest, saying there hadn't been time to do any magic. But then his expression softened, and he added, "However, time was short, and you did real well. You bought me just enough time to allow the others to get away, and, thanks to you, I don't think it had a clue I was there until I attacked."

My shoulders relaxed. Our partnership was still new enough that I didn't want to get into an argument. "Thanks. I'll be more careful next time, though. I think I could have distracted it without getting so close."

He smiled. I turned to look at the monster, wondering what to do about the body. Seeing it was melting into a pile of steaming green and brown goo, I shot a perplexed glance at Paul.

"Yes. They do that. Convenient actually. The police will find it much easier to explain a mess than a monster."

I guess he had a point. Speaking of which, I heard sirens in the distance. "I think it's time to make tracks."

Paul got to his feet, wincing all the way up. "Yes. Let's go. You mind driving? I've got a bag of blood in the car, and I need it to jump–start healing this mess."

I don't own a car, but I do know how to drive, and I keep my license current. I agreed and lent him my shoulder for support.

We made it to the car and drove away just in time. The last thing we needed was to explain our presence or Paul's appearance.

As we drove off, Paul turned around in his seat and rummaged in the back. I risked a glance over my shoulder and saw him reach into a small cooler to pull out a plastic bag full of blood. He ripped open the bag with his fangs and sucked down the contents.

Satisfied, he settled back in his seat and closed his eyes.

"Fasten your seat belt," I said automatically.

He sighed but complied without even opening his eyes.

"You want me to drive you home? I can walk back." It was a long walk from his place to mine, but looking at him, I didn't think he had it in him to drive back from my apartment.

He nodded. "Yes, if you don't mind, drive me home. But keep the car. You can drop it by later."

Good idea. I headed in the direction of the Mount Vernon Square neighborhood, where Paul lived. As I drove, I mentally ran back over the fight. All things considered, I thought we'd done pretty well. Then I remembered that Paul had said he'd fought something like the demon before. "Hey, what was that thing anyway?"

Still with his eyes closed, Paul answered. "Shuggoleth demon." The unfamiliar word rolled easily off his tongue.

"Shuggoleth?" My pronunciation approximated his. Sort of. "Sounds Lovecraftian."

"With all those tentacles? Of course."

I was impressed. Most people don't recognize Lovecraft. I am forever explaining the "Cthulhu For President" button I sometimes wear.

"Are they common?"

He shrugged and finally opened his eyes. "Not really. I've only seen a couple since I was turned."

The question I'd been dying to ask since we first met fell out of my mouth. "How old are you anyway?" I wondered if he'd take offense.

"Old," he said.

I glanced over at him. "Old? Just that?"

Paul looked at me. Exhaustion warred with something in his expression I couldn't identify. "More than a hundred, okay? Can we drop this?" He closed his eyes again.

I got the message and let it go to concentrate on my driving. I drive just often enough to keep the rust off my skills, but I'm not good enough to operate a car on autopilot.

Naturally that's when my phone rang. I checked Caller ID and groaned, but if I didn't take this now, I'd spend way more time later in clean up. I picked up. "Hey, Abby?"

Paul opened his eyes and mouthed, "Isn't that illegal without hands–free?"

I nodded and glared at him to shut up. "Yeah, I'm here. Sorry. Driving now."

I pretended to listen, but I knew why she was calling. It's Friday morning, and she's panicking about her sales. Don't you ever wake up before dawn and panic before work?

Oh, a little background. Did I mention that my day job is as a multi–level marketer? I sell vitamins and other nutritional stuff, and I manage a downline of about 30 people. Three are good. The other 27 are like Abby. They sell just enough to fool themselves into seeing themselves as business owners. What they really are is annoying.

Abby ran down this week's list of excuses. Funny, it was almost exactly like last week's list. And the week before that. "Abby, I hear you. Sorry you're not happy with where you are. You know what to do. Call some people and find out who hasn't placed an Autoship order. You're close. A couple more orders, and you're there. Oh, and do you have any idea what time it is?"

She spluttered an apology for calling.

And I hung up.

Paul looked at me. "Another one of your groupies?"

I rolled my eyes at him. "They aren't groupies. They're associates. And if I can help them be successful, they'll make me successful.

He snorted. "How's that working for you?"

I didn't have a good answer to that, so I didn't even try.

Paul shook his head, leaned back in his seat and closed his eyes.

I know. It sounds lame, but the truth is, warlocking doesn't pay the bills. Maybe someday, but right now the only way to make a living at magic would be brewing love potions. I hate making love potions. Multi–level marketing is as much a family thing as magic. Mom was a Mary Kay Director, and she was really good at it. She put us all through college while Dad managed the coven and ran around the world busting ghosts and stopping the occasional Apocalypse.

I'm getting there, but I don't quite have Mom's knack.

When we reached his house, Paul opened his eyes. He still looked pretty awful.

"You want me to help you in?" I asked.

He smiled. "I think I can make it." He stretched cautiously. I heard the crackling of his muscles and winced when his raw skin ripped. He rolled his shoulders. "I think you need to work on that potion."

Oh. Some of his injuries were the result of my speed potion. I guess I'd made it too strong. "Sorry about that. I made it stronger for you. I thought your body'd be able to take it."

He eyed me. "Oh, it can take it. But I'll need some recovery time." He opened the door and gingerly climbed out.

"What time do you want me to stop by with the car?"

He paused. "Not until after sunset. I think I'll need the whole day to sleep this off."

I nodded, still feeling bad that my potion had caused so much trouble. "Right. See you this evening."

He waved vaguely behind him and limped to his house. I watched until he opened the door and went inside.

And before you say anything, yes I know he's perfectly capable of handling himself, but, well, we're still feeling our way through this friend thing. I'm not always sure where our lines and boundaries are. I mean, we met over a ghost. How often can you say that? She was haunting him, and I figured out how to help her move on. In the process, we sort of became friends.

Arriving home, I pulled into the alley behind my apartment. Parking is killer in this part of town, and I was relieved to find an empty spot that didn't tax my non–existent parallel parking skills. I hopped out and keyed the door lock. I love the little "chirp" it makes when I do that. As I walked toward my apartment, the adrenaline from the fight wore off. I was exhausted.

Turning out of the alley, I noticed a puppy lying on the sidewalk. He was adorable and kind of reminded me of a wolf I'd once seen at the zoo. I glanced around. No owner in sight. I shook my head, wondering how people could just abandon their dogs.

I knelt down a few feet away and held out my hand. The puppy stopped panting, wagged his tail and stood up to sniff me. I scratched behind his ears, looking for a collar. Just as I thought. He didn't have one. The little guy rolled onto his back, inviting a tummy rub. I obliged. I've always been an animal person.

As the puppy squirmed under my hand and tried to mouth me, the sun poked its head over the horizon.

That's when it happened. One moment, a cute ball of fluff. The next moment, a naked boy, about two or three years old. He blinked up at me and smiled.

I jumped back. Sure, I dealt in weird, but I wasn't expecting that! I hurriedly glanced around, figuring, with my luck, this would be the exact moment for a police officer to appear. Young, single guy. Naked little boy. Bad combination. Luckily, the cops were still donut-bound.

I whisked the kid into my arms and hurried into my apartment where we were promptly assaulted by two more fur balls... of the ferret variety, to be precise.

Warlocks need familiars, right? I have two, Gyre and Gimble. Okay, they aren't really familiars, but they are cute, and they keep me company.

The boy squealed and squirmed to be let down. I hesitated. Ferrets play rough, and he didn't have any clothes to protect him. But Gimble nipped at my leg, and the kid struggled harder. Too tired to fight it, I put him down.

I needn't have worried. The three of them got along great. Being nipped didn't seem to faze the boy, and my ferrets were delighted to have a playmate closer to their own size. I left them scrambling across my living room floor while I wandered into my bedroom to find some clothes for the kid.

I rummaged around in my closet. I have a very large family, and one reason I need extra money is that I'm constantly buying presents for all the cousins. One of my older sisters has a son about the age of this kid. I thought I'd remembered finding a cute outfit for him. Hah! There. I pulled out the Gap Kids bag and rummaged around to find a pair of ripped jeans (just like mine) and a blue t–shirt. Nathan loves to dress "just like Uncle Dafydd," and I'm a bad, bad uncle who indulges him. What can I say? I'm gay, and I know clothes. Who better to dress my favorite nephew?

But for now they could be sacrificed to a greater cause. dressing a lost werewolf puppy. I went back to the living room, pulled him away from the ferret melee and dressed him. He struggled the entire time, but I'm used to dressing little kids, and I managed. As soon as we finished, I put him back down, and the mayhem re-sumed.

Time to see about some food. Did I have anything decent for a kid to eat? We were in luck. I still had half a box of Cap'n Crunch (one of my guilty pleasures), and I poured most of the rest into two bowls. I was out of milk, so I hoped he didn't mind his cereal dry.

Heading back to the living room, I pondered what to do with the boy. I estimated his age to be about three. Now, before you say anything about a bachelor estimating ages, I'm actually good at it.

Remember that large family I mentioned earlier? I'm the seventh son of a seventh son of a seventh son. And you wondered where my magical talent came from? My father and grandfather were both accomplished warlocks, and they trained me well. I once commented, in jest, that they've been breeding warlocks for several generations. The flat looks they gave me were … disturbing.

The boy dug into his cereal. I've seen hungry kids before, and the way he tore into his food made me think he'd been out on the streets for a few days. I took a few bites before asking, "What's your name?"

He glanced away from his cereal long enough to give me a puzzled look. Gimble tried to worm her way into his bowl. I'm not the only one who likes Cap'n Crunch. The boy snatched the bowl back and gave a warning growl. I frowned, not expecting that from a little kid. Gimble backed away and attacked Gyre. The kid went back to his cereal.

I dumped the rest of my breakfast in his bowl and pondered some more. I knew werewolves existed, of course, but my studies had focused mostly on demons and ghosts because that's what my dad's coven dealt with. It had, of course, been assumed I'd follow the family tradition.

As I watched the kid eat, dread crawled down my spine. I groaned, knowing what that meant.

I've got limited prophetic abilities, which usually come to me in dreams. It was how I'd known to trust Paul when I saw him in person for the first time. I'd dreamed about him for years. My instincts were now warning me that something ominous was about to happen.

I ran through what had been going on recently: finally meeting Paul, encountering bigger demons and now a werewolf showing up in front of my apartment? Way too much coincidence for me. If this kept up, I'd need to call my dad and see if his coven knew anything. My grandfather insisted something was happening in 2012, and he'd asked me to keep an eye out for weird stuff. Did this count?

Right now however, I had a more immediate concern. Like, what should I do about my "guest"? Before I could decide, I needed more information. I only knew one source that could help, but damn, he was he going to be pissed about the situation.

I grabbed my phone and called Paul's number.

His phone rang 12 times (I guess vampires don't believe in voice mail), and I was about to give up when I heard a click and a sleepy voice say, "Dafydd. Do you have any idea what time it is?"

Apparently they do believe in Caller ID.

"Yeah, sorry about that. I kind of have a situation here."

Paul gave an exaggerated sigh and said, "What's up?"

"What do you know about werewolves?"

"You couldn't wait until evening to do research?"

I glanced at the kid. He'd finished his cereal and was back to playing with the ferrets. Gimble is tough, but I think she'd met her match this time. Fortunately, she seemed to be enjoying it. Not that I would have enjoyed being used as a mop. On the plus side, my place did need a cleaning.

I plunged in. "Couldn't wait. I kind of have a werewolf in my living room right now."

A long pause. Finally, he said, "I must still be asleep. I thought I just heard you say you had a werewolf in your living room."

I nodded. "Yep, that's what I said."

"And you're calling me instead of running?"

I hastened to reassure him. "Well, it's not a full grown werewolf. More like a werewolf puppy."

"A werewolf puppy?" I could hear the confusion in his voice, and I explained briefly. When I finished, I asked, "So, he's cute and all, but am I in any danger?"

Paul chuckled. "A little late to be worrying about that. You might have thought of that before you carried him into your apartment."

"Well, yeah, but—" I couldn't believe I was justifying this to a vampire. Finally, I just said, "Aw hell, he was cute and looked all lost. You would have done the same thing."

"Probably," he said. "How old did you say he was?"

"About three, I think. His puppy form was really

young. Fur still fuzzy, but his eyes were open."

"And you said he shifted right at sunrise?"

"Definitely." Sunrise and sunset are magically power-ful times of day, and I always know exactly when they occur. Useful for casting spells. Not so great for sleeping in.

"Hmm."

I tapped my foot and watched the kid and ferrets play.

"What's he doing now?"

"Wrestling with the slithy toves."

"What? Oh, right. The ferrets."

No Lewis Carroll references this early in the morn-ing. Good to know.

I could hear him shifting in bed. Finally, he asked, "You do know there are two types of lycanthropes, right? Infected weres and natural weres."

Really? "No, I didn't."

He paused before saying, "For what it's worth, the same applies to vampires."

Alarmed, I blinked. "You mean some people … I mean … vampires are born that way?"

"Yes, and Dafydd—" I heard the concern in his voice and braced myself. "If you ever encounter a natural vampire, run. Run as fast as you can."

"That dangerous, eh?"

"They make me look like a child."

This was a real surprise. Of course the thought of a vampire more powerful than Paul was daunting. But the real surprise was his being candid about it. He didn't talk

much about his kind. He'd cheerfully correct my mis-
conceptions, but he rarely volunteered information.

"Good to know." I eyed the kid. He and Gyre appeared to be in a tug–of–war over Gimble. The loud
"dooks" and giggles indicated a good time was being had
by all. "Is it the same with weres? And which kind do I
have here?"

"Yes, but not as much as with vampires. The biggest
difference is that natural lycanthropes have more control
over their shapes. And that's what has me puzzled."

"Why?"

"Because you said the kid shifted at sunrise. That's
usually the sign of an infected werewolf. But I've never
heard of anyone biting a kid. Has he spoken?"

"Nope."

"Hmm. Admittedly, my memories of children are
kind of dated, but I seem to remember that three–year
olds can talk."

I suppressed a giggle. "Usually, the problem with
three–year olds is getting them to stop."

I could almost see Paul nodding in satisfaction.
"Right, then. You've got a natural werewolf. No danger
to you. Although on principle, I'd avoid getting bitten."

"I'll see if I can manage that. Why are you so sure?"

"From your description, he's just a couple months
old. The animal form and human form don't stay in
sync. If he can't talk, he's just a baby, and that means
he's a natural."

"Okay. It still begs the question of what to do with
him."

A long pause on the other end of the line. Finally, Paul said, "That's a good question. I'm not sure I have a good answer. But, I do have some friends who might be able to help us out."

"Would these friends happen to be werewolves?"

"Yes. And I need to warn you. They are kind of a rough crowd."

I snorted. "Isn't that the pot calling the kettle black?"

I heard a stifled chuckle. "Well, okay, vampires can be violent. But most of us are at least well–behaved on our social time. Werewolves tend to play harder than my kind."

"I think I can handle it. What time and where?"

"How about eight? Can you drive my car over here?"

"Sure thing."

Another pause. "Dafydd, have you thought about who'll watch the kid while we meet?"

Another good question. I hadn't gotten that far. I scrambled quickly through options. Sonya, the waitress at my favorite hangout was working this evening. None of my family were in town. Most of my other contacts who knew about the weird side of the world were psychics. Definitely not the folks to deal with a kid. Most of them worked evenings, and some of them weren't exactly stable. That left only one person.

"I'll take him to Laura's."

It wasn't the ideal solution. Laura knows about magic in the world. She's a magician in her own right, but with technology, not with the supernatural. When I need research, she's fantastic. Her black Lab, Billy, would love the kid. So why do I say it isn't ideal? Laura's a quadriplegic. She was in a car accident in high school and has been confined to a wheelchair ever since. It's why she prefers the online world to the physical world. There, no one has to know she's disabled. Of course she'd kill me if she knew I used that word to describe her.

She's also tough, as she reminds me on a regular basis. She hates it when I use her disability as a reason to leave her out of situations, but I can't help it. We've been friends since grade school, and I can't help but be protective of her.

Paul obviously was thinking something similar. "Are you sure that's a good idea?"

I guess Laura has rubbed off on me because I became stubborn. "You said he's safe, right?"

"No, I said he's *probably* safe. There *is* a difference."

"I don't know anyone else who can take him on short notice. And he's too young to be left here by himself."

I heard Paul sigh. "I guess you're right. Okay, Laura it is. Her dog will probably love him, and if anything happens, I guess a Lab can take on a puppy, even a werewolf kind."

I nodded, even though he couldn't see it. "See you at eight then. Err…. Sleep well?"

He laughed. "Assuming you'll let me this time."

We hung up. I headed straight for my bedroom, taking the kid and the ferrets with me. It had been a long night, and this evening looked like it would be more of the same. I definitely needed sleep.

Chapter 2

Friday, September 4, 2009:
Late afternoon

I AWOKE SURROUNDED by small, warm bodies. The boy was curled up against my back, and the ferrets had piled together in the crook of my legs. While cozy and comfortable, it was also cramped.

All my muscles hurt, but that was to be expected. Even the potions I create for my body leave aftereffects. You can't enhance the body without paying for it later. Usually a hot shower and a couple of Advil get rid of the worst of it.

When I shifted, someone, probably Gimble, nipped me in protest. You only hurt the ones you love, right? Ignoring the sharp pain in my calf, I got up, making sure to replace the covers over the boy, who was still sprawled in sleep.

I glanced at the clock on my way to the bathroom. 4:00 in the afternoon. Wow! I had been tired. Fortunately, I still had enough time to run the kid by Laura's before going to meet Paul.

As expected, a hot shower eased my aching muscles. Looking over my clean clothes, I decide it was the right day for a tight t–shirt (pink, with "Cheap Trick" emblazoned on it—the band, not what you were thinking) and ripped dark wash blue jeans. Pretty much standard issue for me when I wasn't working.

I came out of the closet (no comments, please), and saw the kid sitting up, rubbing his eyes and yawning. He looked so cute. I sat down on the bed. "What's your name?"

Like earlier, he just looked at me. I sighed. "I know you understand me, but why won't you talk?"

Again, total silence. I guess Paul knew what he was talking about.

I shrugged and got up. "Want a sandwich before we go?" He nodded and followed me into the kitchen.

Having been to the grocery store a couple of days ago, the pantry was well–stocked with important staples like peanut butter and jelly. I juggled the phone and called Laura while I made two sandwiches for myself and one for the boy. While Gyre liked peanut butter, Gimble didn't, so I grabbed a few raisins for each. Ferrets will do almost anything for raisins, but too many are really bad for them.

Laura picked up on the second ring. "Hi, Dafydd. What's up?"

"I need a favor."

She laughed. "Any chance it will involve seeing that hot vampire guy again?"

I sighed. First she wanted me to hook up with him. I've told her repeatedly he doesn't play on my team, so now I think she's making a play for him herself. "Maybe later, but not now. Although, I think Billy will be pretty happy about it."

"How's that?"

"A werewolf puppy followed me home, and I need a place to stash him while Paul and I try to figure out where his parents are."

Silence on the other end of the line.

"Laura?"

Finally, she spoke. "Uh, did you really say 'werewolf puppy?'"

I grinned. "Yep. Paul says he's safe to be around. Apparently there are lycanthropes who can pass on the disease and others who are just born that way. He thinks the kid is the natural kind, so no worrying about being bitten." Did I sound too much like I was trying to convince myself?

I heard her take a deep breath. "Dafydd, I swear. Being around you just gets weirder and weirder."

"It's part of my charm. So, is it okay to bring him over?"

"Sure. I've never met a werewolf before. Might as well start now."

"Thanks, Laura. You're a champ."

We hung up, and I took the sandwiches and raisins into the bedroom. The boy had managed to get dressed, in spite of Gyre and Gimble's help. He downed the sandwich as eagerly as he had the cereal earlier, and I gave him half of my second one. I made a mental note to tell Laura to lay on the snacks.

"Come on. Time to go."

He glanced at the ferrets, to me and then back to the ferrets.

"Yeah, I get that. They are fun. But right now we need to go to a friend's house. She has a dog. You'll like him."

His eyes lit up at the word "dog."

He really was a puzzle. He clearly understood everything I was saying, and I didn't know if that made Paul right or wrong. My stomach twisted, and I hoped I wasn't making a mistake by leaving him with Laura. I considered calling her back, but my imagination played through the thorough tongue lashing she'd give me. Laura hates it when she thinks I'm protecting her. I told my stomach to settle down. Paul knows his stuff.

I led the kid out of the house, and to Paul's car. Getting him buckled into the seat was a challenge, but I finally managed it. The trip went quickly, and we soon arrived in Crystal City. The kid looked around in fascination as we walked through the underground to Laura's apartment. I knocked at her door, and it opened, as if by magic. It wasn't really magic, but technology can do a pretty good imitation. We stepped in.

A large woman in shorts and a t–shirt with hair dyed electric blue was just leaving. "Hey, Stephanie. Good to see you."

She gave me a big hug. "Dafydd. Been a stranger lately."

I rolled my shoulders. Actually, she was right. Stephanie is an amazing massage therapist. She doesn't usually do outcall work, but I recommended her when Laura's last therapist moved to the West Coast. She said she's do it "as a favor to a friend," and she's been massaging

Laura for more than a year now.

"I'll schedule something soon."

"You do that."

She left, and I turned to Laura, who was just rolling out of her bedroom. I blinked. Laura stands out in a crowd with her candy–apple red chair. But the rest of her usually blends in. Not now. As always, her blond hair was cut short for ease of care, but today it was spiky. And half of it was dyed neon pink.

"Okay, what's up with the dye?"

She did the eyebrow lift that substituted for the shrug she could no longer make. "Stephanie thought it would add character."

"Yeah, it does that."

"You don't like it?"

I laughed. "Of course I like it. I was just surprised. That's all."

"And who's that hiding behind you?" Her voice was soft and reassuring.

I glanced down. The kid was peeking around my legs, and he looked uncertain.

"Say 'hi' to Laura."

He shook his head.

"Where's Billy?" I asked.

She turned her chair and called out, "Billy!"

A black Lab bounded into the room: Billy, her service dog. As I'd suspected, boy and dog became fast friends, and they wrestled their way around the living room.

Laura and I watched them for a moment before she

said, "So he followed you home, and now you want to keep him?"

I laughed. "Well, now that you mention it, that's pretty close to what happened." I quickly told her how the kid and I had met, and I started to fill her in on the high points of my conversation with Paul. Just as I was getting to his explanation of the different types of lycanthropes, Mary came in from the kitchen.

Mary, Laura's live–in companion, and I don't exactly get along. Apparently, her family also has a mystical background, and she doesn't get a good "vibe" off me. Which I don't understand. I only practice white magic, and I've never misused my powers. Even so, she took a dislike to me from the first moment we met. Laura finds the whole thing hilarious, but then she's always been a bit bent.

"Hi, Mary," I greeted cheerfully.

She completely ignored me, instead glancing on the floor at the boy and dog. Billy had brought out his favorite rope toy, and the boy was losing the tug–of–war battle, but, from all the giggling, he didn't seem to mind.

"What's that?" Mary asked, her voice disgusted.

Really? Referring to a little boy as a "what" was a bit much, even for her.

Laura saved us. "Dafydd found him outside his apartment today. He needs me to look after him while he tries to find his parents."

"*That's* no little boy. It's a monster." Her glare made me feel six again.

"No, he's not." I hated the defensive tone in my

voice, but hey, you'd be defensive too if some old bat were calling you on the carpet. "He's just a little boy."

The look she shot me communicated that even she didn't think I was that stupid.

"Okay, he's a werewolf puppy. But he's harmless."

She shook her head. "Nothing of that breed is harmless."

Laura interjected again. "Mary, why don't you go out for a bit? I'm sure there's some shopping that needs to be done." I would have gone for soothing. She went for firm.

Firm worked. Mary "humphed" and grabbed her purse. I wondered again why Laura kept her around.

She left, and Laura and I both relaxed. "Sorry about that. She just gets like that sometime."

I nodded. "Yeah, I've noticed."

"Anyway, what was that about different types of werewolves?"

I finished the story, and Laura thought for a moment. "I don't know, Dafydd. This sounds dangerous, even for you."

"You want me to take him somewhere else?"

She shook her head. "No, that's not what I mean. I'm not worried about the kid, but werewolves? They kind of have a reputation, you know?"

I chuckled. "Like vampires don't? You're not worried about Paul. Far from it. You want to hitch us."

She smiled. "Paul's different. He's not bad."

I hadn't told her all of Paul's background. He used to be really bad. About 30 years ago, he was the kill—

anything–that–had–blood kind of vampire. Then he killed a girl he'd been in love with and changed. I still don't have the whole story, but I'm giving him time to trust me enough to level all the way.

Now wasn't the time to go into all that with Laura. "Well, if Paul can't protect me from the Big Bad Wolves, I don't know who can."

She snorted. "Like he protected you from that tentacled thing last night"

I blinked. "How'd you know about that?"

"There's cameras around the Washington Monument. Didn't you know?"

"Uh, no." My heart sank. Oh God, don't tell me the whole thing was on camera for everyone to see? Generally, humanity is really good at ignoring what's inconvenient. It's how we witches and warlocks have been able to get along all these years (well, except for a few truly noteworthy exceptions. Salem Witch Trials anyone?) If people see something magical, they explain it away. But, eight–foot tall tentacled monsters ripping apart homeless people in the middle of a National Monument? That's pretty hard to explain away.

She grinned at the sudden look of panic on my face. "Don't worry, silly. I altered the video footage to something boring and normal."

I relaxed. Laura was a really good friend to have. She's a wizard with technology. I use her to track down people and information over the Internet. Never thought I'd need her to cover our tracks in the battle against evil.

Then I frowned. "Wait, how'd you even know?"

"A lucky accident, actually. I was awake and scanning camera feeds for fun."

Right. Doesn't everyone? She really is a geek.

"I saw the thing in the grass. Then you and Paul drove up and did your thing." She gave me a stern look. "Next time, duck when the boss monster tries to grab you, okay?"

I had the grace to look abashed. "Yeah, okay. But did you see Paul? He was fantastic!"

Her stern look morphed into a smile. "Yeah, he was. I didn't know vampires could move that fast."

"They can't usually. That was a potion of mine."

"Well, I watched until it was over and then messed with the feed so it just shows the park at night, nice and quiet." Abruptly, she changed the subject. "So what are you and Paul going to do to find his parents?"

"Paul says he's got some contacts at a werewolf bar. We're gonna go talk to them."

"A werewolf bar? I didn't know they existed."

I shrugged. "Neither did I."

Laura got a sort of faraway look in her eye. "Werewolves have bars. Do you suppose vampires do too?"

Uh oh! She was starting to think about landing herself her very own blood sucker. Not a good idea. "Um, never thought about it. Guess I can ask Paul." Time to go before she thought too much about it. I made a point of looking at my phone. "Wow, look at the time. I'm running late. Gotta go meet Paul."

She came back to the real world. "Yeah, okay. When do you think you'll be back?"

"Not sure. Paul and I are meeting at eight. I guess we'll probably be at the bar a couple of hours. I'll get him to drive me here to pick up the kid. Call it 11 or 12. Too late for you?"

She shook her head. "No, I'm running a trace for another client tonight. It looks like an all–nighter. I'll sleep tomorrow."

"Cool." Then I remembered about sunset. "Hey, Paul figures the kid can't control his form really well at sunrise and sunset, so he'll probably become a puppy in about an hour. Can you tell him to take off his clothes before then?"

Okay, that sounded weird, but she took it well. "Yeah, I'll ask him. I hope Mary won't get back early. I doubt she'd take that well."

"Probably not." I said my goodbyes and left.

THE SUN WAS just setting as I pulled up at Paul's house. The Mt. Vernon Square neighborhood was beautiful, lots of old row houses, most of which have been renovated. Paul's house was one of the loveliest. I've still never seen it during the day, but it's three stories, painted a gentle cream color, and it has an awesome header over the top window. It gives the impression of Gothic without being at all out of place. I love his house, and someday I'm going to have one just like it.

But for now, I get to admire his. I trotted up and knocked on the door. It took a while for him to answer, and I wondered if he was even up yet. I checked the

36

time. 7:45. If we were going to meet at 8:00, he ought to be up.

The door opened, and Paul said, "Sorry. Just got out of bed."

I barely heard. His hair was still mussed, and he was wearing just a pair of sweats. Sure, I'd seen him without a shirt before. Last night, for example. But he'd been all covered in caustic goo, and I hadn't really noticed the broad, well–muscled shoulders, tight pecs or narrow waist that ended in a perfect six–pack. His sweats hung just below all that muscle, in a casual drape it would have taken me ten minutes to artfully arrange. With Paul, though, he just threw on sweats, and they look like that.

So not fair that he doesn't play on my team.

"Dafydd?"

Oops. I hoped I hadn't been drooling. "Yeah, sorry. Um, just. Uh." What to say? "Nice sweats," I finally managed. Lame, I know, but, tell me you could have done better under the circumstances.

"Thanks." His eyes twinkled, and I had the sudden urge to come up with an excuse to flee. "Come on in. Make yourself comfortable while I get dressed."

"Yeah, sure."

I followed him into his house and turned to the living room. Where my place is decorated in what my parents call "neo–eclectic," Paul's décor all fits together. Mostly antiques (I think, being no expert). A couple of heavy wing back chairs with cream cushions that I swear match the paint on the outside of his house. On the other side of the room, a chaise longe (I had to look it up) covered in a paisley fabric. Heavy bookshelves, full to bursting with tomes, both leather–bound old books and modern hardbacks. A cherry table with intricately carved legs (dragons and gryphons) was conveniently placed near the chaise. I would call it a coffee table, but he'd probably use some fancy name.

Quiet classical music played in the background. Maybe Rachmaninoff, but I'm no expert.

As always, I was drawn to an ancient pistol and bayonet on the wall between two bookshelves. The weapons seemed to have a place of honor, and I was sure both had history, but I hadn't found the time to ask Paul about them. It wasn't just the antique's evident age that told me there was a story. I pick up impressions from inanimate objects, and something about the weapons, especially the pistol, tugged at me.

I sat down on the leather couch (the only modern piece of furniture in the room, other than the computer desk in the corner) and picked up the hardback on the table. I had to chuckle. *Heat Wave* by Richard Castle, one of my favorite authors. Last Christmas, my family chipped in and bought me all his books, in hardback. I've been watching Castle's website for his next appearance in D.C. I want them all signed.

Paul entered the room, fully dressed. Of course, he still looked good in a gray, loose button–down shirt that I swear was silk. Low–hung blue jeans, artfully and expensively ripped down the left thigh completed the image. I glanced down at my own t–shirt and jeans. "I feel under dressed."

He laughed and glanced down at his shirt. "No worries. This is so old, I probably should toss it soon."

Yeah, right. Old.

"Ready to go?" he continued.

I got up but couldn't resist a nod at the book on the table. "Good choice."

He grinned. "Open it up to the title page."

I frowned and did as he asked. My eyes widened at what was written there.

"To my dear friend, Paul. Many thanks for services rendered."

I looked at him. "Services rendered?"

Paul shrugged. "I took care of a troublesome stalker a couple of years ago. He's sent me a signed first edition ever since. Not sure I'm liking Nikki Heat as a replacement for Derek Storm, but it's not a bad book."

I shook my head and turned for the door. "Someday you're going to have to give me the story of your life."

He laughed and followed me. "That will take a while. Better set aside a couple of days."

In my dreams, I thought.

The sun had just set when we stepped outside. There were still hints of daylight, but enough long shadows for Paul to be safe.

"Where are we going?" I asked as we climbed into his car.

"Green Lantern on 14th."

"Really? That's a werewolf bar?" I've heard of it, of course. It's a gay bar which is known primarily for its "Toolshed," a place for what they call the "bear crowd."

Use your imagination. I'm sure you'll be pretty close.

Paul nodded. "Yes, not that most people know about it. They kind of fit in the Toolshed, though. It's considered neutral ground for all the local packs, so they keep a pretty low profile. Disputes are taken elsewhere. Green Lantern is a place for them to drink and hang out socially."

I had to ask. "Is there a vampire bar?"

"Sure. Lounge 201 near Capitol Hill. I'll take you sometime."

"Did you just ask me out on a date?" I asked teasingly.

He gave me an odd look. "Yes, sure, if you get off on hanging out with a bunch of blood–sucking predators. It's not exactly a date–kind of place for us."

Damn. One of these days, I'll learn to think before opening my mouth. "Sorry. Sure, I'd like to go sometime, as long as you promise not to let me get killed, or turned, or whatever."

He laughed as he slowed for a red light. "No problem. If you're with me, you'll be safe enough. I'm older than most of the vamps in the city."

I bit my tongue before I said something else stupid. Paul seldom let anything slip about himself, and if I said something, he'd just be more careful in the future. Instead, I said, "So tell me more about werewolves. They really do run in packs?"

As he accelerated away from a light, he said, "Yes. Although running probably isn't the right word. There aren't many places in D.C. where they can actually run.

Natural werewolves generally live outside the city. There are a couple of communities in the Shenandoah and one a little closer in, near Gainesville. Sometimes they come to the city to hang out, see the sights and do what everyone else does in a city."

"What about infected werewolves?"

He shifted in his seat. "They are fairly rare. That's another reason I think your kid is a natural. My guess is his family came to the city to sight–see, and they got separated. His parents probably know about Green Lantern, and it's where they'd start to get the word out."

I sensed he was dodging my question about infected werewolves. "Okay, that makes sense. Now tell me about the other kind."

Paul pulled to another stop, and looked directly at me for a moment. "You asked earlier why I knew about a werewolf bar?"

"Yeah."

"Well, several years ago, an elder of the pack out in Gainesville caught me at a kill. He was ready to put me down, kind of like the first time you and I met."

I smiled at the memory. Yeah, coming across him leaning over a body, fangs still in the guy's neck, in a dark alley had been … memorable.

"I convinced him I wasn't a bad guy, and he asked for my help keeping track of the infected werewolves in the city. You see, infected don't have a lot of control. They only change a few days a month, and that holds down the trouble they can cause, but it's still tough for them to keep their kills under wraps. Unlike vampires, they don't have the presence of mind to conceal or make their kills look like something else."

"Something else?" I asked.

Paul shrugged. "Suicide or something like that. Mostly, we prey on prostitutes, gangers and homeless people. Folk who are less likely to be missed or whose deaths are investigated fleetingly, if at all."

Paul really was in an expansive mood tonight. "Go on."

"Natural werewolves don't kill people. They prey on animals only, deer, squirrels and rabbits mostly. Pretty much like real wolves. But they do like being able to come to the city. And they like to experience the city in wolf form. Their senses are keener, and they say it's a real rush to walk the streets at night. They've got a vested interest in keeping the infected under control, and a natural will kill an infected if he sees one killing."

"I can see that a bunch of killer wolves in D.C. might ruin it for everyone."

He nodded. "Exactly. I'm roaming the streets most nights, keeping an eye out for trouble, both of the supernatural variety and otherwise. Stream That Runs, the elder I mentioned, figured I could be another set of eyes for them. I make a point of being very active during the full moon. If I catch a were killing, I kill him. If I catch one just roaming, I 'persuade' him to go home and stay locked up."

I didn't think I wanted too many details on the "persuading" part. Getting back to the topic at hand, I asked. "There's more to this, though, isn't there? This is more than just a lost kid."

"I think so. The last couple of months, I've seen more wolves than usual. I've gotten to where I know most of them in town. I recognize them, and they recognize and avoid me. But the last couple of months, I've seen new ones. They aren't killing, I don't think. But my instincts are telling me they are up to something, and I want to figure it out."

I glanced out the window at the full moon hanging low in the sky. "But isn't it the wrong time of the month to go to the bar? They're all out in wolf form."

"There are always a few there, including a friend of mine who's very plugged in. If anyone knows anything about the kid, it'll be Runner."

Are you sensing that werewolves go in for the odd names?

Paul continued. "If he doesn't know anything, and you're up to it, maybe we can poke around and try to find out what the others are up to."

I nodded. Sure, if there are lots of killer wolves running around my 'hood, I want to figure out why, and what they are doing. And maybe stop them before something really bad happens. "Yeah, let's do that."

Paul pulled onto 14th Street and started hunting for a parking spot. I spotted one and pointed. He nodded and smoothly parked. While I'd struggled to learn parallel parking, he made it look like something he'd done for decades. Well, maybe he had...

We got out of the car, and Paul led the way into the Green Lantern.

The main bar area was a square counter surrounding the displays of liquor. Big screen TVs hung on every wall, with sports on a couple displays and porn on the others. I briefly thought I should get over here a bit more often.

Paul and I found seats at the bar and waved over a waiter. He introduced himself as Scott and said he'd be taking care of us. This was my first time going out with Paul, and I will say it was an experience. Scott was certainly attentive to me, but let's say he gave Paul some special attention. The vampire took it well, flirted back comfortably, but also made it clear he wasn't looking.

Scott left with a grin to get our drinks, and I sat back to look around.

It was a light crowd for a Friday evening. Paul was also scanning the room, and after a moment, he nodded to a tall man sitting on the opposite side of the bar with two other men. The tall man nodded back and walked over.

Guessing he was a werewolf, I examined him closely as he approached. Other than being very tall, muscular, and a bit on the hairy side (he was shirtless, as were several other patrons), he looked normal. He was wearing jeans and Doc Martin boots. As he came closer, I couldn't help noticing his eyes. Mostly brown, they had an oddly attractive gold tint to them. I don't know if I would have noticed if I hadn't been looking for it, but they did not look human.

He greeted Paul in a pleasant deep baritone. "Hey, Paul." He looked me over quickly. "Who's your friend?"

Paul smiled at him. "Runner, have a seat. We'd like to talk to you for a minute. Buy you something?"

Runner sat but looked at Paul with some suspicion. "You never offer to buy me a drink unless you need something. And you still haven't introduced me to your friend."

I glanced at Paul, wondering what game he was playing.

"This is Dafydd. He's a warlock, and he knows what you are."

Runner looked me over thoroughly. I felt like he counted all my teeth and could probably tell me about scars I'd forgotten about. "How do you know him?" he asked me.

I shrugged. "I helped him get rid of a ghost who was haunting him. And now we help each other out with, shall we say, problems."

"What kind of problems?" His voice was a low growl, and I glanced at Paul. His face was impassive, giving me no signs. I took that to mean "be careful."

"Problems of the supernatural variety. Maybe you heard about that demon by the Washington Monument last night? That was us."

The werewolf sat back, shoulders relaxing and gave a hearty laugh. "That was you two? Benny filled me in. That thing damn near ate you two alive." He glanced at Paul. "If this is the kinda help you're getting, wouldn't you be better off alone?"

I started to bristle but then I noticed Paul grinning, and I decided to keep my mouth shut.

"Wasn't his fault. If the lookie–loos had the sense to get outta the way, we woulda had more room to work."

I restrained a blink. That was the first time I'd heard Paul use anything other than proper grammar and enunciation.

Runner laughed again. "Yeah, them spectator's usually more trouble than they's worth." He reached over and clapped my shoulder. "Okay, warlock. If Paul says you're okay, it's cool."

Scott came by then with our drinks, a Pale Ale for me and a glass of red wine for Paul. I hadn't recognized the name when he ordered, which probably meant it was expensive. Paul nodded to Runner. "And another of what he's having."

Runner gave him a look, and Paul chuckled. "Okay, another of what he'd like to have and figures he can make me pay for."

Scott grinned. "Right. The Macallen 18 then."

Paul winced, but there was no seriousness to it. He turned to me. "He always did have a fine taste in spirits." He took a sip of his wine and continued. "Are we done fencing? Can we get down to business here?"

"When the whiskey arrives. Pleasure before business."

I settled in with my ale, figuring we were going to be here a while. I was perfectly willing to be distracted by the scenery around the bar.

Scott arrived a moment later and put down a glass. Paul nodded. "Start a tab, if you will. I think we might be here a while."

"Sure thing."

Runner sipped his drink with a smile. "Ah, that's good. I'd say I owe you, but something's telling me you'll be the one doing the owing."

Paul smiled. "Ready for business?"

The werewolf nodded and waved a hand. "Go ahead. What do you need?"

Paul glanced at me. "It's properly your story, Dafydd. Want to go ahead?"

I nodded and told Runner the basic story about finding the puppy, then boy, outside my apartment. He listened carefully, and I thought his expression grew troubled when I mentioned the change happening at dawn.

When I finished, he didn't say anything for a moment. Finally, he asked, "You're sure about the change at dawn? Right at dawn? Not a few minutes before or after?"

"I'm sure. Dawn and dusk are such powerful times that I've trained myself to feel the energy shift at that precise moment."

Runner frowned, more of a thoughtful frown than an angry or upset frown. I wondered what he was thinking about.

Paul obviously was wondering the same thing. "What's up?"

He shook his head. "Well, that story's really odd. I'd've sworn there were no kids in town."

"Maybe a family visiting the city from one of the farther communities?" Paul suggested.

Runner shook his head. "I don't think so. But let me ask a couple of the other guys. Might be they know something I don't." He got up and moved to the other side of the room. I watched him approach some of the others.

"All those werewolves?" I asked Paul.

He nodded, eyes grave as he watched the brief conversations. All of them ended in head shaking. "They are. Most of them are from the Gainesville pack, but a couple are visiting from farther out." He turned to face me. "It worries me a bit that he's so sure there are no families in town. Runner keeps track of things. I've never known him to be caught unaware."

I felt a chill start to go down my spine. "And what does that mean if there are no families in town?"

Runner came back before he could answer. The large werewolf was shaking his head. "It's what I thought. No families around."

"Then that means," Paul started.

The other man finished for him. "Yeah, that kid ain't no natural were."

The chill settled in my gut. Not a natural werewolf? And I'd left him with Laura.

I started to move. Runner grabbed my arm, and I tried to shake him off. I might as well have been trying to move a tree. "Where are you going?"

"I left the kid with a friend of mine." I heard my voice break, and I fought to get it under control. "She's in a wheelchair. She can't defend herself or get away if—" I couldn't finish the sentence.

Paul nodded and got up. "We need to get there. The sun set almost an hour ago. If he's infected, he's already changed."

Runner was already moving toward the door. "Not sure what possessed you to leave a werewolf, even a pup, with a crippled girl, but let's be getting there as soon as possible." He waved at Scott, who approached quickly. "We gotta run, now. He'll settle the bill when I get back. You know he's good for it."

Scott nodded. "Yeah, sure, Runner." He looked concerned. "What's wrong? Someone hurt?"

"I can't say right now, but I'm hoping not yet."

And we all three rushed outside. Paul led us to his car and hit the remote to unlock all the doors. Runner rolled his eyes when he saw the shiny red Prius. "You still driving this candy ass car?"

Paul grinned briefly. "It gets me the kind of attention I'm looking for."

Runner snorted. "Yeah, I know what kinda action you vamps are looking for. Not interested in getting me any of that."

I climbed in back, being the smallest and easiest to cram into the back seat. Runner contorted himself into the passenger seat, and Paul started the engine before we even had a chance to fasten our seat belts.

"Call her," he said as soon as he'd pulled out of his spot.

My cell phone was in my hand, and I'd already dialed. "On it."

I waited. One ring. Two. Three. My heart pounded.

"Hello?" Laura's voice.

"Laura? It's Dafydd. Everything okay there?"

I could hear the puzzlement in her voice. "Sure. Why wouldn't it be? He changed less than an hour ago, just like you said. He and Billy have been playing ever since."

I let out the breath I'd forgotten I was holding. "Okay. That's good. We're on our way." I held my hand over the phone. "Anything I should warn her about, Runner?"

His voice rumbled in the darkness. "Tell her to keep him calm. Don't scare him. Who's 'Billy?' Another kid?"

I shook my head. "No. A black Lab."

"Okay, as long as they're playing, that should be okay."

I could hear Laura's voice in the distance, saying "Dafydd? Are you still there?" over and over again, sounding more anxious with each repetition. "Yeah," I said to her. "I'm back. Umm, don't get too worried, but we might have been wrong about the kid."

"Wrong how?"

"He might not be a natural werewolf. He might be infected, and we're not sure what he'll do."

"You sure?" Her voice sounded doubtful. "He's just acting like a puppy right now. Billy hasn't had this much fun in ages."

"No, we aren't sure, but just to be safe, keep your distance and don't startle him."

"Okay."

Perversely, I would have felt better if she'd sounded scared. But I guess the crash in high school knocked all the scared out of her. She's not stupid, but nothing ever since has phased her. "We're on our way."

I glanced out the window. Paul was making amazing time. He was already crossing the 14th Street Bridge. I hoped there were no cops around. Or that Paul could do some sort of vampire "whammy" if we got pulled over. "We're already out of the city. Should be no more than 10 minutes, tops."

"We'll be here."

I hung up, sat back and tried not to worry.

Runner glanced back over his shoulder. "If he's not causing trouble now, they should be fine."

"That's what I'm hoping. But if something happens to her, I'm responsible for putting her in danger." Laura has known about my magical abilities since high school. She thinks it's cool, but I know how dangerous they can be. My family is trained to handle themselves, but she's not. And as much as she wants me to ignore her handicap, I can't.

"Any chance you could be wrong, Runner?" Paul asked. "Maybe there's a family in town you don't know about?"

Runner shook his head. "No, every wolf who comes to the city knows about me and knows to check in. If not with me, with one of my pack. We keep a pretty good eye on who's here and who's not. We need to."

"Why?" I asked, glad of the distraction.

"So if we hear of something happening, we know if it's us or the others."

"You mean the infected werewolves?"

"Yep. If one of our kind causes trouble, we usually run 'em out of town. If it's one of the others, we generally kill 'em. Can't have that kind ruining it for the rest of us."

I frowned, still not sure of the distinction between lycanthropes. "That doesn't sound fair. I mean, if one of your kind causes trouble, shouldn't you ... well ... take drastic action too?"

Runner stiffened visibly, and Paul answered for him. "I may not have explained the differences well enough, Dafydd. Natural werewolves have control over their form and their actions in either form. I've only heard of a few ever harming humans. Generally, if there's trouble, it's a youngster playing a prank."

Runner's shoulders relaxed, and he chimed in. "Oh, we've got our bad seeds too. But we handle our own. I've had to kill a couple who thought humans were easy prey. But Paul's right. Mostly it's pranks. When that happens, we run 'em out of town and let their pack know what happened. Pack justice isn't always pretty. That usually straightens them out."

From his grim tone, I decided I didn't need any more detail than that. "Then what about infected werewolves?"

Paul picked up the explanation. "They are a lot like what you see in the movies. On the full moon and the two days on either side, they turn into monsters. And I'm using the word for a reason. They can't control their blood lust. Most are good people who were in the wrong place at the wrong time. Once they realize what's going on, they lock themselves up for five nights a month. The rest? Well, some of Runner's people patrol those nights, looking for those who don't."

Runner made a "humphing" noise. "Not just my people who patrol. You're out most full moons keeping an eye on things."

Paul nodded. "Yes. And when I find one who's killed, I turn him or her over to Runner's people for pack justice."

"What happens to them? You kill them?"

"Not always. We can sniff out the ones who are generally horrified by what they've become. We help them build a strong room to contain themselves. The rest? Those we kill, yeah. You humans are fragile. Someone has to look out for them."

Paul shifted in his seat, and Runner added, "And yeah, we deal with your kind who break the rules too."

"I know you do," came the vampire's quiet voice.

He took the exit for Crystal City, and I hoped Laura was still all right.

As Paul merged onto Crystal Drive, Runner commented, "You know. Now that you mention it, there is something weird going on. We've just heard bits and pieces, but it seems there's more infecteds running around than a few months back. We've been trying to figure out where they're coming from, but no luck so far."

Paul stiffened when he heard that. "What have you heard?"

Runner shrugged. "We haven't actually heard anything yet, but we're worried that someone is making them and using them for some purpose, probably not good. You see, warlock, infected werewolves make good thugs for those who can contain 'em. After infection, they're stronger, even in human form and without the full moon. It's never happened here that I know of, but another pack leader in New York told me about some guy who teamed up with a werewolf to infect people and make his own bully gang. They locked 'em all up during the full moon, but the rest of the time used them as muscle."

"That would work," Paul said musingly. "It's not like they'd have much choice. They couldn't go to the police. Who would believe them?"

Runner snorted. "Until they transformed in a cell."

I blinked. "That's got to have happened before."

"Sure has. The pack took care of it."

His voice was flat, and I didn't want to ask for more information. Besides, Paul was just pulling into a parking spot. Time to find out if Laura was okay.

We rushed into her building, and I cursed when I saw all the elevators were at the top of the building. I pushed the call button several times, knowing it wouldn't help, but needing to do something to burn off nervous energy.

Paul touched my shoulder. "She'll be fine. It's only been 15 minutes or so since we talked to her. Nothing will have happened in that short a time."

"I know. It's just—"

He smiled. "I know. I like her too, you know."

By the time the door "dinged," I was ready to jump out of my skin, and three other people had gathered. Two looked to be a couple, and one was a guy who looked like he'd gotten an early start on the Friday night party. He reeked of cheap alcohol, and he was barely stable on his feet.

We all entered, and I hit 12, Laura's floor. The couple were on 5, and the drunk was on 11. Great, we'd have the pleasure of his company for the entire ride. Not my night.

As if things couldn't get worse, as soon as the couple exited on their floor, the drunk tried, clumsily, to pick me up. Paul was obviously trying to stifle a smile, while Runner didn't even try. His mouth opened wide in a toothy grin that intimidated me. It should have shut up the drunk, but apparently he'd had enough to kill both inhibitions and common sense.

His floor finally arrived, and I pushed him out the door. Paul tapped the "close door" button, and I heaved a big sigh of relief.

"You get that often?" Paul asked with a grin. Probably the one he'd been stifling earlier.

"Not too often, thankfully."

The elevator door "dinged" and opened again, which meant they didn't have any time to tease me further. The three of us dashed down the hallway to Laura's door.

Paul growled as we drew closer, and I glanced over to see his fangs drop. Uh oh. That could not be good. I shot a quick look at Runner, and his eyes were glowing an ominous yellow.

When we got to Laura's door, I could finally hear what they must have picked up earlier. Growls. One deep. Another lighter, almost a yip. And voices. Not quite panicked, but getting close.

I paused, suddenly not sure how to get into the apartment. I didn't want to knock, not wanting to complicate the situation inside. I might have been able to use magic to get inside, if we had at least half an hour to spare. My magic isn't the quick and dirty kind like you see in movies. It's more about the ritual and less about the flash bang.

Paul took care of it by breaking down the door.

By the way, you should know. Laura's door is the reinforced security kind with a heavy–duty deadbolt and a rugged frame. Paul went through it like it was a flimsy interior door. I've seen him do some pretty amazing stuff, and yet again, I was shocked at how strong he is.

We burst into the room, and I glanced around to take in the situation. It wasn't good, but it could have been worse.

Billy and the kid, still a wolf puppy, were facing off. Both were growling loudly, and the Lab was positioned in front of Laura's chair. His intent was clear. Move any closer to his mistress, and there would be trouble.

Laura's attention was split between Mary and the puppy. The companion's hand was raised, and she was pointing to the puppy. She was speaking as we burst in, "… told you there'd be trouble from associating with someone who's sold his soul to the Devil."

Huh, was she talking about me?

Before I had a chance to react, the puppy moved. He was fast. He dodged around Billy, and as soon as he had evaded the Lab, the puppy leaped. Directly at Mary. I felt helpless, unable to do anything.

The puppy yipped. I blinked. I hadn't even seen Runner move, but he had the puppy by the scruff of his neck. The pup struggled briefly and then hung, body limp.

Runner's eyes were still glowing gold, and he glared at the puppy, who wilted under the stare and began to whine pitifully.

I glanced at Paul, who had also moved past me, but not as fast as the werewolf. As I watched, his fangs receded, and he gave me a nod.

Almost everyone started talking at once.

Mary continued her rant about "unnatural creatures and people."

Laura was looking at the door in amazement and asking how we'd managed to break it down. At least she wasn't mad about it. Yet.

Paul wanted to know what had happened.

Billy barked at both Runner and the puppy and went to stand closer to Laura.

Runner and the puppy continued to glare at each other.

I sighed. Apparently it was my job to bring some order to the chaos. "Everyone! Quiet!"

Surprisingly, it worked. Everyone looked at me.

Ever felt like a bug under glass? Well, that was me right then. Paul gave me an encouraging grin, which heartened me to continue.

"Laura, you haven't met Runner yet. He's the other kind of werewolf, and he clued us in that the puppy might not be what we thought."

She nodded at him. Mary's expression was still hostile, but I ignored her. I turned to the two werewolves. "Runner, you've got the pup under control?"

He nodded. "Mind if I take him aside for a quiet chat?"

"Uh, yeah, sure." How exactly did he plan to talk to the puppy? I couldn't get him to talk in human form, much less animal. Maybe lycanthropes have a secret language.

Runner carried the puppy into the next room, and I left them to it.

"Laura, what happened?" I wanted to make some comment about "hadn't we told you not to upset the puppy," but my brain engaged in time to stop the words falling out of my mouth.

Laura took a deep breath and glared at her companion. From the look, I had to wonder how much longer Mary would have the job. "Everything was fine after you called. Billy and the puppy were playing, having a grand time. Then Mary came back."

Mary started to speak, but looks from both Paul and Laura silenced her.

"She saw the puppy and started yelling about unnatural creatures." I knew she was fine when she shot me a grin and a wink. "I think right as you … err … broke in."

"Sorry about that," Paul interjected.

Laura nodded. "Yeah, well, under the circumstances, I'm okay with it. Just, maybe knock next time?"

The vampire laughed. "Sure, the next time you're being threatened by a werewolf, I'll make sure to knock first."

She grinned back at him. "Yeah, you do that."

"Glad you two are bonding and all." I said. "But some of us want to know what happened."

"Right. So, as you all broke in, Mary had moved on from unnatural creatures to warlocks who make deals with devils."

I knew that expression. She wanted me to get all righteously indignant. Not that I wasn't tempted. It's kind of a sore point with me, but I refrained.

"So what set the puppy off? All the yelling?"

Laura raised her eyebrows. "Guess so. As soon as she started yelling, Billy and the puppy stopped playing. As she went on, I could see the puppy getting agitated." She shot her companion another dirty look. "I tried to get her to settle down, but she talked right over me."

I was sick of the dagger–like stares I was getting from Mary, so I turned to her and asked, "Okay, what's your side of the story?"

If anything, her expression hardened. "I've told Laura time and again that nothing good will come of her being friends with you, and look at what happened. She was nearly killed by that … that … creature."

"Actually, I think he was about to bite you, not Laura," I said. "But that still doesn't explain why you started yelling. You knew what he was when you left."

"She knew he was a werewolf?" Paul asked.

I nodded. "Yeah, which reminds me. How did you know anyway? I should have asked when I was here."

"It's none of your business," she snapped.

I was about to snap right back at her when Runner came into the room. "She knows because she is a were. We can smell others like us."

I blinked, and Mary shifted her stare from me to Runner, who just nodded at her. "Hello, Shifting Sands."

I suppressed a laugh. Yeah, that name described her pretty well. But, really, she was a lycanthrope? "Okay, if that's the case, how do you get off calling me unnatural?"

She sniffed but didn't answer.

Runner chuckled. "She's not a werewolf. She's a were serpent. They kind of consider themselves above the rest of us. Something about the serpent in Eden, though I'm not sure that recommends their kind."

I was getting more confused by the minute. Wasn't the serpent in Eden kind of the bad guy?

Mary's shoulders slumped under Runner's amused glance. "Our kind has long been associated with wisdom." She squared her shoulders and added, "Unlike your wolf kind which has always been associated with treachery and cruelty."

I waved a hand to cut her off. "Okay, enough. We're not here to debate scripture. You knew the kid was a werewolf, and you were okay leaving earlier. But when you get back, you go all ballistic."

An expression I'd never thought I'd see passed over

her face. Embarrassment. She cleared her throat and said, "I assumed earlier that he was of Runner's kind, a natural were. When I came back, I realized he was not. And I ... overreacted."

I'll say, but I didn't say it. Instead, I turned to Runner. "You're sure? He's infected."

The big were nodded. "Definitely." His eyes, not all the way back to brown yet, hardened. "And I need to find out who infected him. There is an unwritten code, even among their kind, to leave children alone. It's an abomination to infect a child."

Mary nodded. "That's why I assumed. It never even occurred to me."

I mentally ran back over our conversation earlier, and I realized something.

"What, Dafydd?" Paul asked. "I know that look."

I grinned. "Well, earlier, Mary called the kid a monster. I thought it was because he was a lycanthrope. But that wasn't it, was it?" I turned to her, and I felt my eyes sparkling. "It's because he was a wolf, right?"

She didn't answer in words. The look of disgust on her face said plenty.

Runner laughed heartily. Laura smiled, and even Billy seemed happier as the tension in the room eased.

I could hear the suppressed mirth in Paul's voice as he said, "Now we know what he is." His voice sobered. "But that doesn't answer who did this to the kid. Or why? Or what to do with him now."

Runner cleared his throat. "I don't have answers to the first two, but the last one is easy. My people will take him for now. We are immune to his infection, and we know how to take care of puppies. He'll be safe with us, and we can keep him from hurting anyone."

I nodded. It was a generous offer, and I was grateful. I wasn't equipped to take care of him. With Runner's people I didn't have to worry about the kid hurting anyone. "Thank you. I think that's a great idea. But it doesn't get us closer to finding his family."

Mary interrupted. "Why would you want to? He's dangerous. He should be put down."

I was ready to explode at her, but Paul was faster. "He's a child. I don't know about you, but I've never killed a child. I'm not about to start now."

Her expression was smug. "You're a vampire. We're supposed to believe that?"

Really, this was the kind of person taking care of my best friend?

Just then my best friend spoke up. Her voice was calm, but I could hear the steel in it. "Mary. You are fired. Get out now. I'll have your stuff packed up and sent to you. I don't want you here another minute."

Mary turned, her expression shifting from shock to scorn. She huffed. "You'll change your mind. Once these … creatures … show their true colors, you'll see."

Laura's expression never wavered. "The only true colors I see here are yours. Get out."

Mary gathered what was left of her dignity and left, her arrogance trailing her like a cloak. When she was gone, I felt the energy in the room shift and relax.

"I'm sorry," Laura said. "She wasn't like that before.

Sure, she's always been a bit difficult, but never like that. Never that cruel."

Paul shrugged. "It's not like I haven't heard it before."

Runner shook his head. "You couldn't have known. Her kind is often like that. Some are really good people, but others are fine only as long as they are in control. Take that away, and you see something different."

I glanced around, looking for the kid. Runner nodded toward the other room. "He's in there. He'll be fine until we leave."

"Uh, okay. How did you—" I trailed off, not even sure what I was asking.

He grinned. "I let him know I was alpha male, and we're fine. He'll stay put."

"Well, in that case, I guess the next thing is to figure out who and where his parents are. If they are werewolves too, that could be complicated."

Everyone nodded. Laura said, "If I can help with research, let me know."

Laura's kindness never ceases to amaze me. "Thanks. You know I'll take you up on that when we know what we're looking for."

"I can ask around," Runner added. "Like I said earlier, there's been some rumblings around about more werewolves than usual. I can try to figure out where they are and maybe where they are coming from."

"I can ask my sources as well," Paul offered. "The vampire community keeps on top of the weird stuff. They might have heard something. And they won't share with you." He nodded at Runner. "But they might with me."

I suddenly thought of a question to ask him later, when it was just the two of us. "I can ask around too, but I'm not sure what I'll come up with. Some of my friends believe vampires and werewolves exist and some don't, so I don't know if they'll know anything."

"You might be surprised," Paul said. "They might know something odd is going on without knowing what it is. If they give us some clues, we might be able to follow them someplace useful."

I nodded. "I'll ask around." And then kicked myself. "Uh, I guess I could also do a divination ritual." I'd been so distracted by everything that I'd ignored what should have been obvious to me.

Paul shot me a grin. "Yes, I guess you could do that. I mean, if it's not too much trouble for a warlock to actually do some magic."

I cheerfully flipped him off, and everyone laughed. "It's not my fault you all have been throwing all this stuff at me. Sure I knew lycanthropes existed and all, but it's a long way from theory to actually meeting you."

"It's not magic, but I can do some Internet search-es," Laura added. "The news might have the cause wrong but be reporting on events that might mean something to us."

"Good idea." Laura was good at digging stuff up and seeing patterns other people might miss. "When should we check in?"

"How about evening after next?" Runner suggested.

"My people are distracted tonight with the actual full moon. Tomorrow night, I'll have more luck getting information."

"I agree," Paul said. His expression grew abashed. "I'm afraid my people also take advantage of the full moon period. With all the other crazy things going on in the human world, a few vampire feedings can go unnoticed."

Another uncomfortable reminder that Paul hasn't been human for a long time.

"Works for me." I turned to Laura. "Okay if we meet here? Say 9:00 in the evening?"

Laura nodded. "That's fine. Um, anything I should have on hand? Like refreshments?"

Trust a woman to think of things like refreshments. Before I could say anything, Runner laughed heartily. "Yeah, sure. Have some O–positive on hand for the blood–sucker."

I glanced at Paul, not sure how he'd react to that. I needn't have worried. He had a huge grin spreading across his face, and he said, "Sure, as long as she stocks Wolf Chow for my flea–bitten buddy here."

We all had a good laugh.

"I was thinking more along the lines of soda and chips, but I'll keep the other things in mind for the future, if you'd like," Laura said.

We chatted for a few more minutes before I finally nodded toward the door. "I think that's enough for tonight. Runner, want to grab the kid?"

He headed toward the room where he'd left the

puppy and emerged a few moments later with a sleeping ball of fluff in his arms. He looked so cute, all limp with a tiny snore. It was hard to believe he could be a danger to everyone around him.

Runner smiled. "Don't worry. We'll take good care of him. If his parents aren't werewolves, we'll figure something out."

"And if they are?" I asked quietly.

He shrugged. "Then we'll still figure something out."

I nodded. "Hey, Laura. Can I borrow a pair of scissors? I need a bit of his fur for the ritual."

"Sure thing." She led me to the kitchen and indicated the correct drawer. I used the moment of us being alone to ask, "You going to be okay without Mary?"

She did her eyebrow shrug. "I'll manage. There's someone who fills in for her when she's on vacation. I'll call him and get him to help out until I can find a replacement."

I felt bad about being the cause of her needing to scramble. She must have seen my expression because she added, "And don't you dare feel guilty! You didn't make her like that. I'm glad to have found out sooner rather than later. I'm guessing from what your friend said, she'd have been trouble eventually."

"Yeah, but still—"

She didn't let me finish. "No, that's enough. It's not your fault, and I'll be fine."

"Can you get someone over here tonight to help out?"

"Absolutely."

"Okay." I still felt bad, but if she wasn't going to let me make a big deal out of it, I figured I'd better just get out so she could take care of herself.

I grabbed the scissors and a napkin to wrap the fur in, and we went back to the living room. Paul and Runner were talking quietly, but stopped when we entered. Nothing made me think the conversation was anything to worry about, so I didn't say anything and just snipped a bit of fur from the puppy, who didn't even move. Then I wrapped the fur in the napkin and put it all in my pocket.

Laura looked at me curiously. "I could give you a plastic baggie or something."

I shook my head. "Won't work. There's something in plastic that messes up the aura. Paper is better."

"Oh," she said. "I didn't know that."

I shrugged. "No reason you would have. Even cops keep some evidence in paper bags because plastic degrades stuff. I can't remember exactly what, but I know I read it somewhere."

I recognized the look on Laura's face. Internet research coming up. The next time I saw her, she'd know exactly what evidence could be bagged in plastic and what couldn't. I smiled to myself. She loves stuff like that. If I weren't careful, she'd probably also track down the basics of ritual magic. Good thing she can't actually set up a ritual. I wouldn't put it past her to try it out.

We said our goodbyes, and I led the way to the car. No one spoke on the trip back to Green Lantern. Paul settled the bill from earlier, and we left Runner and the kid there, repeating our agreement to meet two nights hence to share information. Hopefully, we'd all have something.

As soon as we pulled away from the curb and Paul turned in the direction of my apartment, he asked, "What's up?"

I blinked. "Why would you think something's up?"

He shrugged. "You want to ask me something. It's that look you get."

"What look is that?"

"The one where your brow all furrows up and you kind of turn away."

"Oh. That one." I never knew I had that look. But that might explain a lot about how Mom always knew when something was bothering me. Was it the same look she saw?

"Well?"

I sighed. "Yeah, okay, there was something I wanted to ask."

"Out with it, then."

I hesitated. He'd never volunteered too much about his kind, and I wasn't sure how he'd react. But he was looking at me with an impatient expression, and I decided it was better to ask so he'd turn back at the road.

"The other vampires. Do they know about you not killing?"

His eyebrow went up, and he didn't answer right away. When he finally did speak, he didn't answer my question. Instead he asked one of his own. "Is that really your question? Or did you really want to know where I stood with the rest of the vampire community?"

It's uncanny sometimes how he seems to know exactly what I'm thinking.

"Yeah, I guess that's really what I'm asking. Do they hate you? Or think you're weak? Or something like that?"

"Do you think I'm weak for not killing?"

"No way!" I admired him for his restraint. I didn't think we could be friends otherwise.

His smile was knowing. "Good to hear." He thought for a moment. "A couple of centuries ago it might have been a problem. Back then it was hard to get other sources of blood. Killing livestock almost garnered more attention than killing people."

Not a really nice way of looking at the past, but I thought I understood where he was coming from. Farming wasn't big agricultural companies back then. People knew most of their animals as individuals, and the only killers of livestock were predators or enemies.

"I guess I can see that."

"It's different now. Records are electronic. People notice when someone disappears. And death is investigated with science. It's hard for a vampire to make a clean kill as often as he'd like. So we all have to get by with alternate sources of blood. Bagged human blood, willing or unwilling donors or even animal blood in a pinch."

"So they don't think anything about you not killing?"

He laughed. "I wouldn't go so far as to say that. They don't agree in principle with my decision. Most of my kind will kill without hesitation if the opportunity presents itself. They are just careful to avoid anything that will get them caught or attract too much of the wrong kind of attention."

That was kind of what I'd thought. "Then how do you know you can get information? Won't they refuse to talk to you? Like on principle?"

Paul pulled into the alley behind my apartment and turned off the engine. "It's not quite like that. We have a sort of hierarchy. Based largely on age. I'm one of the oldest vampires in the city. That gives me a certain status. Even if they don't like me, they won't push me too far."

I opened my mouth to ask something else, but he held up a hand. "Enough. I'm sure you could ask questions all night."

Probably.

"But," he continued. "It's late, and it's been quite a night. Trust me that I can get information without being in danger from my kind. Good enough for now?"

I nodded. "Okay. Good night then."

"Good night, Dafydd."

I wasn't sure what the tone of his voice meant, but I didn't ask. I climbed out of the car and waved as he drove off. Then I sighed and went in my apartment.

The ferrets were delighted to see me, and I played with them for a little bit before heading to bed. Gimble nipped my feet to let me know she wasn't done playing yet, but I rounded them up and put them in their cage for the night.

Tomorrow was a big day. Obviously I needed to do the location spell and ask around to see if the psychics I knew had heard anything. But I also had a training meeting at the house of my business upline. I couldn't miss that. Some of my team needed a kick in the pants to get selling more.

Even warlocks have to make enough money to eat.

Chapter 3

Saturday, September 5, 2009:
early morning

BANGING IN THE ferret cage woke me the next morning. Gyre has a habit of beating the food bowl against the bars when she wants attention. Maybe they were out of water. I'd been busy the last couple of days, and I couldn't remember if I'd checked.

I groaned and rolled out of bed. Checking the clock, I saw it was 8:30. Damn! Barely enough time to get ready and over to Bob's house for the meeting.

I usually enjoy the meetings, and I had been particularly excited about this one. Our big company meeting and rally had been a couple of weeks ago. I hadn't had enough money to go, but Bob had gone, and I wanted to hear all about the new products and changes. There had been rumors for months about a change in the compensation structure. Anything that might get me more money was fine by me.

Today however, with everything going on now, I wished I could skip. I needed to buy some stuff for the ritual, and two late nights without enough sleep meant I had the beginnings of a pounding headache.

I downed an extra dose of vitamins with breakfast and a couple of Excedrin Migraine for good measure.

Just because I sell vitamins doesn't mean I completely ignore the other stuff.

After breakfast, I showered quickly, threw on old jeans and a plain white t–shirt, gathered up what I needed for the day in my backpack, scratched both ferrets behind the ears in goodbye and headed out.

The weather had been hot recently, even for early September, but today it was cooler. The sky was almost that perfect fall blue, and I felt both my spirits pick up and my headache start to recede. I sensed today was going to work out well.

Even the Metro cooperated. I made all my connections quickly (not always the case on the weekend), and I got off at the Mt. Vernon/UDC stop. Ironically, Bob's house is only a couple of blocks away from Paul's. I've been near his house for years and never even knew.

I walked quickly to Bob's house, and opened the gate to get to his basement apartment. As always, I wrinkled my nose at the odor of cat urine. Bob provides a sanctuary for a couple of feral cats. I said "hi" to Boyfriend, one of them. He meowed at me but declined to be petted, which is normal for him. I opened the door and went in without knocking. It's nice to have a standing invitation.

Bob is a character. Some drag queens are very convincing as women. Watching straight guys try to pick up some of my friends can be hilarious. The look of horror when they realize their mistake is usually priceless.

Bob is not convincing. Start with 6'3" hairy inches. Add about 40 pounds of extra weight and a five o'clock shadow that no amount of shaving can get rid of. Top it off with horrible fashion sense, and you've got a pretty good idea of what Bob looks like in a dress.

Today was no exception. The only thing about Bob that didn't look awful was his hair, pulled back into a neat ponytail. I'm not sure where he found a neon orange short skirt, but it should be burned. And matched with a pink sleeveless blouse? Really? No shoes, since he was home. A good thing. No telling what he'd select to go with that outfit.

But before you think Bob is a buffoon or a fool, he's not. He's got one of the sharpest business minds I know. When he's meeting with potential customers or distributors, he cleans up *very* well. His suits are all perfectly tailored and not the slightest bit feminine. He's also one of the kindest, most generous people I know.

I've learned a lot about business from him, and I attribute most of my success to his coaching. Sales skills don't come naturally to me, and Bob has been most patient in teaching me and helping me close some tough customers.

His attire told me the only people attending today would be current team members. If we were expecting any prospects, he would have dressed appropriately. I relaxed, and my headache receded a bit more.

"Hey, Dafydd. Glad you're early. I could use some help setting up. Any chance you could magic up a spirit to clean up the place?"

Did I mention Bob knew about me?

I grinned. "Not my area, Bob, but I can use mundane means to help."

He smiled, and we started moving around the living room, tidying. Bob's not too messy, and it didn't take long. After it was clean enough, I helped him set out trays of snacks on the low coffee table.

Bob's apartment was pretty nice. The living room was big enough to fit a good-sized couch and four sling-back chairs like mine—I got the idea from him. It's got a couple of cozy book shelves, a cherry end table by the couch and a basket overflowing with magazines he never seems to have enough time to read.

By the time the food was set out, the rest of the people started to arrive.

Abby, predictably, was first. She's just a bit younger than my mom and dresses well. Today was no exception. Her neat pantsuit made her look more professional than she is. Granted, she's always excited about training and learning new things. If only she were so enthusiastic about implementing what she learned.

"Hey, Abby. I noticed you came pretty close on orders. Nice job rallying the team." Okay, pretty close was being very kind. She'd barely made it half-way to the orders she'd needed for the week. Bob shot me an amused smile.

"Well, it wasn't bad, but if only my new team members had made the orders they'd committed to, it would have been a lot better. Hey, did I tell you about the new attraction training I signed up for?"

I sighed. Here we go again. A new training to distract her. And attraction-based at that. I knew this song and dance. Think positively, and everyone you want will "magically" come to you. Come on! I do real magic, and I know better.

I forced myself to be positive. I've learned not to comment too much on Abby's latest seminar craze. "Sounds good, Abby. But don't forget the goal setting you and I talked about last week. If you break it down into daily chunks, you'll get there in no time."

A couple of other people arrived: Sally and Bill, one of Bob's most successful associate pairs. Unlike Abby, they actually do work instead of talking about it. We chatted for a few minutes. I always get good ideas from them, and tonight was no exception. They've been trying social media, and they were excitedly telling me about a new associate they just found through Twitter.

Social media to me is like magic to you mundane folks. I don't get how it works, but everyone tells me it does. I've pretty much ignored it until now, except for a personal Facebook page to keep up with my large, far–flung family.

Bill was just explaining about something called a "hash tag," when the door opened and someone new walked in. I caught the movement out of the corner of my eye and turned to look.

Then I looked again. And wished I'd paid more at-tention to what I was wearing. At least the jeans were tight and showed off my butt.

The newcomer was dressed very simply in light wash blue jeans, artfully ripped along the left thigh and a tight blue t–shirt with an American Eagle logo. I knew the shirt well since I had two of them at home in that exact shade of blue. He was just under six feet tall and couldn't have weighed more than 130 pounds, from the look of it all slim muscle. I guessed he was a swimmer, definitely not a weight lifter. Everything was lean and long instead of bunchy.

His brown hair was worn long and casually tied back. When I say "casually," I mean it probably only took him 15 minutes to get it in that pony tail. Well-sculpted cheek bones and lively brown eyes completed the picture.

Bob saw him come in and hurried over. "Everyone, this is Stephen. He's my newest associate, and I'd like you to welcome him."

Abby barely gave him a glance while Bill and Sally surrounded him in their usual inviting welcome. I hung back, suddenly shy. Bob gave me a wink and said, "Come on, Dafydd. Not like you to hide when a gorgeous young guy enters the room."

He turned to Stephen. "Dafydd's single and looking, aren't you, honey?"

I murmured something even I couldn't hear and stepped forward to shake Stephen's hand. His grip was sure and solid, but not too firm. It might have been my imagination, but I thought he gave my hand an extra squeeze as he let go.

Bob grinned proudly at both of us, and I made a note to get even later. Ever since my last boyfriend left me, Bob had made it his goal to get me hooked up again. This was the third guy he'd run past me, though I had to give him credit this time. Stephen was the best yet, definitely my type. I'd have to see where this might go.

"All right, everyone. Grab some food and a seat. I've got lots of great stuff from the convention to go over. We've got exciting new products and a new compensation plan which you're all going to love!"

Bill and Sally took a couple of chairs next to each other. Abby started for the couch, but Bob artfully redirected her to another chair. That left the couch for me and Stephen, who gave me a wry grin as he sat down. I sighed, and took my place, accepting for the moment that Bob would not be distracted from his match–making.

So much for being excited about the new material from the conference. Sitting beside Stephen was completely distracting. I could feel his body heat, and smell some delightful cologne. Had Bob tipped him off that I'd be here? Not many people wore cologne to these meetings. Or was that just his way?

I spent most of the meeting running over possible ways to ask him out.

"Want to grab some coffee and talk over the new compensation plan?" Way too lame!

Perhaps *"Want to grab some coffee and then grab my ass?"* Tempting, but probably too much for a first meeting.

As it turned out, I needn't have worried about it. As soon as Bob ran out of news, and everyone started to leave, Stephen turned to me. "Want to grab some coffee sometime?"

Yeah, that worked. Why hadn't I thought of that

one?

"Um, sure. I'd really like that." Easy, Dafydd. Not too eager. "Text me when you're free?"

He smiled, warm and inviting, and we exchanged phone numbers. Then he left, and I hung around to help Bob clean up.

"What do you think, honey? Isn't he absolutely perfect?"

I felt the blush rise all the way to my forehead. "Uh, yeah. He seems pretty nice."

"Pretty nice? He's gorgeous. And he just broke up with the most obnoxious twink. Horrible the way it went down. So you're just what he needs right now. I think you two will get along fabulously."

"Yeah, thanks, Bob." I knew if I stayed around longer, I'd be treated to a list of Stephen's best features, in Technicolor if I weren't careful. Not that Bob really knew that much detail, but that never stopped him from making stuff up. And he was strangely accurate most of the time.

So I made my excuses and escaped. Walking back to the Metro, I thought hard. Did I want a relationship right now? I was so over the last guy, but there was a lot going on in my life right now. Did I have time? And what about Paul? What would he think?

I stopped that line of thought immediately. Yeah, I was attracted to the vampire. Who wouldn't be? Strong. Handsome. Good dresser. Mysterious. And with that aura of danger that surrounded him, even though he didn't kill good people any more. But he'd given me definite signs of playing on the other team, and I didn't want to wait for something that would never happen.

Yeah, I'd go out with Stephen. Even if it went nowhere, it'd be fun. And I needed some normal fun in my life.

Just then the phone rang. I looked at the display.

PAUL

Great timing. "Hey, what's up?"

It was early afternoon, and the sun was still high, so I knew he hadn't been out yet.

"Just wondering if you've found anything yet?"

"Not yet. I just finished a meeting. I'm off to buy the supplies for the ritual. I should know something in, oh, six hours or so."

"Oh, I thought you'd have done that by now." I could almost hear the frown in his voice, and it irritated me. Who was he to judge how I spent my time?

"I told you I had a meeting I had to go to first." I could hear the snap in my voice, but I didn't tone it down.

A long pause. "Oh. Sorry. I guess I thought the meeting was with your psychic friends."

I sighed. "No, it was for my business. I do have a life outside of chasing down bad guys, you know. Some of us have to work for a living."

I felt bad as soon as I said it. Tracking down werewolves was important. Paul wasn't wrong about that.

"Sorry," I said. "I'm done with it now, and I'll get right on the ritual. Tomorrow I'll hit up the Psychic network for information. I'm sure I'll have something to report when we all meet tomorrow night."

"Okay. And hey, sorry if I came off too strong. I guess I do forget you have a day job. It's been a long time since I did, and I don't really remember what it was like."

I smiled. Probably not. And I doubted my job was anything like what he used to do. "No problem. I'll give you a call when I finish the ritual, okay?"

"Yes, I'll be up."

We hung up, and I hurried the rest of the way to the Metro. Just enough time to get supplies and get back to my place before sunset. Might as well take advantage of the extra magical power.

D.C. DOESN'T HAVE a proper magic shop. New York has the best. Since one of my sisters lives in the city, I make a point of going at least once a year to pick up supplies and visit family.

For regular stuff, most of what I need can be found in Chinatown. I've learned over the years to make substitutions, and usually they work out fine. Sure, the purists would cringe at using Chinese herbs instead of Western, but my focus is on "does it work?" instead of "is it traditional?"

I got off the train at the Chinatown station and headed a few blocks to my favorite store.

The bell above the door tinkled cheerily as I entered. The wizened proprietor glanced up and smiled at me. I paused for a moment to inhale the spicy mélange of herbs and spices. Ah, that must be a fresh shipment of ginger. I made a mental note to pick up some.

"Hello, Dafydd. What you need today?"

I handed him my list, and he looked it over, clucking at some of the items. "What you doing this time, eh?"

I shrugged. I don't know if he believes I do real magic, but he always asks, and I always tell him. "Pretty basic divination to find someone's parents, Mr. Lin."

He gave me a sharp look at that. "With wolfsbane?"

"It's kind of a long story."

He grinned toothlessly. "And you in big hurry right now. You come back and tell me how it work out, okay?"

"Sure thing." Suddenly it occurred to me that Mr. Lin always seemed to keep on top of things happening in the neighborhood. He'd be good to ask about strange occurrences, but I wasn't sure how to ask without mentioning werewolves? He seemed tolerant of my magic, but that didn't mean he believed in the supernatural.

Mr. Lin puttered about the store, gathering my stuff.

I took a stab. "Hey, I was wondering. Has there been any trouble around here? You know, more violence? Unexplained attacks? That sort of thing?"

The old man turned around from the shelf where he was bagging some sandalwood chips. "Why you ask?"

I shrugged casually. "Oh, I'd just heard about some stuff happening near me, and I wondered if it was just my neighborhood, or if it was everywhere."

He shook his head. "Not near here, but my grandson say there have been threats against shop owners over on 14th."

I perked up. "What kind of threats?"

"He not say exactly. But apparently someone wants to tear down small shops and build big ones." He shook his head. "No good for business. Plenty large shops in city. Need more like mine. People like."

I smiled, trying to envision buying what I needed in Pentagon City or Tyson's Corner. "Yeah, I know what you mean."

He handed me a bag with my stuff. It smelled bitter, and I frowned. It wasn't right. These ingredients should smell earthy and rich. I usually get a feeling from the very first stages of a ritual, even just from buying the ingredients. Something here wasn't right.

Mr. Lin must have noticed my frown because he asked, "Something wrong, Dafydd?"

I glanced through the bag. "Are you sure you gave me the right stuff?" I was thinking more about what was wrong than my tone of voice. Many shopkeepers would have taken offense at my implication that they'd made a mistake, but Mr. Lin just took my list and dumped out the contents of the bag.

We compared. Everything was there and correct, including the ginger I'd smelled earlier. "That's funny," I said. "Something's not right, but you gave me everything I asked for."

"Are you sure ingredients are right?"

I was sure. Location rituals are my bread and butter.

You take something that forms a link to what you are trying to find. The principles of sympathetic magic say that if you establish the link properly, you can find anything. I had the kid's fur, which has his DNA. His DNA should form a link to his parent's, which would allow me to create the finding through the ritual. Hey, science and magic aren't completely incompatible, you know.

I ran through the formula again. "Yeah, I also need bay leaf, but I've got plenty of those at home. A missing bay leaf shouldn't make it smell like this." I shook my head. "I don't know why, but I don't think the spell's going to work."

I straightened up. "But I still need to try." I made my voice confident. "And you've given me everything I need."

I paid Mr. Lin and thanked him. "I'll let you know how it works out."

He nodded, and I left to return home and try the ritual. I hoped it would worked.

RITUALS CAN BE tricky things. You have to set everything up just right, use the correct ingredients and apply your will appropriately. It's not strictly necessary to have magical talent to perform a ritual, but if you don't have talent, you need to substitute something for the missing power. Certain times of day, and days of the year, have inherent power, and the non–talented can perform working rituals at those times. Why do you think Wiccans do their magical workings at Samhain or the solstices? There's power at the turning of the seasons.

There are other ways to create ritual power, but I don't recommend blood magic. Sure, it works, but blood magic is dangerous. Someone or something has to die to create enough power for big workings, and, as a white warlock, I'm duty bound to hunt you down and bring you to justice. Besides, killing is just wrong.

If you're like me and have magical talent, you can perform rituals any time, and they will work, assuming you did everything right. Even so, I like to take advantage of powerful times. The ritual will take less out of me and probably be even more effective. So there was every reason for me to take advantage of sunset.

Why are sunrise and sunset powerful times of day? They are times of change. During times of change, the barrier between our world and the world of spirit is weaker, allowing energy to seep through to our world. Ritual magic allows us to harness that power and direct it to do what we want.

Once, when I was telling Laura about rituals, she asked a great question. "If rituals are just a way to direct power, and you've got power available, why do you need all the ingredients?"

I'd been impressed because it was one of the first questions I asked my dad when he started teaching me magic.

My dad told me that technically, the ingredients aren't needed. If you have enough power, a strong will and complete focus on the outcome, you can do ritual magic without all the trappings.

Very few, maybe only a handful in history, have ever been strong enough and sufficiently focused to make that work.

For normal ritual casting, the ingredients have symbolic meaning. For example, I planned to use a magnet as a symbolic link to what's missing. St. John's Wort is a good herb for divination (in other words, it's good for helping to find stuff). Mugwort helps enhance magical power, and sandalwood chips are the best thing I know for granting wishes. It's not that any of the ingredients have power in and of themselves. It's their symbolic meaning that gives us the means to focus our will and make things happen.

I'm probably not explaining it well. Laura gave me some pretty odd looks when I tried to tell her about ritual magic. What can I say? Teaching isn't in my blood. It was one of Dad's gifts that he didn't pass on to me.

I could certainly have performed this ritual in the middle of the day. Finding rituals are pretty basic, but something about this one had me on edge. Like the ingredients not smelling right, which is never a good sign. So I figured taking advantage of the extra power at sunset seemed prudent. Finding the kid's parents was important. I didn't want to mess around with doing this thing twice.

As soon as I got home, I let the ferrets out for a quick romp while I prepared. For obvious reasons, they'd need to be caged when I actually did the magic.

While they tore up the living room, I went into the

tiny second bedroom to get set up. Affording even a postage stamp–sized second bedroom strained my finances, but I needed someplace I could close off and keep just for magic to prevent influences and energies that could get in the way of magical workings. Don't believe me? Try concentrating in a room where you just had a big fight with your spouse. Pretty tough, isn't it? Stuff in the room reminds you of the fight. It's easier to focus someplace else.

Using a room just for magic means that the only memories and energies in the room are about magic. That's important when you're throwing around power like I do.

I closed the door behind me just in time to stop Gimble charging in. She's convinced the ferret equivalent of the Holy Grail is behind this door, but ferrets and magic do not mix.

There's not much in this room. Just a small altar, a couple of boxes of stuff, two shelves with books, a work table and a small rug.

The rug is one of my most prized possessions, partly because Mom made it for me but mostly because it makes my working so much easier. Magic requires a circle to keep out energies and influences that might interrupt my ritual. Most warlocks have a permanent circle set up in their working room. Dad has one in the basement which was made of silver permanently embedded in the floor. Seriously cool, and pretty expensive. Mom had to sell a lot of makeup to afford that.

I live in a rented apartment, and my landlord has

been very cool about ferrets, but I figured he'd draw the line at me etching a permanent circle in the spare bedroom. When I moved in, I'd casually asked about painting. He thought I meant the walls, but he still said no. So for a couple of years, I used chalk to draw my circle each time, which was a major pain.

Then three years ago Mom gave me the rug for Solstice (we don't celebrate Christmas). It's black with a silvery white circle. Best present I ever got. I'm still trying to figure something even close to give back to her.

Preparing for a ritual is almost as important as the actual performance. First, the ritual space needed to be clean. I'm so glad I live in the 21st century. Vacuum cleaners are so much easier than brooms. I paid special attention to the rug because the ritual circle needs to be unbroken. I once flubbed a working because I hadn't vacuumed carefully enough and left some fluff on the circle. Nothing bad happened, but I was pissed that I had to do the entire ritual over again.

When I had everything spotless, I laid out the ingredients and ritual tools on the altar. They're pretty much what you'd expect. I have two knives, one with a white handle and one with a black. The black–handled knife is an *athame*, and it's used to direct energy. The white–handled knife is the one I use for cutting and slicing ingredients during the ritual. Candles, a saucer and a small cast–iron cauldron completed my tools.

I arranged the ritual ingredients on the saucer, ready to be chopped, burned or waved around. Finally, I grabbed a laminated map of D.C. and laid it out on the floor next to the altar.

Once everything was set up, I carefully opened the door and went back into the living room. Luckily, Gyre was dragging Gimble across the room by her neck, and the white ferret was too distracted to try to make a break for the magic room.

I broke up the tussle and tossed them in their cage, with a few raisins as a bribe. They took the bribe but still shot me dirty looks. I promised them a good run later and headed for the bathroom for a cleansing bath.

Yes, ritual purification is a part of the process. Dad insists that showers work perfectly well, but I always draw a hot bath. Sitting in the tub and relaxing in the warm water is as important for me as actually getting clean.

Dad says you can't ever get properly clean in a tub, sitting in soapy, dirty water, but it works for me. And I cheat. After soaping up and washing, I drew a second bath for the final cleanse.

Bath done, I dried off with a fluffy white towel I keep just for these occasions. I don't use the washer for it. Hand washing only. And I store it in my ritual room. Probably overkill, but it works for me.

Naked, I padded to my bedroom to put on my robe. Yes, we really do wear robes. Well, except for the warlocks who do their workings "skyclad." You know what that means, right? If not, try Wikipedia.

My robe is deep red and very soft. It's made of a kind of velour material, but it's not tacky. Also a gift from my mom. I'm not sure exactly what she made it from, but it's warm and rich. Putting it on always makes me feel good. It's soft against my skin and puts me in the right mood to perform.

And yes, before you ask, I only wear it for ritual magic. I have another robe for when I'm performing in other arenas.

All the set–up done, I was ready to do the ritual. I felt so good and ready that even the bad omen at the store seemed minor. This was going to work and work well. I knew it.

I checked my internal sense. I was right on schedule. Sunset was in about 15 minutes, which was plenty of time to cast the circle and make my final preparations.

<hr />

AS I WENT from my bedroom to my work room, Gimble gave me a dirty look, but I ignored her. Negative energy from a ferret isn't enough to stop a working.

I closed the door behind me and took a deep breath. Like I've said, working magic is as much a frame of mind as the right use of tools. I checked my altar one last time. Everything was in place. It's a real bummer to have closed the circle and be half–way through a working only to realize you're missing something.

The first step of any ritual is to close the circle. It allows a warlock to focus his energy, and it keeps out negative influences. My teachers work with a modified Wiccan formula, so if you're familiar with that, you'll recognize some of the stuff.

I started by placing white candles at the compass

points. Even though the circle is outlined on the carpet, it's still helpful to light the candles. Sort of focuses everything.

I lit a smaller, white candle at the altar and took a moment before the altar, calming my thoughts. Then I leaned to the eastern candle, lit it with the small candle and said, "Here I call forth the power of air that I may be unfettered and pure."

Next, I lit the southern candle and said, "Here I call forth the power of fire, that I may endure all hardships to become strong."

Moving to the western candle, I invoked more power and said, "Here I call forth the power of water that I might support and protect all that I encounter."

Finally, the northern candle. "Here I call forth the power of Earth, that I may be grounded at all times."

All the candles burned with a soft light, and I was ready to complete the circle. I closed my eyes, gathering my will and visualizing a soft light around me. As I concentrated, the light of the candles melted together, forming an actual light around me. The circle was almost closed. I sent my will into the light surrounding me and said, "Welcome Air, Fire, Water, Earth. Shine your light and lend your strength to this my circle tonight. Now is my circle cast, unbreakable and without harm. Thus is sacred space decreed, and no act goes unnoticed. So mote it be."

If you've ever cast a Wiccan circle, you probably noticed that I skipped some steps. That's because, I've got the power to actually close the circle instead of only doing it symbolically. That allows me to cut to the chase, if you will, draw on the power and make it happen.

Circle cast, I could feel a soft thrumming of power around me. Outside sounds were muted, and the thrum seemed to settle in my bones, soothing away small aches and pains from my battle with the creature yesterday morning. I was ready to move on to the actual finding ritual.

I lit two more candles on the altar, one black (for solving mysteries) and one orange (for luck, which I figured I'd need since my link to the boy's parents was indirect). I put the bay leaf, the St. John's Wort, wolfsbane and mugwort on the small plate and got out a sandalwood chip. Oh, and a stub of pencil.

I lit the bay leaf and put it in the cauldron to smolder. The smoke heightens clairvoyant powers.

Then I mixed the St. John's Wort, wolfsbane and mugwort together on the plate and slowly chanted:

Bound and Binding
Binding Bound
See the Sight
Hear the Sound
What was lost now is found
Bound and Binding
Binding Bound

Then I carefully unwrapped the boy's fur from the napkin and rubbed it three times over the magnet.

Finally, I wrote "parents" with the stub of pencil on the sandalwood chip and lit it with the flame from the black candle. I tossed the chip into the cauldron to burn with the bay leaf.

So far everything I'd done was within the ability of a non–talented practitioner. Now it was time for the actual "magic" to begin. First, I reached out with my senses to feel the approaching sunset. I'd timed it perfectly, and the surge of power was no more than seconds away. It's hard to describe exactly what I did. I touched the power from the outside and drew it in, mixing it with the energy within me. I felt energized and ready. Once I had it gathered and under my control, I prepared to use it.

Focusing my will on the flame of the black candle, I visualized a man and a woman. They both had brown hair and eyes, like the boy, and they were smiling, arms open, as if to welcome a loved one.

I placed the magnet between the two candles and stroked it towards me as I recited,

By the wavering flame of this black light,
Grant to me of lost parents a sight.
By the power of this orange flame,
Give me luck to find the same.
On this map, their location I see
Make the magnet draw them to me.

I put down the magnet, and, still concentrating on my vision of the parents, I took the orange candle and held it over the map, moving it back and forth slowly. I shaped the power within me and concentrated on the link between the boy and his parents. After a moment, I felt something. It wasn't what I'd expected. I'd anticipated feeling a burst of life energy as I made the link. What I got instead was a blast of gray light in my vision. As I blinked to clear it, the candle dropped a blob of wax onto the map.

I sighed and sat back on my heels. I hadn't expected that. Now I knew where his parents were, but the blast of gray light meant they were dead.

I carefully marked the location on the map with a grease pencil. Then I extinguished the smoldering sandalwood and bay leaf. I pinched the orange and black candles with my fingers to put them out.

Finally, I turned my attention to the circle. I raised my *athame* and drew in the power. Then I thanked the guardians for their service. I pinched out the candles in the reverse order of lighting them and chanted:

North. "I release the power of Earth and thank you for the grounding you gave this working."

West. "I release the power of Water and thank you for your support and protection in this working."

South. "I release the power of Fire and thank you for the strength and endurance you granted the working this evening."

East. "I release the power of Air and thank you for the purity you brought to this working."

I felt the power settle in me, reviving my spirits from the disappointment of learning about the deaths. I took a deep breath and concluded with, "Farewell Earth, Water, Fire and Air. Your light shone on this working, and protected my circle. Thus is sacred space released and no act went unnoticed. So mote it be."

With that, the ritual was ended.

I gathered up all the materials I had used and put everything away. I had expected to feel a sense of urgency when I was done, wanting to find the boy's parents and arrange a joyful reunion. Now, I was left with telling him his parents were dead and that he was now an orphan.

Coming as I did from a large, loving family, I couldn't even imagine what that would be like.

As I put things away, and the peace and goodwill of completing a ritual faded, I found myself growing angry. I didn't know who had bitten the kid. From some of Runner's comments, I was starting to wonder if there was more to this and if someone was behind the increase in werewolf activity. Was that same person responsible for the kid's parents dying? Had he (or she) or a minion murdered them?

I'd never thought of myself as a vigilante. I guess that's more Paul's thing: keeping the bad werewolves off the street and the like, but right now I wanted to have a direct part in righting a wrong. I'd never felt this way before, but something burned hot inside me.

It was time to call Paul and tell him what I knew.

Chapter 4

Saturday, September 5, 2009:
just after sunset

I CHANGED OUT of my robe and into jeans and a t-shirt. I also let the ferrets out of their cage. They danced around me, and their antics calmed my mood. A bit. I was still angry, but I was calm enough to see that doing anything hasty would likely just make things worse. We still needed more information, and my network of psychics might know something.

But right now, finding the bodies of the kid's parents might yield even more.

I called Paul, and he picked up quickly.

"Hey."

"Hey, yourself." I could hear loud music in the background. "Where are you? Sounds loud."

He chuckled and said, "I'm at Lounge 201, seeing if any of my people know anything. It's Saturday night. What do you expect in a bar?"

"Yeah, okay. Heard anything useful?"

"Not too much. But it's still early. Mostly just young ones here now. The old vampires don't usually show up until later."

I checked the time. Just after eight. Early for vampires, maybe.

"What about you?" he asked. "Anything from the ritual?"

I must have paused too long because he said, "What? You found something, didn't you?"

"Yeah. I found his parents. Only thing is, they're dead."

"Oh." His voice was grave. "How can you tell?"

I shrugged, even though I knew he couldn't see it. "I just know, okay. It's how the energies came back."

"Do you know where the bodies are?"

"Yep. Want to go take a look?"

"Definitely. I'll be right over. See you in a bit."

He hung up, and I went to grab a jacket and few other things. I recognized the area I'd marked on the map, and it wasn't the nice part of town. I figured having a couple of potions on hand, just in case, would be a good idea.

I'VE LEARNED THAT with Paul "right over" means exactly that, so I wasn't surprised when, less than fifteen minutes later, I heard a car pull up. I grabbed the map I'd used during the ritual and stepped outside to see Paul's red Prius. His car always made me smile, even with everything bad happening.

When I'd first met the vampire, I'd figured him for driving something large and black, with a huge trunk in case he got stuck somewhere close to dawn. His car was pretty much the opposite of everything I'd imagined. He said it was a chick magnet which, if I weren't convinced that he didn't drink human blood, would be disturbing. As it was, it was just Paul.

I hopped in the car. Paul, as usual, was dressed—if you'll pardon the phrase—to kill. He had a black silk shirt, casually unbuttoned to about the mid–point of his chest, white slacks and a tailored white blazer. His black hair was neatly trimmed and gelled into place. I'd never seen the length of his hair change, and I wondered if he was just obsessive about getting it cut or if vampire hair just stayed the same length all the time.

Motioning to his slacks, I asked, "Getting in your last couple of days to wear white slacks?"

When he answered his voice was serious, but I caught a faint hint of amusement in his eyes. "Of course. Labor Day is Monday. Even vampires know that rule." The amusement left his eyes. "So what did you get?"

I unfolded the map and pointed to the spot where the candle wax had dripped. I had circled it in red grease pencil. "Right here."

Paul humphed. "Nasty part of South East."

I was pleased to note that he didn't ask me if I was sure about the location. I liked that he trusted my abilities. To this day, some people who'd known me for years were always suspicious when I said I'd found something or that, yes, you really do have a ghost in your apartment.

I nodded. "Yeah, I brought a couple of things along, just in case."

He cocked an eyebrow at me.

"You know. Potions."

He nodded. "As long as you're not going to shrink me again."

He'll never let me live that down, will he?

"What do you think we'll find there?"

I settled back in the seat as he pulled away from the curb. "I'm not sure. Obviously, I hope I'm wrong about them being dead, but—"

"You're probably not." His voice sounded sad. "I'd been afraid that's what you'd find."

That stirred my interest. "What have you found out?"

He sighed. "Not as much as I'd like. The younger vampires don't pay much attention to anything outside their circle. Young ones are usually concerned with their looks, getting away with the occasional kill and moving up in the pecking order."

"You make them sound like a bunch of homicidal high school students."

He glanced over and gave me a quick grin. "That's not too far off, actually."

Once again, I was glad I'd been home–schooled. A kid like me would not have fared well in a traditional high school.

"So what did they notice, other than the latest fashions?"

"I was able to confirm Runner's story that there's increased werewolf activity. Most vampires and lycanthropes get along about as well as cats and dogs. The young ones were quite contemptuous of the 'amount of wet dog smell' in town."

Make that *snooty*, homicidal high school students.

Yeah, I know I shouldn't be cracking jokes while we were driving to find dead bodies, but I couldn't help myself. My sense of humor, twisted as it is, gets me through stuff like this.

"Why'd that make you think the kid's parents are dead?" I asked.

"Because I've seen this sort of thing once before. A long time ago."

Silence. That didn't surprise me. Paul was practically phobic about talking about stuff from his past.

I gently prompted him. "What happened back then?"

He sighed and shifted lanes. The buildings outside the window were looking shabbier. I didn't get into this part of town much. Even with the car windows up, the air started to smell funky, sort of a combination of stale beer and mold. I was glad I wasn't alone.

The vampire finally spoke. "It was in the early 1900s. I was in Chicago, right around the time of Prohibition." He glanced at me. "You do know what that was, right?"

I snorted. "Yeah. I did study at least a bit of history."

He looked abashed. "Sorry. It seems like schools teach less and less history the older I get."

I could sympathize. The other reason I'd been home–schooled was that Mom had no faith in the public education system.

"Anyway, one of the mobsters found out about werewolves. I never could track down how. He used them as muscle, but he didn't have very good control over them. Sometimes they'd leave their victims alive to come back as wolves. And sometimes they'd just go on a killing spree and leave lots of bodies behind."

I didn't want to think too long on the images that generated.

"The mobster was on his way to becoming a major player on the Chicago mob scene. Al Capone wouldn't have been able to touch him. It was getting ugly on the streets. People were dying. No one knew how. Bodies would just show up, chewed like they'd been killed by animals. People started shooting stray dogs, and then even dogs that weren't strays. The town was on its way to a major panic."

"What did you do?"

He looked at me sharply. "What makes you think I did anything? I wasn't hunting evil doers at the time."

I snorted. "An environment like that would be bad for vampires. Sure, you could hide your kills in the general mayhem for a while. But, if the humans got panicked enough, well, I don't know what the Roaring Twenties equivalent of a mob of torch–wielding peasants looked like, but I bet you didn't want to find out."

He smiled grimly. "Pretty much. The older vampires bullied the younger ones into taking action. We started killing werewolves and eventually found the mobster who'd started it all. He just disappeared one night, and it was over."

"Funny. I don't remember reading about that in the history books."

"Not surprised. There's a lot that didn't make it into your books."

I looked over, the tone of his voice intriguing me. In the dim light from passing street lamps, I could just make out his features. Something about them looked haunted, and I wondered exactly what he was thinking about that hadn't made the history books.

I was about to ask when he pulled over to park by the side of the road.

"We're here. Let's see if we can find those bodies."

When we got out of the car, I wrinkled my nose. Every city has bad areas, and D.C. is no exception to the rule. The stale beer odor I'd smelled in the car was even stronger here, along with an undertone that seemed to scream "crime and poverty."

I noticed that Paul's body was tense, and his eyes swept back and forth in a scanning pattern. I stayed close to him, confident he could handle most anything here.

"Let me see the map," he said. I handed it over. The dim light didn't seem to bother him. He looked at it closely, then lifted his head. It took me a moment to realize he was sniffing the air. Okay, that was gross. Especially here.

"Anything?" I asked him, forcing my voice to stay cool.

He nodded. "This way, I think. I smell death, and it's fairly recent." He started off, and I hurried to follow.

He smelled death? This was definitely not my first choice. I get weirded out watching *Bones*, and this sounded like it was going to be a lot more up close and personal than seeing something on TV. Of course I couldn't admit to that, so I tried to walk like I looked for bodies every day.

As we approached the looming sides of a building that looked identical to all the other buildings, I wondered how their owners told them apart. Paul spoke, and I stifled a startled jump. "Don't worry. I won't think less of you if you throw up when you see the bodies."

"Huh? No way. I'm cool." Something clanged in the distance, and I couldn't stop an instinctive flinch. I peered through the gloom. Was that something moving over there?

Paul chuckled. "Sure, you're cool. That's why your heartbeat is over 120 a minute, and you're breathing heavy while trying not to smell anything. Not to mention jumping at the sound of a raccoon knocking over a trash can lid."

Was that what it had been? Suddenly I felt foolish. "Oh. Okay, yeah. I've never seen a dead body before." Well, there was my great–aunt Mildred who had insisted on an open–coffin service. And ghosts don't count. They don't smell. "Outside of a funeral home, at least."

He put a hand on my shoulder. "It's okay. The first time it's horrible."

"And then I get used to it?" Surely not.

Paul glanced around before answering. As he spoke, he strode confidently in the direction of a building. "No, you never get used to it. At least, not if you're a normal human."

I drew myself up to my complete 5'6" height. "I'm a warlock. By definition, not normal."

His voice sounded absent. "Well, if you put it that

way." Suddenly he held up a hand and stopped.

I could smell it. Even thought I'd never seen, or smelled, a dead body, I knew what that sickly–sweet odor had to be. Sort of a mixture of the coppery stench of blood mixed with shit and rancid garbage. Dinner threatened to come back up, and I started to hold my breath.

"Don't," Paul said.

"Don't what?"

"Hold your breath. Just breathe it in, slowly. In a few minutes you'll get used to the smell. If you hold your breath, it'll take longer."

Words of wisdom from a vampire. I guessed he knew what he was talking about, so I breathed in slowly, talking firmly to my stomach the whole time. I hoped he was right. The stench was awful.

Paul took a few steps forward, and I followed. The smell grew stronger, and I was sure I was going to have to throw up. Even though he said it was normal to feel this way, I desperately wanted to maintain control. For some reason, being more than normal in his eyes was important.

"Got a light?" Paul asked.

"Huh?" The question distracted me from my rebellious stomach.

"A flashlight? I think this is it."

Oh great. As it happens, I do keep a flashlight on my key ring, but if I handed it over, I'd have to look at the bodies. Sight plus smell might be more than my stomach could handle right now. I wasn't about to admit that to the vampire, so I gave him my key ring.

He clicked the small light, and illuminated two bodies a few feet away. I felt dinner start to come up, and I firmly set my will to keeping it down. Come on. I can cast spells. Mastering a rebellious stomach should be a piece of cake, by comparison.

On second thought, that wasn't the best analogy to use right now.

Somehow I managed to keep dinner in its place. Then I really looked at the bodies.

Flies swarmed over them, and the light revealed something moving in the soft tissue of their faces. My stomach rebelled yet again when I realized they were maggots. The bodies were bloated, which I thought meant they'd been there at least a couple of days. That fit with when I found the kid.

Paul knelt over the bodies, shining the light up and down the corpses. I glanced away. The moving light plus the moving bugs was more than I could take.

Suddenly, I realized something. He'd been right about the smell. I must have been getting used to it because it wasn't as overwhelming. Small favors.

"What do you think? Is it them?"

He shook his head. "I can't be certain of that. My guess, from their clothes, is that they were homeless." He pointed to a couple of places, pointing out details I wasn't sure I wanted to notice. "Look here and here. Obviously they were killed by something with teeth."

"Like wolf teeth?"

He nodded. "Yes, that looks about right. Too big for

dogs or coyotes."

"So they weren't just gnawed by strays?"

"Oh, yes, they were." He pointed out a couple more wounds. "That's what these are. But those wounds are postmortem." He pointed to a large slash that had nearly ripped off a leg. "That's the fatal wound for her."

Comparing bite marks on a corpse was just weird. And wrong. They'd once been as alive as I am, and now they were dead. It made me realize how thin the line was between life and death.

"How long do you think they've been dead?"

He looked them over once more. "My guess is 36–48 hours or so."

"So they were killed the night before I found the kid."

He nodded. "That sounds about right."

I wondered if the kid had seen their deaths or if he'd been somewhere else. Seeing your parents murdered was the kind of trauma to leave scars that never go away.

While Paul might not be sure if these were the right bodies, there was a way I could be. I took out the magnet I'd used in the ritual. I'd taken the precaution of slipping it in my pocket when I left.

I knelt down, reminding myself that while these objects had once been people they weren't now. That made it easier to control the nausea. I hoped that, wherever they were, they'd understand. It wasn't personal, just practical.

Paul watched me curiously while I passed the magnet over each body. I concentrated on the energies in the magnet. Again, it's hard to explain if you don't practice, but when I did the ritual, I'd formed a link between the bodies and the magnet. What I was looking for now was a resonance, for want of a better word. And I felt it. These were definitely the bodies of the kid's parents.

I stood up and nodded. "It's them."

Paul looked them over one more time and then glanced at me. "All right. You're the warlock. I'll contact Runner and tell him where they are. He'll see that they are buried decently someplace where no one will find them. Those wounds raise too many questions for mortal police."

I looked around. "I guess I'm surprised they haven't been found before now."

Paul shook his head. "I'm not. Cops don't come here any more often than they have to. And the homeless aren't generally big on reporting murders. They tend to be suspects."

"Oh."

I started to turn away, but paused when Paul didn't move. It looked like he was sniffing deeply, like he was trying to imprint a scent in his memories. Finally, he nodded and turned away. "There. I'll recognize their killers if I smell them again."

"Can you, like, track them from here?"

He moved slowly away from the bodies, towards the street, but away from his car. "Maybe. That's what I'm trying. I doubt I'll be able to follow it far though."

I stayed behind him, not wanting to get in his way. "Why not?"

"I've got an excellent sense of smell, but it's not as good as a dog's. The smell was very strong by the bodies. Fear and excitement make an odor stronger. The parents had been afraid. The wolves had been excited. But once the kill is over, the emotion dies down. Something about the kill makes me think it was just business. Nothing personal."

I got it. "So once it was over, no real emotion. Not like if it had been, say, a crime of passion."

He turned to me and nodded, but his expression was puzzled. "Exactly." The word was definite, but his tone was uncertain.

"What?"

He shook his head. "That's odd."

"What's odd?"

"The trail. It just stops here."

I shrugged. "Maybe they got in a car. We are right by the street."

Paul nodded. "That's possible, and, if they had been human, it's what I would have expected. But werewolves don't usually drive cars."

"True. What about the people who hire were-wolves?"

"That's quite possible."

Suddenly Paul stiffened beside me, and he raised his head, again smelling the air.

I looked around, but even the dim light from nearby street lamps didn't show me anything. I couldn't hear anything either, and there was no way I was going to inhale deeply.

"We've got company," Paul said.

I looked again. Still nothing. "Where?"

The word had barely left my mouth when two things happened. One, I heard a low, menacing growl, maybe 20 feet from me. Two, Paul picked me up and threw me, hard. I must have flown 30 feet, in the opposite direction from the growl.

I hit the ground and skidded several more feet. If I'd had a bit more warning, I might have been able to turn my skidding slide into a controlled roll, but as it was, I hit my head and saw stars for a moment. I forced myself to shake it off, knowing, even in my confusion, that I didn't dare stay down for long. Paul was good, but I didn't know how many there were, and I couldn't rely on him to protect me.

Forcing my legs to work, I scrambled behind a near-by dumpster—Paul had good aim and presence of mind—and, hidden for a moment, glanced around to see what was attacking us.

My heart sank when I saw my friend fighting three large wolves.

Have you ever been to the wolf enclosure at the zoo? If so, you might think you have an inkling of what I saw. Zoo wolves have a wildness about them, even in captivity. They pace back and forth, with a smooth motion that you just know could spring into a hunting charge at any moment. They just look dangerous.

Let me tell you that there is about as much similarity between zoo wolves and these creatures as between a wolf and a poodle. Sure, similar species. Fur and fangs.

That sort of thing. But wild wolves are tame house pets in comparison to these.

The three creatures attacking Paul were almost half again as large as even a big wolf, almost all of it muscle. Their fur was long, shaggy and probably offered decent protection, even against small arms fire. And the way they moved? Pure killing power. I've read that man is the top predator on Earth. No way. These things were way above us.

Fortunately, vampires are also above us on the predator scale, and, for the moment, Paul was holding his own. He whirled with easy grace, his claws extended to slash first one wolf, then another.

While I'm certain he could have handled two wolves with relative ease, three were too much. As he tossed one wolf aside with what looked like a casual back–handed blow, another slid underneath his guard and snapped at his ankles, aiming to hamstring the vampire. Paul twisted at the last minute, and lowered one leg to catch the blow on his thigh. Then he glided to one side, positioning himself so that he faced all three wolves. He was facing in my direction, and I knew he was trying to keep their attention on him and off me.

I appreciated the effort, but I could see he wouldn't last long. Another wolf timed his motion to slash at Paul's side, and the vampire gasped, loud enough for me to hear, even at this distance.

Time for me to get into things. Normally, I'm not the kind to get into a dust up like this, but ever since I met Paul, I knew I was going to have to be prepared to get physical, so I've been working on some things I can do quickly. First, I reached into my coat pocket and pulled out a potion. Keeping an eye on the fight, I unscrewed the bottle top and gulped it down. (In case you were curious, small water bottles are a great way to carry around potions. Much better than the glass vials used in most high fantasy novels.)

I felt the effects almost immediately. My vision sharpened. Sounds were clearer, and I could hear the hitching breath of one of the wolves Paul had wounded. The night air moving on my skin felt like it had weight. I nodded. Good. It worked the way I'd hoped.

I pulled out another bottle and yelled, "Paul. Heads—up!"

He truly is amazing. While still holding off three wolves, he hopped back, putting a few feet between himself and the furred buzz saws. I threw the bottle, trusting my enhanced reflexes and senses to get it moving in the right direction.

Paul did the rest. With one hand, he slashed through the foreleg of one of the wolves. It yelped and hobbled to one side, out for the moment. The biggest wolf leaped for Paul's throat, but the vampire spun one way in a quick feint and then reversed the other way, leaving the big wolf off balance.

The bottle flew, one end over another, seemingly in slow motion, closer to the fray with each rotation.

The final wolf saw it and changed direction, hind legs bunching for a leap.

I yelled. "Hey! Fur face. Over here."

The wolf's head moved to look at me, and I grinned, catching his gaze directly. I tamped down my fear, letting none of it show in my eyes or expression.

It shifted its weight slightly, preparing to leap in my direction.

The bottle rotated once. Twice. Three more times.

Paul dodged the big wolf and slashed at the smaller, which had recovered and jumped back to attack.

The bottle spun again.

Paul reached out with his right hand and caught it neatly. With a smooth motion, he lifted the bottle to his lips, and, not bothering to open it, sank his fangs into the smooth plastic and drank it down.

Immediately, his motions were faster, and his strikes had more power behind them. I nodded. Now he'd be fine. Especially since he only had two wolves to deal with. The other was just starting to leap my way.

I'd planned to draw off one of them, so I was ready for it. I reached back into my pocket and drew out a small container. I held it ready. The wolf leaped. It was moving fast. Without my potion, I'd never have been able to follow the movement, much less react. Under the influence of my magic however, I saw the wolf's leap in slow motion, and I was able to time the action for the top of its arc.

I actually moved closer to the wolf, wanting to show that I wasn't afraid (even though I was). Plus I needed the distance to be just right.

When the wolf was in position, I held up my container and triggered it.

I'd timed it perfectly. The spray hit the wolf directly in the eyes, just as I'd wanted. I jumped back as the wolf let out an anguished howl. Its precise leap devolved into a helpless tumble, and it fell, hard on one side. If it hadn't been so big, its whimpering would have sounded pitiful.

I smiled as I ducked back behind the protection of the dumpster. I held my pepper spray container in front of me, ready to hit it again.

The huge canine continued to whimper, and I peered out from behind the ripe–smelling metal structure. The wolf was frantically pawing at its eyes and letting loose pitiful whines and whimpers, in between racking coughs. It tried to look in my direction, but its eyes were screwed shut and watering profusely.

After a moment, it stood up and staggered away, apparently out of the fight for good.

I nodded in satisfaction. I'd gone all the way and purchased the Triple Action spray, a mix of pepper spray, tear gas, and a UV dye, for good measure. Not that I thought he'd be sticking around for identification.

I turned my attention back to Paul's fight, while still keeping some of my attention on the retreating wolf.

My efforts had helped. Paul was bleeding freely from several wounds, but the smaller wolf was retreating, tail between its legs with one paw held up while another dragged the ground in an obvious limp.

The larger wolf was attempting a fighting retreat, but its movements were slow. As I watched, it turned tail and ran.

Paul started to chase after it but then sagged, coughing. I recognized the effect of the potion wearing off, and I hurried to him. My own potion was fading too, but I could still see well enough to watch both wolves backing away. I held up my pepper spray and motioned in the direction of the third wolf, whose pained howls could still be heard, moving in the opposite direction.

Both wolves snarled but continued to retreat.

Paul kept his feet until all the wolves were out of sight, and then he slumped to the ground. I caught him halfway down, staggering under his weight.

"You okay?" I asked.

"Are they gone?" he asked weakly in return.

I looked both ways. The wolf I'd wounded was barely visible, lurching around a corner. The other two were completely out of sight.

"Looks like it," I said as I eased him to the ground and stripped off his shirt to get a better look at his wounds.

He started to protest the familiarity, but I hushed him.

It was bad, but he'd had worse the other night, so I wasn't too worried. One of the wolves has bitten him just under the throat, but it was already starting to close. He also had assorted slashes and gashes on his arms and a particularly nasty one that had come close to disemboweling him. I could also see blood on his legs, and his white slacks were badly ripped and stained, but I wasn't about to take off his trousers.

"You'll live," I said.

He managed a weak grin. "In a matter of speaking."

I shrugged. "Okay, then. Your undead state will continue until further notice." I smiled at him, and he winked in return.

"Okay. Stick with the 'live' part. Less of a mouthful."

I nodded. "Like I said. You need help making it to the car?"

He attempted to stand, almost made it and landed back on the ground. "Guess so."

I put a shoulder under him, and, between the two of us, we managed to get him standing and back to the car. I helped him to the passenger seat, figuring I was driving again. Without him asking, I reached into the back seat and found the cooler still there. I opened it and found one bag of blood. I handed it to him.

He took it and said, "Seems we're making a habit of this."

"No worries. Just drink."

I went to the other side of the car and opened the driver's side door. While I didn't expect the wolves to come back soon, I also didn't see any reason to stick around.

Of course, that's when my phone rang. I really have to remember to turn it off when I'm working. Glancing at the display, I couldn't help smiling.

Paul glanced up from drinking and raised an eyebrow. "Downline?" he asked.

I shook my head. "Give me a minute." I took the call. "Hey."

"Hey." It was Stephen. "I hope this isn't a bad

time?"

Well, yes, it was, but I certainly didn't want to say that. "Hang on sec. Let me get my headset on." I fumbled in my pocket for my ear buds, put them in and started the car. As soon as I was driving, I said. "No, I've got a minute. What's up?"

I studiously ignored the curious looks I was getting from the vampire. I waved him back to his blood. Paul grinned and went back to drinking.

"I was wondering if you wanted to schedule some time to get together," Stephen said.

I had to think for a minute. There was a lot going on right now, but guys who look like Stephen don't come along every day. Hoping Stephen would turn out to be good boyfriend material, I decided I could handle one more thing in my life. I glanced over at Paul, who had finished the bag but was politely looking out the window, giving me the illusion of privacy. "Sure. What did you have in mind?"

Even as I listened to him, I was looking for wolves. So far so good.

"Tomorrow night, maybe?"

Darn. That wasn't going to work. We'd all agreed to meet tomorrow evening to compare notes. As much as I wanted a boyfriend, figuring out what had happened to the kid came first. On the other hand, maybe I could propose an alternative? I ran through some things quickly. Yeah, I think I could just about make it work.

"Dafydd? You still there?" Stephen's voice sounded nervous, and I realized I had waited just a little too long to answer.

"Yeah, I'm here. I just had to think things through. I can't meet tomorrow night. I've got something else I have to do, but what about breakfast tomorrow?"

I held my breath, hoping he'd say yes. I'd planned on sleeping in tomorrow. The psychic crowd never budged before noon, and I knew tomorrow evening would be late, but hey, I'm young. I can afford to short myself on sleep once in a while. I ignored the fact that I'd been shorted several days recently.

"Yeah, sure. I can do that. Anyplace you have in mind?"

I turned onto Pennsylvania Avenue and started to relax. We were getting back to the better part of town. "How about Annie's?"

Annie's is a well–known restaurant in the gay community. I was sure he'd know it. I grinned for a moment. Sonya, my favorite waitress there would be thrilled to see me coming in with a guy. She's been trying to hook me up ever since my last boyfriend left me. Maybe now she'd stop bugging me about asking Paul out.

Stephen chuckled on the other end of the line. "Sure. That works. Sonya'll be thrilled. She's been trying to hook me up for months."

I laughed. "You too? Sure you want to go there? If we're not careful, she'll take out a half–page ad in the *Blade* to celebrate."

"I think I can handle the press."

"Cool. Nine o'clock then?"

"Yeah. See you in the morning." A pause before he

added. "I'm really looking forward to it."

"Me too," I said, and we both hung up.

I glanced over at Paul, who was reaching into the back seat to toss his empty bag back into the cooler. "That sounded like you were setting up a date."

I nodded. "Yeah, someone Bob kind of set me up with."

"Is he cute?"

This was a very weird conversation to be having with a vampire. "Yeah, he's cute."

Paul grinned, but something in his eyes didn't match the smile. "Good luck then. You've been … alone for a while."

Now that was odd. Paul was always so certain in his speech. He didn't usually pause like that. I wondered what it meant, but I knew he'd never answer if I asked, so I just said, "Yeah, it'd be nice to have a boyfriend again, but this is only a first date. We might not even like each other."

Paul shook his head. "Anyone who wouldn't like you is just crazy."

I blinked, but before I could say anything, Paul changed the subject. "You handled yourself really well back there."

I nodded, pleased. "Thanks. I'm trying to be more prepared."

"That potion you gave me was good. Nice if it lasted a little longer, though."

He was right. So far I hadn't been able to make an enhancing potion last longer than a couple of minutes. I didn't know if it was a limitation on the magic or the body it was enhancing. But I was thinking it was the magic. Our bodies should have different tolerances, but it didn't seem to matter. His weren't lasting any longer than mine.

"I'm working on that. But so far, a few minutes is the best I can manage."

He shrugged. His motions were already more fluid, and I knew the blood he'd ingested was working. "What was the one you used on yourself?"

"Umm. Sense and reflex enhancing. Super strength kind of got me in trouble last time, so I decided to try something more subtle."

He snorted. "Pepper spray was hardly subtle."

I could hear the approval in his voice and didn't take offense. "Well, it seemed like a good idea."

I decided not to mention my worries that it wouldn't work on werewolves. It had worked this time.

He echoed my thoughts. "It won't work on everything supernatural. But werewolves are definitely the right things to use it on."

"What about vampires?"

He shook his head. "We don't breathe." He thought for a moment. "Although the stuff in the eyes might slow us down for a bit. But not for long."

"I'll keep that in mind for the future," I said. "Now, the important question. Why were the wolves there tonight? Do you think they were keeping an eye on the bodies?" That seemed kind of gross, even for werewolves, but I didn't have any better ideas.

Paul nodded. "I think that might be it." He frowned. "And yet—" He trailed off.

"And yet what?"

He shook his head. "It doesn't really make sense."

"Why not?" I asked.

"Because they just dumped the bodies. They didn't leave that much evidence behind. Why would they need to watch and see who found them when they could guess it would probably be the police? Or another homeless person."

He had a point. I thought about it while I drove. "Well, you said they didn't leave much evidence, but those teeth marks have got to be pretty distinctive."

"True, but there have been were kills before, and the police are really good at explaining them away."

Just like with vampire kills, I couldn't help thinking. But he was right. Both he and Runner had indicated that infected werewolves had killed before. I've never seen "Werewolves killing in D.C.. Update at Ten!" on the news, and it didn't seem likely some journalist would suddenly pick up on them now.

I passed the Mt. Vernon Metro station. Only another couple of blocks to Paul's house. "Then there's another reason for them to be hanging around."

"Yes. And a good enough reason to make them attack a vampire. Unless they are very newly infected wolves, they'd know I would be a tough opponent."

"So they are young, stupid or guarding something really important." I parked in front of Paul's house.

"Probably. It's late, for you at least, so I think we'll

save figuring it out for another time. Maybe Runner or Laura will have something else for us to look at."

"At least tonight, we confirmed that the kid's parents are dead."

"And who killed them." Paul stretched. "Not bad for a night's work." He looked at me. "Guess we're making a habit of this."

"Of what?"

"You driving me home."

I shrugged. "Yeah, I guess. Well, just make sure the bad guys don't beat you up. Then there won't be any need."

"I guess it's not so bad."

I chuckled. "Which one? The getting beat up? Or me taking you home?"

His voice was quiet. "The latter one." His tone lightened, and I could hear the hint of humor in it. "I could do without the first one."

"Yeah, me too." We sat for a moment in silence. It wasn't uncomfortable. I wondered what Paul was thinking. I knew where my thoughts were going. This was my first experience with death like that. Ghost hunting didn't count because by the time I was called in, the mess was long gone.

But those bodies. It was all wrong. No one should have to experience the fear and pain of being torn apart. I didn't know what we'd do when we found the responsible party, but I'd worry about that later. Right now I just wanted to find them. And fast.

"I'll check in with the psychic network tomorrow," I

said. "They might know something."

Paul nodded. "I probably should head back to the bar and see if any of the older vampires have shown up. They might know something."

"You sure you're up to it?" He looked okay now, but the wolves had gotten him pretty bad.

He flexed his shoulders. "I'll be okay. Come in for a minute while I grab a quick shower and change? Then I'll run you home."

"Works for me." We got out of the car, and I followed him in. He immediately vanished, and I moment later I heard the water running in the shower. I settled on his couch, thinking hard. Why were the werewolves there tonight? Paul was right. It didn't make sense unless there was something they didn't want anyone to see. I frowned, trying to think it through. There had to be something to get Laura researching on. She's a whiz at it. If I only knew where to aim her.

Something was tickling at the back of my mind. I relaxed, closed my eyes and let my thoughts go blank. Maybe that would pull it through. It took me a while, but I finally got it.

Paul was just coming back into the living room, showered and dressed in fresh clothes. He looked fabulous in a black silk button down and tight black jeans. I looked at him. "I just thought of something."

He walked into the kitchen but motioned to me to continue. "What?"

When I'd closed my eyes and drifted, I remembered my conversation earlier today. Mr. Lin's voice saying "…

my grandson say there have been threats against shop owners over on 14th."

It might be unrelated, but then again, maybe not.

"When I was shopping for ritual stuff today, I asked Mr. Lin—he owns the store—if he'd heard of anything happening. He mentioned hearing about threats on 14th street. Something about threats against the store owners."

Paul's voice was distant in the kitchen but still clear enough to understand. "What kind of threats?"

"He didn't say, but I could have Laura check for something happening in the area."

Paul was nodding as he came back to the living room, carrying a couple of bags of blood. I guessed he was restocking the cooler in his car. "It's something to check out. Maybe when we talk to our folks, we'll get something else to work on."

I sat back. It wasn't much. It might be nothing. But it was a place to start.

We headed out to his car, and he drove me home. We rode in silence, not much else to say. We'd covered everything, and I needed a minute to think about what Paul had said earlier about not minding me driving him home. What did that mean exactly? And what did I want it to mean? How did I reconcile that with my upcoming breakfast with Stephen?

Paul dropped me off at my place with a casual "Want me to pick you up tomorrow evening?"

"Yeah, thanks." I dragged my mind back to business. "I'm going to call Laura before I go to bed. See if I can get her working on the 14th Street angle. Maybe she can dig up why the wolves were there."

"You sure? It's pretty late."

I shrugged. "Yeah, but she usually keeps weird hours anyway."

"Sounds like a plan." I started to close my door but stopped when he added, "Give me a call tomorrow after you've talked to the psychics?"

I nodded. "Sure thing. Until then."

"Until then. Sleep well." With that, he drove off.

Kind of weird for a vampire to wish me a good sleep, but I shrugged and entered my apartment. Naturally, the ferrets wanted my attention, but I ignored them and called Laura.

"Hey, Dafydd. What's up?"

There was no good way to say it. "We found the kid's parents."

"Really! That's great." Her voice was excited.

"Actually, no. It's not so great. They're dead."

Silence on the other end. Then. "You're sure it was them?"

"Yeah, I'm sure." I couldn't get the image of the torn bodies out of my head. "But that's not all. A couple of werewolves attacked us at the dump site."

Her voice sounded worried. "You okay?"

"Yeah, we're fine. Paul took care of two of them, and I maced the other one."

She chuckled. "So that was a good tip?"

The mace had been her idea. One night, while we were hanging out and watching movies, I'd mentioned I was looking for a way to deal with supernatural bad guys. I tended to look for magical answers and was stumped. That's when Laura suggested pepper spray.

"Yes, it was good."

"Why didn't you have it on the Mall?"

I'm not sure it would have worked on the shuggoleth thing, but I just said, "Forgot it. Paul was kind of in a hurry, and it slipped my mind."

"Well, okay then. Sorry about the parents, but I guess that wasn't a big surprise."

"No, not really. Hey, I've got something I want you to look up."

"Sure," was her immediate response. Laura is very good at compartmentalizing. She has to be.

"When I was getting ritual materials in Chinatown, I heard about threats against shop owners on 14th Street. It might be nothing, but—"

"… it might be related," she finished for me. "I'll look into it. See what I can dig up." She paused then added, "Where did you find the bodies? If there's any nearby cameras, I might be able to find something."

It wasn't a bad idea. It made sense that warehouses in a lousy part of town would have security cameras. I told her the location.

"I know the area. I think there are some. I'll see if I can pull any footage. Figure two or three days ago, based on when you found the kid?"

Her businesslike tone was reassuring. "That's what Paul thought. He's better at judging time of death than I am."

I heard her chuckle. "Yeah, I guess he would be. I'll see what I can find."

"And," I added. "… see if you can dig up what's in the area. We're thinking there was something there they don't want us to see."

"Sure thing. And Dafydd—" Her tone grew soft.

"Yeah?"

"I'm sorry they're dead. And I'm sorry you had to see it."

"Yeah, me too. Thanks. We'll talk tomorrow." I forced some lightness into my tone. "And I may have good news to report."

"Really?"

"Yep," I said. "I have a date tomorrow."

"Call me afterwards! I'll want to hear all the details!"

She was still laughing when I hung up. Women! Gotta love their priorities.

Chapter 5

Sunday, September 6, 2009: early morning

W HEN MY ALARM went off the next morning, my first impulse was to ignore it and go back to sleep. Then I remembered why I'd set it. Right. Date with Stephen. Can't miss that.

I hurriedly showered and fed the ferrets before rushing out the door. Fortunately, Annie's is a short walk from my apartment, so I got there in plenty of time. I walked in and Sonya, my favorite waitress, greeted me. "Hey, Dafydd." She frowned slightly before adding. "Alone again, as usual."

I shot her a grin. "Not today. I'm meeting someone."

She showed me to a table by the front windows. "Someone. As in—"

I nodded. "Yep, an official first date."

"For breakfast? Seriously, honey, if he'll only spring for this, he's not worth it."

I shook my head. "Breakfast was my idea. He wanted to meet later, but I've got stuff going on all day."

She poured me some coffee. "Well, okay, but I'm still going to reserve judgment."

I saw Stephen open the door and walk in. "Okay," I said. "Turn around tell me what you think."

Her squeal said it all. She gave Stephen a big hug when he approached. "Why didn't I think of hooking you two up? You're perfect for each other!"

Stephen managed to shoot me an "I told you so" look over her shoulder, and I stifled a smile.

Letting him go so he could sit down in the chair opposite me, Sonya asked, "Whose idea was it?"

"Bob's," we said in unison.

She nodded. "Of course. Tell him it's been too long since he came in to see me."

She gave us both menus and a bit of privacy.

"Hey," Stephen said, his voice soft. He laughed, sounding nervous. "I was afraid you wouldn't show up."

I smiled back at him. "No way. I wouldn't miss it." I nodded in the direction of my apartment. "Besides, I just live a couple of minutes from here."

He glanced in the direction I'd pointed. "Really? I'm not too far either. Funny we've never seen each other here."

Now that he mentioned it, that was odd, but I didn't think too much of it as I tended to keep strange hours. "Anyway, glad you came."

We avoided awkwardness for a few minutes by examining the menu. I didn't want anything too fancy, so I decided on oatmeal and fruit. It's not on the menu, but when you're a regular like I am, you get special treatment.

Sonya came back, and we ordered. Stephen went for a full breakfast, which I liked. I prefer guys who aren't obsessive about food.

"Not hungry?" he asked.

Oops. Maybe ordering oatmeal and fruit made *me* look obsessive, so I nodded. "This is early for me on a weekend. My stomach needs time to wake up."

He smiled. "So what do you do, besides sell vitamins and stuff?"

This is where things always get awkward. Do I tell a possible boyfriend about being a warlock? It's a dilemma. I don't want to look too weird in the beginning, but if we start going steady, he'll find out. However, finding out after we've been seeing each other for a while can be even more awkward.

I decided to avoid it for now. "I dabble in this and that. Mostly, I'm focused on building my business."

He grinned. "All work and no play—"

I grinned back. "I never said anything about not wanting to play, did I?"

He blushed and looked away for a moment before meeting my gaze. "No, seriously, what do you do? Bob kind of hinted at something, but he didn't really say. Just said you had 'special skills' and said I needed to ask you if I wanted to know more."

That surprised me. Bob can be a gossip, as well as a terrible flirt, but he didn't usually reveal anything significant. I made a mental note to say something to him.

"Well—" I hesitated. Like I said, revealing stuff too early has killed relationships. But if Bob already gave him a hint.

"Go on," he said in an encouraging tone. "Whatever it is, it can't be, like bad, right? You haven't killed anyone, have you?"

I shook my head. "No, nothing like that. It's just not something I tell everyone." I finally decided to just spit it out. "I'm a warlock. A *real* warlock. I do *real* magic."

There. It was out. Now I'd find out if this would be a very short date.

He blinked and sat back in his chair but didn't say anything for a moment. I started to get worried and took a gulp of coffee. Damn! It was still really hot.

I spluttered, and Stephen asked, "You okay?"

"Yeah. Just burned myself." I didn't know what to say after that. Saying, "Okay, so I can do magic. Still want to date me?" didn't seem to cut it.

Finally, he asked, "By magic, do you mean cast spells? Like fireballs and stuff like that?"

I shook my head no, relieved. Being asked questions was always a good sign. "No, not flashy stuff like that. I don't know anyone who can do real elemental magic. I make potions, do finding rituals and stuff like that. Useful, but lots more subtle than blowing stuff up with magic."

He looked relieved. "Okay. That's not so bad. I was afraid for a minute if I pissed you off, you'd fry me. Or turn me into a toad."

I grinned. "Well, technically, I could brew a potion that might turn you into a really big toad. But the potion tastes so bad there's no way I could trick you into drinking it."

His eyes lit up. "Really? You can turn people into animals and other stuff?"

I shook my head. "No. I was just winding you up."

He mock–frowned. "So what can you do?"

"Oh, brew potions, find stuff magically and some-times see the future." I gave him a sly grin when I said that.

He grinned back and started to say something, but just then Sonya came over with our food. We could have kept talking. Sonya is one of the people who knows about me, but I didn't want to give her any reason to stick around.

"Having a good time?" she asked as she put down the plates.

I knew what she was really asking. "Is this date going somewhere?"

I said something noncommittal, and Stephen just dug into his food. Sonya glanced at each of us, grinned and left.

"What was that grin for?" Stephen asked around a mouthful of omelet.

I shrugged and speared a piece of fruit. "Not sure. Anyway, enough about me. What about you? What do you do when you're not selling vitamins and nutritional shakes?"

I wondered if he'd let me get away with the topic change. Most people at this point would have asked for a demonstration, which wasn't really practical.

To my surprise, he answered the question. "I've got another job as a waiter."

Okay. Weird, but it made things easier on me, and he wasn't making excuses to leave suddenly. "Where?" I asked.

"Little bar and grill over in North East. Nothing special. I'm really working hard to build my business so I can get out. I want to just work for myself." He ate another bite and then added. "Nothing as exciting as what you do."

Honestly, I didn't think of what I did as "exciting." I know. I probably should. Not many people can cast spells, deal with ghosts or hang around with hot vampires, but it's what I've done all my life. Well, except for the vampire part.

Conversation lagged for a bit. Then Stephen asked what kind of music I liked, and everything flowed from there. We talked about music, TV shows and books we liked. It turned out we had a lot in common. I grew cautiously hopeful that this could actually turn into a real relationship.

Finally, I pulled out my phone to check the time and said, "Wow! I had no idea it'd gotten so late."

He glanced at his phone. "You're right." His voice grew hesitant. "I really enjoyed this."

I smiled at him. "Me too. Want to, maybe, I don't know, do it again sometime?"

He smiled back, and I noticed the muscles in his shoulders relax. Okay. I hadn't been the only nervous one here. "Yeah, I'd like that. I'd like that a lot."

I thought quickly. I wanted to spend the next couple of days focused on the kid and solving the mystery of his parents' murder. As excited as I was about maybe having a new relationship to explore, my simmering anger at the injustice of murder was still there. However, I hoped by next weekend we'd have that wrapped up. "I've got something keeping me busy this week, but maybe we could get together Saturday night?"

A look like disappointment flashed across his face, but Stephen simply said, "Sure. Maybe we could hang out at Apex?"

I nodded. Apex is a gay dance club, and I hadn't been there in a long time. My ex didn't like dancing, but I did. "Sure. I haven't been in a while." I lowered my voice. "I've been told I'm a pretty good dancer."

His eyes sparkled. "Well, I'll have to be the judge of that." His expression grew serious for a moment. "And don't think I won't ask for some kind of demonstration of... you know..."

I nodded. "Yeah. I can manage that somewhere less public."

Sonya came back with our check. We paid and got up to leave. Suddenly awkward, I wasn't sure what to do. Should I kiss him goodbye? Shake hands?

Stephen made it easy. He ducked in for a quick kiss, just a brief heated contact that definitely left me wanting to learn more. Then he smiled, and we left Annie's. I could feel Sonya's eyes on us as we exited. I knew her well. She was cheering us both on.

We went our separate ways, agreeing to talk during the week to finalize plans for Saturday.

I headed back to my apartment to grab what I needed for the rest of the day. As I walked, I realized I was smiling and feeling better than I had in a long time. If it hadn't been for the pall of the murder over me, I'd say things couldn't have gotten much better.

BACK AT MY apartment, I quickly checked the ferrets' food and water and topped them off. Gimble gave me a hopeful look, but I shook my head. "Not now, little one. I've got more errands to run."

She gave a little sigh and snuggled back down with Gyre, who hadn't even awakened.

I threw some stuff into my backpack and headed out the door.

I know most people think psychic readings are just a scam, and, honestly, many are. But I do know a few people in the profession who have a touch of magical ability. It's a weaker version of my ability to read people's auras. The good ones know how to use their ability to entertain and inform. Occasionally they can even see something significant in someone's present or future.

Most of the reputable psychics in town know me. They hear about ghosts and other weird things in their client's lives, and sometimes they bring me in to consult on occurrences that do seem supernatural. I've dealt with a few hauntings, including a particularly nasty poltergeist.

Because I help them, they are willing to help me, and the psychics are a good source of information. Part of their job involves listening and watching people. I was pretty sure if anything weird was going on in my town, one of them would know about it.

I started close to home. There were several psychics

in the Dupont Circle area, and I knew them the best.

Unfortunately, I struck out. Oh, they were glad to see and chat with me, but they hadn't heard anything. Even the two I chatted up on M Street could only confirm werewolf activity by telling me they'd heard howling, but they couldn't give me anything new to work on.

Discouraged, I stood on the street for a moment, deciding where to go next. There were a few psychics I knew on L St, near 14th. And there was one more, way north on 14th, but that was farther out than I'd hoped to go.

My phone rang. I took it from my pocket, glad for an excuse to avoid making a decision, at least for the moment.

It was Paul. I was surprised to hear from him so early, but when I looked at the time, I realized it was almost 3 pm. Talking to my friends had taken longer than I'd thought.

"Hey," I said.

"How was the date?"

His question made me feel warm deep down. While there's no question Paul and I are friends, most of our interactions so far had been about stuff we were investigating. We talked shop, but not much about personal stuff. Having him ask about my date made me hopeful that our friendship was evolving. I really liked Paul, not just because he's attractive, but because I've sensed a depth there and a wealth of knowledge and experience. I wanted to get to know him as a person and know more about what he knows.

"It went really well. Turns out we have a lot in common. We're tentatively getting together next Saturday at Apex."

"Sounds good. Glad it went well." A pause. Then he added. "I guess I'd like to meet him some time."

"Sure. I'd like you two to meet. But don't tell me you just called to ask about my date."

A chuckle on the other end of the line. "No, not really. I was just checking in to see if you've learned anything from the Psychic Friends Network."

Paul can be an enigma sometimes. I know he's old maybe even over a hundred, if not older. He's pretty up on popular culture, but some references go right past him. Then occasionally, he'll come up with something like "Psychic Friends Network." I remembered those ads on late night TV. Makes sense that he'd watch late-night TV. What else can you do when you're active while most people are sound asleep? Hunting down evil-doers and monsters can't take up all his time.

"I haven't learned much yet," I said. "More confirmation about werewolves, but nothing else."

"Oh." I could hear the disappointment in his voice. "Maybe Runner will have turned something up. I got a little from the vampires last night, but nothing that will really help us."

Too bad. I'd hoped the vampires would know something. Even so, we couldn't give up yet. "I still have a few hours before I need to head home and grab some food before you pick me up. There's still a couple places on 14th Street I can try. Give me a little more time?"

"Sure. Still want me to pick you up at eight?"

"That works. Thanks. See you then."

"Okay. Until then."

We hung up, and I shouldered my backpack. I couldn't give up yet. Surely something would turn up?

I HIKED OVER to 14th St and struck out at the first place, though Evelyn and I had a nice chat. She's my favorite psychic, with more than a touch of real talent. Unfortunately, she wasn't able to give me what I needed, and I went to the next place on my list.

I love Jessica's place. It's in the middle of a little row of old brownstones that have been converted to commercial space. Her place is right over a comfy neighborhood pub, you know, the kind that's in a basement with an awning over the stairs leading down.

The bells on the door tinkled as I opened it, and the interior was dim and comforting. Crystals hung from just about every surface. The color scheme was soothing greens and blues. It just felt like the kind of place where you'd learn your future.

Jessica was just finishing up with a client. She nodded to let me know she'd be with me in a minute.

"So, Mrs. Cohen, same time next week. I just feel like your husband has more to tell us."

I suppressed a grin. Another dead husband communication. Jessica is one of the more successful mediums in D.C.. She doesn't have a lick of talent, but she knows how to put on a show.

"Mrs. Cohen" was an elderly lady with blue hair that exactly matched the color of her mop dog's fur. How'd she manage that? The dog growled at me on the way out, and the old lady smiled. Great, one of those people who likes it when their dog is obnoxious to strangers.

As soon as she left, Jessica gave me a grin. "Are you sure you can't turn the dog into something nasty? He tries to pee in the store every time she brings him."

I lifted an eyebrow inquiringly. "Then why do you keep letting her bring him?"

She waved at the cash register. "Because she tips very well."

I nodded. "Makes sense." Then I shrugged. "But if I turned her dog into something nasty, she might stop coming."

"True." She chuckled. "But it might be worth it to see the look on her face. No wonder her husband died. He probably did it to spite her."

"Or escape the dog," I added.

"That too." Her voice turned businesslike. "So what can I do for you today, Dafydd?"

I got down to business. "There's something weird going on in the area, and I'm checking to see if anyone knows what's up."

She frowned. "Weird how?"

Because she does know that the supernatural is real, I knew I could tell her what was happening without her laughing at me.

"Paul and I found a couple of murdered homeless people."

She snorted. "Not to be insensitive, but murdered homeless people in D.C. hardly constitutes 'weird.'"

"It does when they've been torn apart, probably by werewolves."

She shot me an incredulous look. "Werewolves are real too? I thought vampires were a bit much to swallow."

I nodded. "I've met a few recently. One is just a little kid. We think it was his parents who were murdered."

"How'd that work? A family of werewolves?"

Shaking my head, I said, "We're not sure yet. That's why I'm trying to learn more."

She frowned, obviously thinking hard. "Yeah, I guess that's weird. Assuming you accept werewolves in the first place."

I started to protest, and she waved me silent, continuing, "Oh, I believe you about the werewolves. That's not my point. I'm just saying that weird is relative here."

I shrugged. "Yeah, guess you've got a point there. Anyway, have you heard anything weird? Maybe heard about shop owners being pressured?"

She visibly jumped when I mentioned shop owners. "What's that got to do with werewolves?"

"You've heard something then?" I was excited. This was the first hint of a lead I'd gotten all day.

"Maybe. It might not be related."

Caution was evident in her voice, and I suppressed my growing excitement. I didn't want her to clam up. "What did you hear?"

She paused. I was afraid she wasn't going to answer,

but finally her body relaxed, and she said, "It might not be anything, but a couple of shopkeepers at 14th and P were talking. A couple of them mentioned that there was some big developer moving in, wanting to tear down the old shops and rebuild them into some big shiny mixed–use development."

It's been happening in D.C. for years now. Mom and Pop shops were being torn down and replaced with big chain stores. The government has been claiming it's all part of "redevelopment" and that it's good for the city and the neighborhoods. Most people, myself included, prefer a thriving small business economy. The big buildings have no character. Local shops thrum with energy. Shiny modern buildings are just, well … dead.

"Okay, I'm not into that kind of urban renovation, but what does that have to do with werewolves?"

"I'm not sure it has anything to do with werewolves. That's why I almost didn't say anything. But Mr. Perez, who owns a bodega down there, said he'd been threatened by some pretty big guys. He was pretty freaked out. Said one the guys growled at him 'just like a wolf' when he said he wasn't interested in selling out and moving."

She made air quotes when she said it.

A chill went down my spine and I flashed back to what Runner had said. … *another pack leader in New York told me about some guy who teamed up with a werewolf to infect people and make his own bully gang.*

Okay, I'm not gonna say normal people can't "growl like a wolf." Or that just because the shopkeeper was scared by a big guy who sounded like a wolf, we should automatically assume they were werewolves, but it sure opened the possibility.

It was the kind of thing Laura could check on. She could do some searches on land developers in the area to see if any of them were likely to use questionable tactics.

I nodded. "Thanks, Jessica. That actually helps."

She looked surprised. "Really? It wasn't much."

"True, but it's something we can check on. Sometimes it's the little things that can break a case."

She snorted. "Now you sound like a cop, or private investigator. Would that 'we' be you and that sexy vampire?" There was a definite sparkle in her voice.

I groaned. "Doesn't anyone see him for more than his sex appeal? I mean, he's also smart and environmentally conscious." Okay, he really drives a Prius because it's a chick magnet, but Jessica didn't need to know that.

She grinned. "Yeah, okay, he might be all of those things too, and maybe more. But his hotness is the part I pay the most attention to. How about maybe introducing us someday?"

I rolled my eyes. "Get in line, Jessica."

Her delighted laughter followed me to the door. Then, just as I was opening the door, she said, "Let me know what you find out, okay?" Her voice sounded scared, so I turned around. She added, "I mean, just because I don't have talent doesn't mean I don't know that stuff exists. And is dangerous."

I gave her my best reassuring smile. "I'll let you know. I'm sure you'll be fine. Just ...." I hesitated, wanting her to be safe but not wanting to frighten her anymore.

"Just what?"

I decided to say it. "Just try not to go out at night alone. The full moon is almost done, so it should be okay, but still—"

She nodded. "Yeah. I think I'll close up the shop early and head home before dark. My schedule was pretty light this evening anyway."

"Good idea. See you around, Jessica."

"See you around, Dafydd."

And I left. Time to call Laura. With any luck she could check out this new lead and have some results by the time we all gathered later this evening.

Laura answered on the second ring, and I filled her in on what Jessica had told me. "I was hoping you could do some digging around. Maybe find out something about local developers. Especially ones that are doing work around 14th Street. With what Mr. Lin told me and now Jessica, everything seems to be pointing to that part of town."

"I've already done some poking into the 14th Street angle. This gives me something to work on. There are a couple of developers working that area. I can see if there's anything suspicious about them."

Finally we might be onto something! "That's great. I doubt we'd get so lucky as to find a news report entitled 'Local Developer Hires Werewolves to Terrorize Shopkeepers,' but you might find something useful."

I noticed a passerby shoot me a weird look when she overheard my made–up headline, but I ignored her.

Laura was saying, "Doubtful, but we'll see."

"Great," I said. "Anything might help. Jessica didn't think what she told me was worth much."

"But it gives me something else to research," Laura said.

That's why I like her so much. We think alike.

"Exactly."

"I'll get on it. With any luck I'll have something to report. You all are still coming by, right?"

I could hear the excitement in her voice and sighed inwardly. I know, Laura's an adult. She can take care of herself, but I can't help it. This was one of those times I regretted bringing the weirdness of my world into hers.

"Dafydd, if you're having second thoughts, stop thinking them right now!"

And that's the downside of Laura thinking so much like me.

"We'll be there. I've spoken to Paul, and he's picking me up at eight. I don't have any way to get in touch with Runner, but Paul hasn't said he's not coming, so I assume he'll be there too."

"Good." Her voice softened somewhat. "I know you want to protect me, and you're a dear for it, but I swore after the accident that I'd still live as fully as I could. I need you to accept that."

Laura didn't talk about her condition very often, so I knew what this meant. If we were going to stay friends, I'd have to stop wanting to protect her. Okay, I don't have to stop wanting. I just have to stop being so damn obvious about it.

"Dafydd?"

I cleared my throat. "Yeah, I'm still here. Sorry. It's just —"

I heard the laughter in her voice. "You have to find some way to express the testosterone."

I snorted. "Yeah, that's definitely it."

"See you tonight then."

"Yep. See you then." I added a mock growl in my voice. "And you'd better have something to report, girl, or you're off the team."

"Yes, sir. You bet."

I could still hear her laughing when we disconnected. I sighed, and checked the time. I had gotten some useful information, but my instincts told me there was still more to learn. I nodded. Just enough time for one more meeting, if I hurried.

I got lucky and made all my Metro connections. Half an hour later I was standing in front of St. Patrick's Catholic Church. I'd met Father Eyler soon after moving to D. C., and he'd become a good friend.

You know how all the horror movies have priests performing exorcisms, chanting Latin phrases and tossing around incense and holy water? Well, that's the movies. Yes, exorcism is still part of Church doctrine, but very few priests are allowed to perform one. And I'm not sure most Catholics really believe in its effectiveness.

Fact is ghosts, demons and other nasty things do exist, and a proper exorcism can help when needed. Soon after I moved here, I got called in to banish a particularly nasty poltergeist. It was strong, beyond my abilities, and

I needed a priest. The psychic who called me in recommended Father Eyler. I was skeptical, but I talked to him and was surprised to discover he was open–minded and had a touch of magical talent, just enough to make his rituals work.

With his help, we got rid of the poltergeist, and we've stayed in touch ever since. I call on him when I need a bit of faith–based help, and he's asked me to teach him how to use his minor talent more effectively.

Although it was Sunday, the last Mass was long over, and Father Eyler was still in.

"Dafydd! Good to see you." Then he frowned. "Does this mean you need help with another poltergeist?"

Father Eyler just looked like a priest. His black suit fit well, but didn't look expensive. I've never asked his exact age, but I'd guess mid–40s. His brown hair is receding a bit, but the well–trimmed beard (with just a hint of gray) draws attention away from his hairline. His kind green eyes are always ready to sparkle with a bit of humor or to comfort, when needed.

I shook my head. "No, nothing like that. I've been hearing about some weird stuff, maybe around 14th Street. You always seem to know stuff, so I wondered what you might have heard."

"Weird how?"

"Like werewolf weird."

His eyebrows shot up. "You mean werewolves exist?"

I nodded. "As real as ghosts."

His fingers idly fingered the crucifix hanging around his neck. "No. I haven't heard anything about werewolves, but now that you mention it, I have heard of some mysterious deaths."

Great, I thought. More mysteries to solve. "What kind of deaths?"

"It's hard to say, actually. I haven't heard many details, but there seems to be some sort of odd fever going around. I had to bury two of my parishioners recently. They had been ill for a few days, growing very pale and faint before dying in the night."

Well, I thought. Anyone who's read *Dracula* ought to be able to figure that one out. I wondered if Paul knew anything about this.

"I know what it sounds like," he went on. "But I'm having a hard time believing that vampires are preying on Washington."

You've probably guessed by now that I hadn't filled Father Eyler in about Paul. Obviously I was going to have to rectify that, but for now, I said, "You might be surprised, actually."

He gave me a look. "Are you saying vampires are also real?"

Nodding, I said, "Yep."

"Something tells me you have more than a passing acquaintance with the subject?"

"Well, actually, yes. We need to sit down sometime for coffee, and I'll fill you in." I glanced at my phone. "Thanks, Father, but I need to go. I'll see what I can find out, and I'll let you know."

I could tell he wanted to ask more, but he just nodded, and we said our goodbyes.

I hated leaving him like that, but my time really was short. I'd have to ask Paul if the Father's story triggered anything.

Chapter 6

Sunday, September 6, 2009: early evening

I HAD JUST enough time to heat up some soup and gulp it down while I gave the ferrets some attention, and time out of their cage. Their sheer joy at being out reminded me that I hadn't been giving them quite enough attention lately. Ferrets don't need lots of time to play. They have two speeds. Fast and Stop. These two are still young, less than two, and so their "Fast" is very fast, but they can't sustain it for long. About an hour (maybe two) of mad play, and they are ready to sleep. Unfortunately, I haven't been home long enough lately to let them have much play time.

Tonight they made me pay for it. Paul's knock at the door came as I was scrambling for the third time to haul Gimble out from behind the couch. She knows she's not supposed to be there, but she punishes me by disobeying the rules. Repeatedly.

"Come on in," I yelled, flat on the floor, arm trying to simultaneously grab a wiggly weasel and avoid being nipped by needle–sharp teeth.

Not exactly the way I wanted to appear to my partner, but what could I do?

I heard the door open and Paul start laughing. I gritted my teeth and grabbed for Gimble one more time. Again, she slipped out of my grasp and this time rewarded my efforts with a sharp nip.

"Ouch!" Damn her! That really hurt.

"What the heck are you doing? Is this a new game you forgot to tell me about? Or perhaps this is a new way of conducting magical research?"

At the sound of his voice, Gimble forgot about disobeying and dashed out from behind the couch to dance at the vampire's feet.

Dogs and cats might be wary of vampires, but ferrets are fearless. Apparently that fearlessness extends to supernatural beings as well.

Gyre raced out of the bedroom, and both ferrets begged shamelessly to be picked up.

As I levered myself off the floor, Paul obliged them, cuddling Gyre in one arm and juggling Gimble in the other. The white ferret was almost incapable of being still while awake, but she actually settled down in the curve of his arm for some serious ear scritching.

"Thanks. I forget how much she likes you. If I'd remembered, I'd have just let her stay under there until you got here."

He scratched both ferrets one more time and put them down. They danced at his feet for a moment until Gimble attacked Gyre, and they were off again to play.

"What was she up to this time?" Paul asked.

I shrugged. "With everything going on, I haven't given them as much time outside the cage as they'd like. Gimble makes her displeasure known by breaking every rule she can think of."

Paul laughed. "She's a clever one. Bet she can come up with lots of rules to break."

I nodded. "Pretty much, yeah."

I tossed my dishes in the sink and headed to the door. "I'm ready."

Paul held the door for me and we went to his car.

As he started the engine, he asked, "Did you learn anything more from the psychics?"

I was itching to ask him about vampires, but werewolves were the focus right now. "Maybe. It might be nothing, but some shop owners over on 14th have been threatened by some guy who wants to develop the area."

"Pretty thin."

"Yeah," I agreed. "But I remembered what Runner said about some guy in, I think it was New York, who was using werewolves as muscle. And didn't you tell me about the same thing happening in Chicago?"

"Chicago was a long time ago. I doubt there's any connection."

"Okay. Maybe you're right about that. But what about New York?"

Paul frowned, and I waited. "Yes, now that you mention it, I do remember Runner saying that. You think this developer might be doing the same thing?"

I shrugged. "Hard to tell, but I called Laura, and she's looking into it. She said she'd try to turn something up in time for the meeting."

Paul raised an eyebrow. "She really does work fast then."

"You have no idea."

We shared a grin for a moment, and then I asked, "You get anything more from the vampires?" I'd worried about him going back to the Lounge after having been beaten up, but he looked fine, so I guessed no one had hassled him.

He didn't answer right away, so I glanced over, concerned. "What?"

He shook his head. "I don't think it has anything to do with this case, but something is going on, and it troubles me."

"Troubles you? How?"

Another long pause. Finally, Paul sighed. "I've told you that vampires mostly keep a low profile, at least these days. CSI has cramped our style. Even though vampires don't leave behind DNA, we're just as likely to leave behind other trace evidence as you humans do."

"You mean like clothing fibers someone can use to track down a lair, or something like that?"

He snorted. "We don't usually call them 'lairs' anymore, but yes, just like that. A police officer tracking us down can turn out bad for everyone. Cop finds vampire. Vampire strikes back and probably kills cop."

I nodded. "Which leaves more dead bodies, pissed cops and another trail to follow."

"Exactly. So we police our own, when we can, to stop young, headstrong vampires from going too far and bringing too much attention to us."

I thought I saw where he was going with this. "So the vampires are concerned the werewolves are drawing too much attention, but they aren't sure how to 'police' another supernatural race?"

Paul shook his head. "No, it's not that. The D.C. community knows I have contacts in the were community and that the werewolves do a good job keeping tabs on the infecteds." He drummed his fingers on the steering wheel. "No, what the elders in the vampire community are worried about are reports of a rogue working the area. And we can't find him or her to put a stop to it."

"A rogue?"

"A rogue vampire who's killing indiscriminately and leaving the evidence behind in plain sight. The D.C. cops are looking for a violent serial killer. We know it's one of ours."

"How do you know? Maybe it is a human nut job."

"Definitely not. The eldest among us has contacts in the police and coroner's office. He's seen the reports. It's definitely the work of a vampire. Even some of the cops are starting to call it that. The press hasn't picked up the story yet, but it's only a matter of time."

I sat back. I could see why he was troubled. The supernatural has coexisted with the natural world for as long as there's been life on earth. When humanity was still ruled by superstition, it didn't matter much when things happened without rational explanation. They thought the world just worked that way.

Then the Renaissance happened, and humans started looking for explanations. As long as humans believe we don't exist, we're fairly safe. But if our world gets too close to their world, no one can predict what would happen. And I'm in no hurry to find out. I'm content to be a "normal" guy to most people, with a few friends who love me and know the truth. I've got no ambition to be in a modern day freak show, even if it meant I miss the chance to appear on Oprah.

"I think I've heard about it too." I filled him in on my conversation with the Father. "But if it looked like his parishioners died of disease, maybe it's not the same thing."

Paul shook his head. "No, it just means he's varying how he kills. That's not good." I could almost see him itching to reach for his phone. After a moment, his shoulders relaxed fractionally. "But that's a problem for another day. Right now we've got werewolf problems. There's plenty of vampires working on finding the rogue. They don't need me."

"You sure? A rogue vampire sounds pretty bad too."

He nodded. "I'm sure. One problem at a time."

Right about then, we arrived at Laura's apartment, and Paul, as always, found a parking spot, as if by magic.

As we got out, I tensed. Something was watching us. All my senses were suddenly on alert.

Paul stopped and glanced at me. "What's wrong?"

"Something's out there." I turned slowly, scanning with eyes, ears and my intuition. I heard a low chuckle and whirled around to see Runner stepping out of the shadow of a nearby building.

"You're sharp, warlock."

I relaxed and looked at Paul. "You knew he was

there, didn't you?"

One side of his mouth quirked. "Yes. The smell of wet dog was overpowering. I just assumed you smelled it too."

Runner laughed. "Not as strong as the smell of fresh blood all over you."

I half expected Paul to stiffen, but he just smiled.

The werewolf snorted and put a heavy hand on my shoulder. "Seriously, kid. Your senses are sharp. That'll keep you alive."

I felt oddly pleased at the praise, and we all entered the building in companionable silence. It seemed we all had, without speaking about it, decided to save our news until we were all together.

Even so, there was one question I had to ask. "Runner, how's the kid? Did you find someone to take care of him?"

The werewolf nodded. "Yes, I did. There's a family out near Gainesville that just lost their son. They were glad to have a little one to fuss over." He looked at me sharply. "Something tells me they just got a new son."

I nodded, still saddened by the remembered memory of the dead bodies. "Yeah, we found his parents. They're dead."

Paul made a silencing gesture. "Not now. Let's wait until we're in Laura's apartment. Walls can have ears."

Arriving at Laura's apartment, I noticed the door had been replaced from the encounter a couple of nights ago. Paul gave me an abashed look. "I arranged to pay for having it replaced."

I knocked and expected the door to slide silently open, like it usually did. I frowned when it didn't open right away. Paul stiffened beside me, and Runner glanced back and forth between us. "Trouble?"

"I'm not sure. Laura usually opens the door right away."

Runner shrugged. "She's in a chair. Maybe she just needs a minute to get over here."

Paul shook his head. "No, she opens it by voice remote. And, if I remember correctly, she has hidden cameras on the door, so she can see who is here. I don't like this."

We all tensed. Doors can be replaced, but friends can't, and if Laura was in trouble—

The door opened, and a pleasant looking man waved us in. "Sorry for the delay. We were taking care of some personal things."

"Who are you?" My voice was harsh.

The young man blinked and stepped back. "Umm, I'm Jim. I'm Laura's new caretaker."

Laura's voice sounded from inside the apartment. "It's okay, guys. Jim's cool. Come on in."

She sounded fine, her tone amused, and we entered slowly. Paul didn't relax, however, until we saw Laura, safe in her chair by the computer desk.

"Sorry about that," she said. "I should have let you know there was someone new here. With everything that's been going on, it just slipped my mind."

I grinned crookedly. "No need to apologize. I should have figured it was the new guy." I glanced from Jim to

Laura and cocked my head questioningly.

She got it and turned to Jim. "We'll be a couple of hours, I guess. Why don't you head out and come back around, say 10:00? We'll take it from there."

Jim looked at each of us. His expression made it clear he thought she was nuts to be alone with us, but he finally shrugged. "Whatever. I'll see you in a couple of hours."

He grabbed his jacket and walked past me to the door. I could just hear him muttering under his breath. "They told me she was weird, but they had no idea."

I chuckled as he closed the door behind him. "He's going to take some housebreaking."

Laura snorted. "Not the word I'd have used. Come on guys, look at it from his point of view. You all looked like you were ready to tear him limb from limb."

I looked at the floor, suddenly embarrassed. "Yeah, I guess I see what you mean."

Her voice softened. "On the other hand, it's nice to know I have such dedicated protectors."

Billy came out of the bedroom, and we all gave him some attention, except for Paul. The black Lab still hadn't gotten over his mistrust of the vampire.

After a few minutes, the dog settled down nearby, and Laura said, "Let's get started. But first, how about some snacks? Dafydd, I've got plenty of Coke in the fridge, and I had Jim stock up on baked Ruffles."

My stomach suddenly growled as if I hadn't just eaten. I loved baked chips.

"There's also some cookies in the cupboard." She

turned to look at Paul and Runner. "Um, I didn't really know what werewolves like, but something about you said dark ale, so there's some good imported stuff in the cupboard by the fridge."

Runner's eyebrows rose, and he turned to me. "You've got some friend there." He turned back to Laura, thanked her and headed to the kitchen.

Laura flushed slightly as she looked at Paul, and I decided to wait a moment to raid the fridge. Something told me this was going to be good.

"Maybe you were kidding, but there's a bag of O-positive in the fridge. I hope that's okay."

For the first time since I'd met him, the vampire looked surprised. And pleased. "That wasn't needed."

"I know," Laura said. "But I wanted to. And, there's red wine in the cupboard by the ale."

He blinked, and she hastily added. "I mean, if you like to mix it with wine or something."

Paul bowed slightly. "Yes, I do like that. Thank you." He turned to me. "Runner's right. She is a good friend."

Warmth rushed through me. I was happy for Laura. From the way her eyes were shining, I knew she was thrilled by their approval.

We all trooped into the kitchen for our respective snacks. Runner waxed eloquent for a moment over the ale. He could have it. I've always thought dark ale was nasty stuff. Paul poured some blood and wine into a glass and carefully mixed it. It didn't look too odd that way. He surprised me by also grabbing some chips. When he caught my look, he grinned. "They're good."

"I didn't think you went for solid stuff."

"All–liquid diets are pretty unsatisfying. Even for my kind."

Back in the living room, we all settled down. Paul and I took the couch while Runner flopped down on the floor. He'd also taken some chips, and the three of us munched companionably for a few minutes.

Finally, I said, "Guess we'd better start. Paul filled me in on the way over about what he got from the vampires. It's not much, but—" I turned to Paul. "Go ahead and fill them in on what you do have." I hoped he got my hint that he didn't have to tell them anything he didn't want to.

I noticed Runner giving me an appraising look, and I wondered if he picked up on it too. After a moment, the big werewolf shrugged and turned his attention back to Paul.

The vampire was saying, "My kind is focused on another problem. They haven't been paying attention to much beyond that. A couple of the younger vampires did say they'd noticed more werewolf activity but beyond the expected 'wet dog' comments, they didn't have much useful to add."

Runner snorted. "I'll show them what a 'wet dog' can do, if we've a mind to."

Paul didn't laugh at the attempted joke. "My advice is to stay away from them right now. The community is on edge, and I don't want there to be any misunderstandings."

Runner looked surprised, but said nothing.

Paul continued. "Anyway, I was hoping for more, but I struck out."

I glanced at Runner. "Paul can you fill everyone in on what we found on the bodies?"

Laura interrupted. "What about the kid? Who's going to tell him?

Runner answered. "Soon as we're done here, I'll call the family watching the kid. They'll let him know as gently as possible."

I winced. There was no good way to tell a kid his parents were never coming home again.

"They're good people," he added. "They'll take good care of him. And I'll keep an eye on him, make sure he grows up well and knows how to control his change."

We all sat in silence for a moment. Just like that, the kid was in and out of my life. I'd found him just a few mornings ago, and I doubted I'd ever see him again. I missed him already. But his parents were our concern now. Someone needed to avenge their death, and human authority would never be able to do it, assuming they even found the bodies.

I took a deep breath and looked at Paul. "Bodies?"

Runner leaned forward. "Yes, do tell. Any clues to who did this?"

Paul shook his head. "The bodies don't tell us much. They were definitely killed by something with large teeth. It fits with a werewolf killing."

"Only one, or a pack?" Runner asked.

"More than one, by the size and shape of the wounds."

Runner frowned. "That's strange. It's odd for infecteds to be working together."

"Why is that?" I asked.

"Infecteds usually roam alone. Since we natural weres are in control of our transformation, we don't try to hide what we are. We pass that trait on to our children, and we form family groups and packs. Infecteds don't have a pack structure, and they usually hide what they are most of the month. That tends to make them loaners. So for more than one infected to work together is very unusual... although it does tend to make sense if someone is using them as thugs."

I nodded. "That goes along with what I learned from the psychics. And with what happened after we found the bodies."

Runner's eyebrows shot up, and he looked from me to Paul and then back again. "What happened?"

I let Paul answer. "We were attacked. By three werewolves."

Runner sat back, eyes wide. "You're sure? Not just big dogs?"

Paul snorted. "Runner. I've been doing this long enough to tell the difference."

The big werewolf looked abashed. He glanced at Laura. "From your lack of reaction, I'm guessing I was the only one who didn't know about this?"

Laura did a kind of shrug with her eyebrows.

"Always the last to know." Runner thought for a moment. "Okay, yeah, you have been dealing with my kind long enough to know the difference. Sorry for doubting you, Paul. It's just … for three werewolves to attack a vampire—" He looked at me and at Laura. "We don't consider that good odds. For us."

I nodded. "I think if Paul hadn't been trying to protect me he would have taken them down fast. As it was, he was hampered by worrying about me."

Runner nodded, but Paul shook his head and said, "Don't be so sure." A grin lit up his face. "And it's not like Dafydd didn't handle himself well. Pepper spray works pretty well on your kind."

Runner winced. "Yeah, it does." He said it like he knew it from personal experience. "Nice job. Glad you had it on you, kid, but that still doesn't explain why they attacked you. A vampire plus an unknown should have made them keep their distance."

Paul nodded. "I've been thinking about that. I've played back the fight in my memory a few times, and I'm pretty certain they were young. Maybe only their second or third change. No more."

I did the math. "That means they were infected within the month."

They both nodded, and Paul said, "Exactly."

Runner frowned. "Well, that would explain why they didn't know better than to attack a vampire."

"They might not even have known what I was," Paul said. "I bet they smelled I wasn't human, but it's unlikely they've run into many of my kind in the last month."

"Wait a minute. How can you tell they were young?" I asked.

Paul shrugged. "From the way they moved. Just turning into a wolf doesn't automatically mean you know how to work the new body. I've fought new wolves and experienced ones. The more you change, the better you get at using the body. These guys weren't really clumsy, which told me it wasn't their first change, but they weren't as smooth as they're going to get later."

Great. I thought we'd been pretty amazing, and now I learned they were just newbies.

I must have scowled or something because Paul laughed. "Don't sweat it, Dafydd. You did great. Just because werewolves don't think three to one odds good ones doesn't mean they couldn't take a vampire. They can. It's just not guaranteed and werewolves tend to avoid anything that isn't a sure bet."

Runner nodded. "Unless they're too young to know better. How'd they fare, by the way?"

"They all lived. One of them was pretty big, and fast. He took a big piece out of me before Dafydd took down one. Once the odds were two against two, and they knew Dafydd could defend himself, they packed it in."

"I'll send a couple of my people out to see if they can pick up a trail." The werewolf shrugged. "Probably too late, but it's worth a try."

"Give it a shot," Paul said.

"Okay, so you all were attacked. You're thinking it's the same ones what killed the kid's parents?"

Paul shook his head. "No. They didn't smell the same. I got a good scent of the ones that killed the parents. I'd know them anywhere, and these weren't the same ones."

Laura chimed in. "You sure? I mean, you were in the middle of a fight?"

Runner answered. "Yeah, he's sure. Vampire sense of smell isn't as good as ours, but he's better at keeping track of multiple things in a fight. Easy enough for him to be mixing it up while a part of his brain analyzes what his nose is telling him."

Laura looked impressed. "So if they weren't the same ones, what were they doing there? And why'd they attack you?"

"That's still the question," I said. "The best we've been able to come up with is that they are watching or protecting something there." I turned to Laura. "That's where you come in. Any chance you turned up anything? Either on the 14th Street angle, or the warehouse?"

Before Laura could answer, Runner asked, "What 14th Street angle?"

"It's pretty thin so far, but there have been some shopkeepers on 14th who've been threatened. No specifics, but one of them had heard howling, and I kind of put the threats together with what you'd said about someone in New York using werewolves as muscle."

Runner nodded. "Okay. Do we have anything else?"

"Maybe," Laura said. She rolled over to her computer and started to give it some commands. After a moment, she said, "Dafydd, can you come over here and turn the monitor around so everyone can see?"

I obliged, peeking at the screen as I did so. It looked to be some sort of video, paused now. I wondered if it was footage of the night of the murder. If it was, I wasn't sure I really wanted to see exactly what had happened.

Paul and Runner came closer to look. "What's this?" the vampire asked.

"It's footage from the night of the murders. A couple of the nearby warehouses have video cameras on the outside."

Runner whistled. "And you were able to hack in?"

Laura nodded. "Easy stuff." She shot Paul a wry look. "Much easier than covering your traces on the Mall."

I snorted. I'd forgotten to pass that on to Paul.

The vampire gave her another bow, deeper this time. "My gratitude, lady." His eyes twinkled. "It's nice knowing someone has our back in the tech world."

She gave him a stern look. "Just don't think I'll cover up, you know, vampire kills, or anything like that."

He smiled. "No worries. I'm good at avoiding cameras for those."

Laura looked worried for a moment before Paul added, "Just kidding."

"Yeah, these days he's careful about who he kills," Runner said. "Just the real bad dudes."

Laura glanced back and forth between werewolf and vampire, both of whom wore carefully bland expressions.

I cleared my throat. "Laura, don't worry about them. Obviously you can't put two supernatural creatures in a room without them nagging each other. For now, can we get back to the video?"

Laura nodded and said, "Play."

The video started rolling. At first it didn't look like much: a grainy black and white shot of a parking lot. I looked closer and saw two people huddled next to the side of one of the buildings. They were dressed in several layers of clothing, even though the temperature was still warm. I guessed they were the kid's parents.

Movement to the side caught my attention, and I watched in fascination as three large wolves padded on-screen and approached the two people. The man must have seen them because he stood up and pointed. There was no sound, but I could see him yell something, and the woman stood up and started to run.

"Bad move," Runner said. "Running'll set them off every time."

"Doubtful it would have mattered," Paul said.

I ignored them, horrified, but unable to tear my eyes from the screen. Two wolves went for the man while the third raced after the woman. Then the real horror began.

All I can say was that it was over quickly. Within moments, both people were dead, and the wolves loped off as if killing homeless people was something they did all the time. No hesitation. No moment of regret. Just kill and go.

I felt sick to my stomach. When I looked at Laura, I could tell from her expression that she felt the same.

Paul and Runner, however, seemed unmoved by the violence. "Play it again," Runner said.

Paul looked at me, sympathy on his face. "You don't have to watch it again. But he and I need to see if there's anything that will help us find them."

"Or at least identify them so my people can take care of them," Runner said.

I nodded. "Yeah, I understand. Look at it as many times as you need. I'm gonna use the restroom a minute."

I left the room, feeling useless. I knew I shouldn't, but somehow I felt like I'd betrayed everyone by not being able to watch the video again. I'd never seen real death before, and what was on that screen was very different from TV and movie fare. In the movies, you always know it isn't real. This was different because it was.

In the bathroom, I splashed water on my face and washed my hands several times. Even though I hadn't touched anything, I still felt dirty. I wasn't sure I'd ever feel clean again.

I heard Laura's wheelchair hum in the hallway, and I remembered I hadn't closed the door. I turned to see her sitting outside the door.

"It was pretty bad. I didn't want to watch it again."

I tried a grin, but I doubted it was convincing. "That's why you had me turn the screen, right?"

She blushed. "Yeah, actually."

I thought of something. "What about the thing by the Monument? It killed several people."

She cocked her head. "Not sure. That didn't bother me as much. I guess it was more like a monster movie. And I didn't know any of them. Not that I knew those people either, but I know the kid."

I nodded. "Yeah, that makes a difference." I glanced

over my shoulder. "Think they're done watching it?"

"Dunno. Ready to go back and see?"

I wasn't sure I was. But did I have any real choice?

WE WENT BACK to the living room, and Paul and Runner were back in their chairs.

"Did you get what you needed from the video?" I asked, hoping I wouldn't need to watch it again.

Runner nodded. "I'll recognize them if I see them again."

"As will I," Paul said.

"Do either of you know any of them?"

They both shook their heads. "And that's odd," Paul said. "Until now, I thought I knew all the infecteds in town. I didn't recognize any of their scents when we found the bodies, but I thought maybe they were newcomers." He turned to Runner. "I was sure you'd know them. You definitely know everyone in town."

"You don't know them because they are also pretty new werewolves," Runner said.

"As new as the ones who attacked us?" I asked.

He shook his head. "I don't think so, but not too much older. Maybe their second or third full moon phase. They were pretty good, but older ones are more comfortable with four legs. You probably noticed that on the video."

I hadn't noticed anything of the kind. But that might have been because I was trying not to see too much.

Paul was nodding slowly. "And it's not just the four

legs. Did you see the big male? He looked like he still didn't quite know what to do with all those teeth."

"Exactly. Didn't stop him from killing, but there was no elegance to it."

I wasn't sure that "elegance" was a term I'd ever apply toward killing, but I decided not to mention it.

Runner continued. "They also weren't acting as a pack, but that's normal for their kind. The woman almost got away. Never would have happened if they'd been working together."

"What about the ones that attacked us?" I asked. "I admit I wasn't noticing the finer points of their attacks, but they were working pretty well together, I thought."

Paul frowned and nodded. "Now that you mention it, you're right. They did work together well." He looked at Runner. "Not quite like you would with your pack mates, but they definitely fought as a team."

Runner thought for a moment. "It might be because they have worked together, before they changed. That's possible."

"Then they might have been, say gang members or something like that?" I asked.

They both nodded. "That would make sense," Paul said.

I turned to Laura. "That give you something else to research?"

She nodded slowly, obviously already thinking through where she'd look. "Yes, I can see what gangs generally work that area. And I've got more than just the video. I don't know how it fits into the werewolves, but

Dafydd tracked down some information about shop owners being threatened, specifically in the 14th Street area, so I did a little research."

"What kind of research?" Paul asked.

"I checked into who is developing that area. As you might expect, there are several. Douglas Development is one, and I thought for a minute, he might be the one we were looking for."

I nodded. Douglas Jemal, the owner of Douglas Development, had been in the news in recent years. "If I remember correctly, there was something about him not paying small contractors?"

"Pretty much. And some other things, but I don't think he's our guy. Lots of people don't like him, but I couldn't find anything linking him to violence. I can dig more if you want, but I think the person we're looking for is Mark McDonald."

I thought for a minute, but nothing about that name came to mind. "I don't think I know him."

"Not surprising. He's fairly new in town. He arrived in in the D.C. area just a couple of years ago."

"Any stories about violence?" Paul asked.

"Not here, no. But—" She drew it out, and I knew she was enjoying a bit of suspense.

"But what?" I asked, playing along.

"He came from Chicago. And I did some news searches. Although he was never charged with anything, there were a number of reports about 'mysterious injuries and even deaths' associated with his projects."

Runner nodded. "Okay, that's something, but by itself doesn't mean he's our guy."

I shook my head, remembering Paul's story from earlier. Granted, that was a long time ago, but if it can happen once.

Runner noticed my gesture. "You got a reason to think otherwise?"

Paul answered for me. "I've seen something like this in Chicago before. A long time ago, but …." He shrugged.

Runner frowned. "How long ago?"

"Last century."

"Seriously? You think there's a link between now and something that long ago."

Paul shrugged. "I don't believe in coincidence. You heard of any recent werewolf activity in Chicago?" Paul asked.

The big werewolf nodded, the gesture casual. "Of course. There's packs there just like anywhere." He frowned. "Well, maybe a few more than other places. Chicago does have a lot of weird stuff. Doesn't the oldest vampire in the States live there?"

Paul nodded. "Yeah, she does. I've never met her, but her reputation does get around." He turned to Laura. "Is that all?"

She smiled and shot me a look. I grinned back.

Paul and Runner looked at us and then at each other. "What?" Paul asked.

"Well, McDonald did just start buying up land around the 14th Street corridor."

I knew there had to be more than that. "Okay,

you've given us the dribs and drabs. What's the really good stuff, Laura?"

Her smile grew broader. "Well, it wasn't much of a story, but buried in the middle of a longer piece on him, it was mentioned that McDonald was fascinated with wolves, owned several wolf hybrids and even a few purebreds and was always accompanied, especially at night, by at least one very large wolf."

Runner and Paul sat up in their chairs. Paul was nodding. "That could mean something. He might be our guy."

I looked at Runner, whose expression was thoughtful. "It might be nothing. Unless he's got one of my kind with him, he'd only be able to have an infected with him during the full moon. Plenty of people are foolish enough to mess around with wolves and hybrids, and it might be no more than that."

"Sure, lots of people own hybrids," I said. "But how many of them are also developers with a history of associated violence who are also buying and developing land near 14th Street, where there are stories about shopkeepers being threatened?"

"And where people have heard howling at night," Laura said. "Don't forget that part."

Paul looked at Runner. "And what if he has recruited one of your kind? That makes him even more dangerous."

Runner shook his head firmly. "No way. None of my people would work with someone who goes around infecting people."

Paul's voice was quiet and sympathetic. "Runner. You've got bad seeds in your kind, just like humans do."

The werewolf snorted. "Yeah, and like your kind occasionally has a good seed."

Paul smiled. "Yes, that too. Can you ask any of your people if they know anyone in Chicago?"

Runner nodded, his reluctance plain. "I can. There's a family unit who just arrived from the Midwest. If anyone knows anything, it'd be them."

His tone made it obvious that he didn't expect to learn anything. I was sympathetic. I didn't like the fact that there were warlocks who used their power for evil. But I didn't deny that they existed. And it just made me more dedicated to using my powers to help people.

I turned to Laura. "Can you do any more digging?"

"Of course," she said. "That was just what I turned up in a couple of hours. Give me a day, and I'll know a lot more. I'm going to see if I can find some video of McDonald and these wolves. Runner, would you know a werewolf from a regular wolf if I found video?"

His answer was still reluctant. "Yeah. I know you humans can't tell the difference, but it'd be obvious to any of my kind."

"I know you don't want to believe it, my friend," Paul said. "But you've seen it before."

Runner nodded. "Yeah, I have. And I don't ever want to see it again. Thinking about it makes me sick."

"A couple of the vampires in town are from Chicago," Paul said. "I can ask them if they've heard anything about this McDonald guy or werewolf activity."

Everyone else had a job or something to check out. I was left feeling kind of like a fifth leg on, well, on a wolf.

Paul turned to me. "Dafydd? Are you doing anything after this meeting?"

I shook my head. "Nothing planned, no. Why?"

Paul looked uncomfortable, and my attention was definitely piqued. "Well, I'd like you to come with me when I talk to the vampires."

I hadn't seen that coming. "Sure, but why?"

I could see that Laura and Runner were also eagerly awaiting the answer to the question.

"If you and I are going to keep working together on weird stuff, the vampires need to know about you and that you are under my protection."

Okay, that was interesting, but something told me there was more to it than that. "That sounds good, but why now? Wouldn't it be better to wait until this was all over? Make it more of a social visit?"

I could almost feel Laura willing me to shut up and not ask too many questions. I ignored her and focused on Paul. All my instincts were telling me to push this one.

Paul's shoulders slumped slightly. "Maybe, but—" His voice trailed off, and I just waited.

"But I think I need your help," he finally said.

I raised an eyebrow. "My help? How?"

"I need you to read the auras of some of my fellow vampires."

I frowned. "Well, sure I can do it, but what are you looking for?"

"Can you tell if someone is being truthful?" Paul asked.

Ah, that's what he was looking for. A mystical lie detector test. "I should be able to. Worried your vampire informants are going to be less than truthful?"

The vampire gave me a toothy smile. "You should always assume a vampire is going to be less than truthful."

I wondered how seriously I should take that but decided to let it go for the moment. "Well, I can't promise anything since I haven't done much aura reading on vampires." Kind of an understatement. Paul was the only vampire I'd ever read, and I hadn't been reading him for truthfulness. "But I should be able to give you something."

"Whatever you can give me will be fine."

"Anyone else have something to add, or should we go our separate ways and regroup tomorrow evening?" I looked at Runner. "That give you enough time to talk to your people?"

The werewolf nodded. "Yeah. I should be able to catch the family before they turn in." He grinned. "Werewolves usually stay up pretty late." He inclined his head toward Paul. "Just like vampires."

The joke wasn't much, but we all needed it and laughed. We all said our goodbyes and agreed to meet at the same time tomorrow night. I felt like we were finally getting somewhere, and I didn't want to lose the momentum.

Outside, we waved Runner on his way and headed

for Paul's Prius.

We drove in silence most of the way. I thought about the video and my reaction to it, but I wasn't ready to talk about it yet.

Paul drove across the bridge into D.C. and took Constitution Avenue. When he stopped at a light, he turned to look at me. "There was another reason I wanted to take you to the bar."

I roused myself from idle contemplation of the street lights. "Yeah?"

"Yes." He was silent for a moment. "You know how I said I'd understand if you wanted to have nothing to do with the more violent side of my life?"

"Yeah." I wasn't sure where he was going with this.

He paused and finally said, "I think it's time for you to see what the other side looks like."

I got it. "Want to see if I could handle that side of you too? From what you've said, you're … kind of tame? Compared to the rest of your kind?"

He chuckled. "I've not really thought of myself as 'tame,' but yes, I think it's a good idea for you to meet vampires who have no qualms about killing."

"I can see that." I felt up for the challenge. If I can learn to look at dead bodies, I figured I could handle vampires. As long as I didn't have to be in a dark alley alone with them. I indicated as much to Paul.

"Let's definitely not have you alone with them in the dark. You'll be fairly safe when I indicate you are under my protection, but no need to take unnecessary risks."

"Works for me. Let's find out what vampires are really like, then."

Chapter 7

Sunday, September 6, 2009:
late evening

W E FINISHED THE drive to Lounge 201, which was located near Union Station. There were a number of neighborhood lounges, bars and grills and the like in the area, mostly catering to the staffers on the Hill. Not exactly my type of people, which is why I've never been there.

As we got close, my phone rang. I groaned, figuring it was Abby again. She often calls me Sunday night to try to get focused for the upcoming week.

Paul gave me a curious look as I took out my phone. When I blushed, he grinned but politely turned away to give me the illusion of privacy.

"Uh, hi, Stephen."

I listened to him for a moment before saying, "Yeah, that sounds good, but hey, now really isn't a good time to talk. I'm kind of in the middle of something."

Right then, Paul found a parking place.

"Uh huh. Yeah, sure, I'll call you tomorrow."

I hung up, relieved that it hadn't taken long. Yeah, I know. There's something not right about wanting to get rid of your (almost) boyfriend quickly, but I do try to keep business and pleasure separated.

"Boyfriend or downline?" Paul asked.

"Boyfriend. He had an idea for Saturday." I hoped if I kept it short, he'd get the message that I didn't want to talk about it right now.

Paul started to open his door, but I motioned him to stop.

"What?"

"I need to prepare my sight, assuming you still want me to check auras."

"Right," he said, as he settled back.

I closed my eyes and settled back into the comfortable seat.

Aura sight isn't significantly different from regular sight. Almost everything has an aura, even objects. People project something about who they are. Objects pick up the energy of people and events. I can see both. Interpreting auras is more of an art than a science, but I'd had a good teacher in my aunt, and I get by.

I put myself into a light trance and concentrated. Some people visualize aura sight as being sort of a third eye that is located in the middle of the forehead. Not so for me. My aura senses are located near my stomach. Hence the saying "gut feeling."

Yeah, I know. It doesn't make sense that you "see" something with your stomach, but it's how it works for me. I still "see" with my eyes, but something deep inside me senses the aura, and then my brain interprets what it all means. It's hard to explain if you've never experienced it.

I felt something settle in place deep inside me, and I

knew I'd achieved the right level of concentration. Carefully, I opened my eyes and glanced around.

Everything looked pretty much the way it did normally, except for a riot of colors surrounding everything. I studied Paul for a moment. I'd read him right after we'd first met, and not much had changed. As before, the colors surrounding him swirled in a kaleidoscope of green, purple and blue, all shot through with black and red streaks.

He frowned. "Any change?"

I shook my head. "Nope. You're still pretty balanced. Maybe a bit more purple." I frowned. "Been working through spiritual stuff, it looks like." I shot him a quick grin. "Attending church maybe?"

He snorted. "Hardly."

"Just teasing, though there really is a bit more purple."

"Is that good or bad?"

I shrugged. "Hard to say. I don't think it's either. It's not a bad color. You're still who you are."

"Good to know. Ready to go?"

I looked around again. Having aura sight active is always a bit disorienting until I get used to it. "I think so. I'm not used to having it active for more than a few minutes at a time. Steady me if I get wobbly?"

He nodded. "Definitely."

"Let's go then." I opened the door and got out. The ground seemed to waver below my feet, but I concentrated and got it back under control. This was going to be interesting.

Paul locked the car doors, came around to the side-walk and stayed close as we started for the lounge.

And of course that's when my phone rang again. Paul raised an eyebrow as I answered. This time the groan was deeper and more heart felt. "Downline," I mouthed at Paul, and he nodded.

I stopped. I never was very good at talking on the phone and walking at the best of times. With this vision, trying to do both was a disaster waiting to happen.

"Hi Abby," I said when I answered.

As I expected, she launched into her grand and total-ly unrealistic plans for the week. Funny how they sounded an awful lot like the plans from last week. And the week before that. I said "yep" and "uh hum" in all the right places and closed with, "Sounds good, Abby. You do that, and you'll definitely have a great week."

She began to launch into the latest crisis in her per-sonal life, and I cut her off. "Sorry, Abby. I really have to go. Got a meeting with a potential client. We'll talk later." And I hung up. I learned two things about Abby a long time ago. One, never let her talk long. She's capable of wasting an entire day on the phone. Two, she's so self–absorbed that she'll never remember that I cut her off every time. Maybe not nice, but it does work and keeps my interactions with her controllable.

Paul was grinning as I pointedly turned off my phone. "Meeting with a potential client? Really? You do know that vampires don't really do the vitamin thing, right?"

I smiled back at him. "You really should, you know.

The right vitamins can greatly extend your life."

He laughed. "Blood does that for us, thanks. And it tastes better."

I shuddered. "If you say so." Then I turned serious. "So, anything I should know before we enter the lion's den?"

"Stay close to me."

"That's pretty obvious. Anything else?"

He thought for a moment. "Yes, don't let anyone get you alone. Don't make eye contact. And don't be startled at anything they ask or say. My kind likes to test humans, and they'll say pretty shocking stuff to see if they can get a rise out of you. It's part of how we select our prey."

Great. "Okay, play it cool. I can do that."

He smiled, the expression reassuring. "You'll be fine." He paused, and his eyes shifted away from mine. "Do you mind if I touch you? Like have my hand on your shoulder or back?"

I frowned. "No. Why?"

"Because it's a way we show someone's under our protection. It'd be even better if I could mark you, but obviously that's not possible."

"Mark me? Like give me something to wear?"

"No. Like bite you."

My hand unconsciously went to the side of my throat. "Oh. Right. No, I'd rather you didn't do that. Touching works for me."

I'd been feeling pretty confident about this, but now my stomach was churning. Paul gave me a reassuring smile. "Don't worry. I'm probably being over cautious.

The Lounge isn't really a place to pick up prey. Humans who know about us do gather there, but they are looking for vampire action, and they're usually pretty obvious about it. Other than those types, we leave humans alone here. I guess I'm just worried because of the rogues."

I nodded. "Okay. Well, let's get in there before my nerves get the better of me."

We went down the short flight of stairs that led to the Lounge. A chalk sign by the stairs told us that tonight was closed for a private event. I stopped. "Are you sure? They say they're closed."

"Don't worry about that. They're only open for private events Saturday through Monday, so we have the front bar reserved every week on those days." He flashed a quick smile. "They love us. We're their best customers. We've been here for, oh, I guess five years now. Almost as long as they've been open."

My eyes widened. "Isn't that expensive?"

Paul gave me a look of honest curiosity. "Yes, so?"

Once again, I was struck by the difference between vampires and humans. Money just didn't seem to have the same impact for them as it did for us. "Never mind," I said. "Let's go in."

We entered the lounge, and a burly gentleman at the door checked our IDs. I glanced around, trying to keep the two parts of my sight (aura and human) separate for a moment. I wanted to get a feel for it as a physical place before I "looked" at it with my other senses.

It was a nice enough place. The bar was circular and large, with three bartenders busy serving the crowded front area. Small tables and round chairs dotted the room. Three big screen TVs dominated the far wall, tuned to sports channels and news. Loud music hammered through speakers. Mostly 90s rock. Not quite my taste. I was more into dance and electric.

The color theme was red, which I thought explained the attraction to the vampire crowd. Lighting was dim enough to be comfortable while still allowing you to see. And, trust me, there was plenty to see.

I immediately recognized I was in the presence of a group of predators. Mostly they seemed to be restraining themselves, but I saw the occasional flash of overly long fangs. Women prowled by in flowing dresses, except for the ones in skin–tight clingy black things. The men ranged from formal wear to jeans and t–shirts. Not surprisingly, black and red were the dominant colors, though a few were daring in blue or deep purple.

That was just the colors of the clothes. When I looked at their auras, I saw even more. A dark, vibrant green flashed from the aura of a male vampire, arguing with another. A female vampire, her expression smug, looked on, her aura shifting between an unwholesome red and a sickly green–yellow. Near the bar, another vampire's aura caught my eye. It was shot through with purple and blue, and I guessed he was young and not yet completely lost to evil. Or he was like Paul and didn't completely embrace everything about the vampire lifestyle.

Paul nudged me down the short flight of stairs to the front room. "What do you think?" he asked, his voice pitched low.

"How can the humans here fool themselves into thinking this is normal? Can't they feel the atmosphere here? I mean, even without aura sight, I'd know this place was a hunting ground."

He sighed. "And we're actually on our best behavior here. You should come by a private meeting some time."

I shuddered. "No offense, but I'd rather not."

He smiled briefly. "Back to your question. You know humans are infinitely capable of rationalization."

"True, but still —"

"And think about this," he continued. "Many of the humans who come here like the sense of danger. It's part of the appeal. Since most of them can't identify what the danger actually is, it intensifies their desire even more. It's really quite like a drug for them."

"That is wrong on so many levels."

Paul's only response was a shrug.

"Fine, but what about the owner and employees? Don't you guys weird them out?"

Another shrug. "Probably. But the money is good."

Looking around, I could see money was definitely flowing. It continually surprised me what people would do for cash.

Feeling a chill down my back, I turned, suddenly aware that I was being watched. Across the room, a man was looking at me. His pale skin and black and red attire marked him as a vampire. He smiled, showing long white fangs and tried to meet my eyes. Remembering what Paul had said, I flicked my eyes down to his mouth, which curved into a broader smile.

I admit I was seriously freaked out, but I remembered what Paul had said about vampires trying to intimidate humans, and I was damned if I was going to let that happen. I glanced up, meeting his eyes briefly, just to show him I could, and then I pointedly looked away and put a possessive hand on Paul's arm. I let my fingers roam briefly and was rewarded with a quick shiver.

Paul's attention had been on the other side of the room, but it quickly turned to me. "What?"

I made a point of looking deeply into his eyes as I answered. "One of your friends over there is making a play. I figured if you could warn them off by showing possessiveness toward me, it might work the other way as well."

Paul's eyes slid from me to the other vampire. Figuring my point had been well made, I looked as well. My gaze was rewarded by a frown, but this time no teeth. Paul laid a hand on my shoulder and met the other's gaze directly. Apparently it wasn't a problem for other vampires. The other bowed his head slightly and moved deeper into the crowd.

Paul nodded and said, "Good move."

"It was?" As soon as the other vampire moved off, I realized how nervous I had been.

"Yes, it was. You're right. Vampires aren't the only ones who are possessive of their humans. It can go the other way as well, though it's not as common. You sent a very clear message." A smile moved across his face.

"Naturally, we've been under observation from the moment we entered. They'll make assumptions I hadn't intended them to make."

A sinking feeling in my stomach. "Um, what does that mean, exactly?"

His smile broadened. "Well, vampires use touch and other subtle signals as an unspoken language. I was planning to send the message that you and I were exploring possibilities. By touching and looking at me the way you did, you told them all we're together."

"And by together you mean?"

"A couple."

That's what I'd been afraid of. "And exactly what does being a couple mean in this situation?"

"That I'm drinking from you. And not sharing."

Automatically, my hand started to rise to my neck. I stopped it before it did more than twitch. "But you've never bitten me. Won't they notice that?"

He laughed. "No worries. We don't just bite necks. They'll assume I'm taking you somewhere else. Like the inside of your elbow, where it won't show."

That wasn't as reassuring as it should have been, and the inside of my arm suddenly itched.

I glanced around, idly letting my eyes roam the crowd, and I'd just manage to relax a little when a deep, resonant voice spoke behind me.

"Paul. Perhaps you'd like to introduce me to your friend."

I turned to see who had arrived. He was short, maybe even an inch or so shorter than I am, but his presence made him seem much taller. His hair was black and cut loose, unlike many others in the lounge. Slicked–back–from–hair–gel seemed to be the vampire hair style of choice. His, however, fell straight down to the middle of his back, almost giving the impression of a cape. His features were even, and he'd be attractive if it weren't for the air of menace surrounding him. His gray eyes held no hint of warmth, though they didn't seem particularly unfriendly either. It was hard to put any emotion to them. Also unlike his younger brethren, his clothes weren't black or red. Tailored gray slacks draped legs that were long for his height, but his presence made up for it, and he didn't seem out of proportion. A cobalt shirt under a gray blazer, matching the slacks, completed the outfit. He wore only one piece of jewelry, an intricate silver Celtic cross around his neck. Paul had explained once that the prohibition against religious symbols was another thing the legends had got wrong, and this vampire's comfort with such a symbol confirmed it.

That was just his physical appearance. To my other sight, he was even more intimidating. His aura was almost completely black. Even the red was muted and swirled so completely in the black as to be more deep maroon than a proper red. I saw a hint of light blue, usually curiosity, which made sense considering his question. But that was it. Also unlike the other auras, which moved and shifted constantly, his was virtually still, the difference between a deep pool and a running brook.

I'd never seen anything like it, and I was suddenly

grateful that Paul had been my first introduction to vampires. I doubted I would have survived a meeting in a dark alley with this one.

Paul inclined his head. "Lucius. A pleasure as always."

I knew my friend well enough to sense the irony in his tone.

"Pleasure, Paul? I doubt that." His smooth voice should have been soothing, but it wasn't. All the hairs on the back of my neck rose, and I restrained the urge to run.

Paul placed a gentle hand on my shoulder. Lucius' eyes tracked the movement, and he gave an enigmatic smile.

"What brings you this evening? And with a friend?"

Paul answered smoothly, little emotion in his voice. "I'd heard there were some newcomers in town. From Chicago. I have a small matter to ask of them."

Lucius raised a slender eyebrow. "It's not like you to socialize with our kind. Or ever ask for help."

"I never said I needed help."

"And yet, you did say you have a matter to ask of them. If that's not help, what might it be?" I sensed amusement in his tone. The same kind of amusement a cat might feel right before pouncing on a hapless mouse.

Fortunately, Paul was neither. "Information."

The single word hung between them. Lucius waited a moment, but Paul added nothing more. Finally, the older vampire shrugged. "As you wish. But—"

The hairs on the back of my neck suddenly stood up

straighter.

"What of this one? It's been a while since you took a … *Companion*."

Yes, you could hear the capital in how he said the word. I was pretty sure what he meant by it, and I didn't like it. I wanted to protest that I wasn't any kind of "Companion," but I trusted Paul, and waited to hear what he'd say.

Paul raised an eyebrow fractionally and glanced casually at me. "This one? He's not a Companion."

"Really?" Disbelief dripped from his tone, but he shrugged. "It's no matter to me who you take for Companionship." A wry glance in my direction. "Or what you choose to call it."

Okay, that did it. I really don't like being mocked. While flashy magical effects aren't my thing, nor generally used outside of fantasy novels, I did have one trick up my sleeve, and I decided to pull it now.

Auras work two ways for warlocks and witches. We can see them. We can also let other people see ours, if we want.

I deliberately flared my aura. For just a moment, a halo of swirling greens, blues and purple, with a flash of yellow and just a hint of red and black (no one's perfect) surrounded me.

Lucius face expression didn't change at all, but something flickered in the depth of his gray eyes, and I smiled inwardly. *Didn't expect that, did you?*

Keeping my voice level and casual, I placed a hand on Paul's arm. As I had done before, I ran my hand up and down in a possessive caress. "What makes you think I am *his* Companion?" (I can capitalize in my speech too.)

Then I let my aura fade before we attracted too much attention. A couple of patrons had already noticed and were pointing our way, but most of the lounge was still oblivious. Better to keep it that way.

For just a moment, I allowed myself to meet the elder vampire's gaze. Probably a stupid thing since I didn't know exactly why Paul had warned me from doing it, but right now, I needed to make it clear that he didn't intimidate me. I just hoped he didn't notice the sudden sweat dampening my shirt.

Paul murmured something that sounded approving and slid an arm around my waist, leaning into me for just a moment.

The other vampire finally spoke. "Warlock?"

I nodded.

Lucius directed his next question at Paul. "And you agreed to this?"

"Of course," Paul replied. "I'm old enough to resist a bond, if I choose to."

The next question was to me. "And is this a companionship of equals?"

Dangerous question, but when it came right down to it, there was only one answer. I kept my voice smooth and confident. "Equals, of course. No one in their right mind would …" What was the word Paul had just used? Right, *bond*. "… bond a vampire against his will."

Lucius laughed out loud, brief and harsh, but with

honest amusement. Nearby conversation halted as vampires glanced at us. After a moment, they went back to their business, voices subdued.

The elder vampire spoke. "Little do you know, young one. Many have tried."

With an effort, I maintained an even tone. "And I'm sure they regretted it."

"Assuredly."

I shrugged casually. "My point remains. Then the fools weren't in their right minds. Either before they tried and certainly not afterwards."

Lucius raised an eyebrow and looked at Paul. "I think I like this one." He nodded slowly. "I approve." And with that final comment, he moved off to join another group. I blinked. I'd seen writers describe people as "gliding across the floor," but this was the first time I'd actually seen it. His feet hardly seemed to move as he entered another conversation. I noticed the other vampires shift, seemingly without being aware of it, to make room for him.

I glanced at Paul, who was looking at me with an expression made of equal parts amusement, satisfaction and frustration.

"What?" I asked. "Didn't I do it right?"

Paul chuckled. "Oh, you did it right." He shook his head and nodded toward a nearby alcove where a female vampire, accompanied by two young humans, bowed her head as they vacated the table. "Come on. I think I need to explain what you just told him."

I followed him, and sat down.

"A moment," Paul said before walking to the bar and ordering a couple of drinks.

I glanced around while I waited for him to return. Several vampires and a few humans were eying me curiously, but none of them came over, for which I was grateful. Contrary to Paul's evident opinion, I did have some idea of what I'd just told Lucius, and I was quite sure the word would spread to the other vampires. In fact, from the looks I was getting, I think it had already spread to most of the bar.

And they say words travels fast in high school. Kids have nothing on vampires.

Paul returned with a couple of beers and sat down. I took one and sipped. Ah, the good stuff. I took another satisfying swallow. "Before you tell me what I did, want to fill me in on who that was?"

Paul put down his mug. "Of course. You wouldn't know. That was Lucius, the eldest vampire in D.C."

I almost choked on my drink. "You mean I just baited the big boss in town?"

He smiled, a mixture of approval and amusement in his eyes. "Yes."

Talk about diving into the deep end. "And I just told him, and by extension, the entire vampire community, that you're my, let me see, what's a good word? Escort?" I let my eyes twinkle wickedly. "Boy toy?"

If vampires could blush, Paul would have right then. "Yes, something like that."

I smiled wryly. "And something tells me you were going to let them think the opposite. That I was on my way to being your boy toy?"

Paul sighed. "Yes. In hindsight, perhaps not the best plan."

I decided to let him off the hook. "It's okay. Though it would have been nice to know in advance that I was doing my act in front of the local equivalent of the Godfather."

Respect filled his eyes. Not an emotion I'd seen in him much, at least not directed at me. "I'm sorry. I should have warned you. But flaring your aura. That was very well done."

I quirked a questioning eyebrow at him.

"I hadn't intended to let on that you were a war-lock," Paul said. "My kind generally doesn't like your kind."

"Why not? Supernatural birds of a feather and all that."

Paul chuckled. "In case you hadn't noticed, vampires aren't much for flocking with those not of our kind."

I made a point of taking in the room, vampires and humans shoulder to shoulder. And in a couple of corners, other body parts pressed together.

He nodded. "Oh, we need humans, so we let them think we're associating with them."

"When what you're really doing is feeding on them."

"Exactly." He paused. "Don't take this the wrong way, but to my kind, your kind are little more than cattle."

Unaffected by the put–down, I nodded. "Got that." A sudden thought. "Most people don't, um how do I put this, 'bond' with their livestock."

Paul calmly took a sip of his beer before answering. "Perhaps cattle isn't the right term. More of a combination of livestock and cat. You amuse us at the same time you give us sustenance."

"But you don't treat me that way." I blurted it out, hoping I'd like the answer. The more I saw Paul with his own kind, the more I wondered why he hung around with me.

He shook his head. "True, but I don't share all the inclinations of my kind. I rarely feed from humans."

"Just the bad ones," I said, my tone challenging.

"And I don't even think of that as feeding."

I continued the farmyard analogy. "That's culling the herd."

He smiled. "Yes. That's fairly apt."

"So then what's the harm in letting them know I'm not just another human."

He gave me the look that means I'm supposed to figure it out myself.

I suddenly got it. "You're not the only one who knows what we can do, and my aura reading might not be as useful if they know what I am."

He nodded. "Exactly. My kind knows that you can see us for what we are."

Damn.

"But don't worry too much," he continued. "We do know that warlocks aren't usually as good at it as witches, so they might not be too guarded." His eyes twinkled. "Besides, the fact that you've captured me will make them curious, and they might let more slip because of it."

I blushed suddenly.

"What?" he asked.

"I just realized that I let them think you're involved with me. But you're straight. Won't that be a problem for you?" Coming out in human society was difficult enough. I had no idea what it would mean to vampires. And since Paul wasn't gay, I suddenly worried that I had caused him big problems.

He snorted. "Don't worry about it. Sexual orientation doesn't mean much to us in our relationships with humans."

My eyebrows shot up. "Really?"

He nodded. "Although we do sometimes have sex with our Companions, it doesn't mean the same thing as it would to you."

"What about with other vampires?"

He looked at me sharply. "Right now that's not something I'm prepared to talk about."

I sat back, feeling chided. "Okay, so I haven't messed anything up for you." I couldn't help the chill in my voice.

His eyes softened, and I realized it was as close to an apology as I was going to get. "No, not at all. Although we don't usually associate with warlocks, there's no stigma to it. And everyone will tread lightly around you, which was what I wanted anyway."

I frowned. "Why will they step lightly around me?"

He smiled. "To have captured someone of my age and standing, you'd have to be quite the powerful practitioner."

Oh. I hadn't thought of that. "But won't that make them less likely to reveal something?"

Paul shrugged. "We'll worry about that later." He finished off his beer and glanced around. "For now, let's mingle and see what happens."

I agreed, and we stood up to join the crowd.

Mingling and greeting is not one of my favorite activities. Bob is always bugging me to get out and do more networking to promote my business, and I keep telling him that I'd rather get a root canal. Bob is fantastic at these sorts of things. He enters a room, works it and walks out with tons of business cards to follow up with. It's not my thing. Even when I don't have my aura sight active, I can feel the press of people in a crowd as an almost palpable thing. I go to a few LGBT networking events, and that's about all I can manage.

I soon realized networking with humans had nothing on hanging out with a bunch of vampires and vampire wannabees. Auras pulsed around me: red, black and sickly green predominated, but here and there I glimpsed the yellow and pale greens of a few auras that hadn't been completely tainted by association. I wanted to walk up to the untainted and beg them to leave, before it was too late.

But I couldn't. I'd established myself as a warlock to be reckoned with, one who could ensnare and fascinate one of the oldest vampires in D.C. Almost everyone in the room found a reason to drop by and chat with us for a moment. I let Paul do most of the talking. It didn't hurt my reputation to be seen as aloof.

I'm amazed anyone was fooled by our supposed "relationship." I'm not that tall or terribly muscled. Plus my hair was in sad need of a cut, and I had to keep tossing back a persistent lock that fell into my eyes every couple of minutes. Not the most desirable package.

Paul gently squeezed my arm. "You're doing great," he said, very softly. I hoped he knew what he was doing. Vampire hearing was keen, and I was afraid most of the room had just heard him reassuring me. But apparently he was right on because the next two vampires to approach bowed respectfully to me before chatting with Paul.

I watched these two closely. Something about their auras piqued my interest. There was the usual swirl of red and black, but these two also had a healthy mix of blue, lots of yellow, a touch of green and some of their black shaded closer to gray. Not certain what it all meant, yet, I resolved to listen closely.

"Paul," one of them said. "It's been a while."

Paul nodded. "Damien, Darlene. I understand you're recently in from Chicago."

Ah, these were the vampires Paul had mentioned earlier. I examined them, while feigning indifference, not an easy task.

Damien was an inch or two taller than Paul, which meant I needed to look up sharply to meet his gaze. While most of the vampires in the lounge wore more formal attire, ranging from well–tailored business suits to a few tuxedos, he was dressed casually in black jeans, a maroon silk shirt and a denim jacket, also black. The denim wasn't heavy, and the cut was like a blazer, so on first glance it looked more formal. He looked good in it. The jeans clung to his hips and fell straight down to black leather boots peering out from the boot–cut cuffs. A heavy black belt, with a succession of silver studs, completed the image. He wore no jewelry.

Damien made an interesting contrast to Darlene, who wore a red and black dress which clung to every curve, leaving nothing to the imagination. The neck scooped low down, revealing perfect breasts.

Hey, I may be gay, but that doesn't mean I can't appreciate beauty, in any form.

Anyway, the dress was slit high on the thigh, high enough that as she shifted, her red thong underwear was alternately revealed and then concealed. Her long, black hair swirled to the middle of her back, and her dark eyes and full red lips promised delights to keep a man interested all night...for many nights.

Paul, however, seemed immune to her charms and stood quietly, head cocked, waiting for their answer regarding Chicago. With difficulty, I dragged my eyes away from Damien's solidly muscled shoulders, and disciplined my thoughts, which kept wondering whether his ass matched the flat stomach and taut chest.

Damien answered. "Yes, we left several months ago. Boring place, really. It's far more interesting here."

Great, his voice was deep, resonant and just as sexy as the rest of him. My thoughts started to wander back to the ass query, and I firmly corralled them back to the matter at hand.

"Yes, really," Darlene said in a rich contralto. "The weather was horrible, and the night life dead and boring. Nothing like this place." She waved a hand to indicate the crowd around us. "I bugged Damien for months to come back here."

Damien grinned and leaned forward slightly, his voice low. "Not exactly how it went." His eyes sparkled. "Darlene here found herself a tasty morsel that she just couldn't leave. That was the real reason we didn't come back earlier."

The female vampire slapped him in apparent vexation, but her aura never shifted, and I knew she wasn't annoyed with him. In fact, as he spoke, something shifted in the pulsing blue, and it shaded more to gray.

Interesting. As I've said, aura reading is far more art than science, but if I wasn't mistaken, Darlene wanted to steer the conversation in this direction. A quick check of Damien's aura seemed to confirm it. Blue slid down his body, from over his heart to near his groin, and as it slid, the colors melded from blue to a dark purple. I suppressed a grin. Darlene hadn't been the only one to sample the delights of the aforementioned "tasty morsel."

I wondered where this would go and continued to listen. Interestingly, Damien's attributes no longer held an attraction for me.

"What about you, Paul?" Darlene's eyes shifted to me as she spoke, and I got the meaning clearly enough.

Paul shrugged. "A bit of this and that." He glanced

around the room. "I haven't been here in a while. Anyone interesting in town?"

Darlene's eyes flashed, but her voice remained cool. "Oh, a few, I suppose. Annabelle Rice might be stopping by later."

I couldn't help myself and choked at the name. Paul grinned at me. "Yes, you heard that right."

"Annabelle Rice? That's her real name?"

Damien shook his head, his eyes sparkling with mirth. "Of course not. And she's a stuck up bitch too. Thinks the name is 'oh so original.'"

"She's just full of herself because she's Lucius' child. Thinks that makes her better than the rest of us. As if he hasn't produced hundreds of children in his centuries."

Paul hadn't always been forthcoming about his kind, but I'd caught him in a relaxed moment a while back, and he'd said that "child" was the term for a vampire created by another. He'd also said that a long time ago, the terms had been "master" and "slave." Apparently even vampires could learn to be politically correct. He'd also told me, with some disdain, that the more pretentious vampires spelled it "childe."

I was curious to hear more about this "Annabelle Rice," but I sensed undercurrents here, and Paul was better able to navigate them. I settled for concentrating on the vampires' auras, seeing what I could read.

Both of them were eying me and making no effort to hide the fact. Their auras swirled in what looked like frustration, while Paul's remained smooth. I thought I spied a bit of cobalt blue in his, which I thought indicated amusement.

"Anything interesting happen in Chicago? It's been a while since I was there."

Darlene frowned. "That's right. You haven't been there since—" She glanced at Damien. "Have we really not seen him since Prohibition?" She languidly waved a hand. "I swear that was the last time anything interesting happened there."

Damien patted her shoulder. "Oh, it's not been that bad." He glanced at Paul, and his aura steadied. "I suppose you want to hear about the werewolves?"

I carefully kept my face impassive, not an easy task for me. From the way they were fencing, I'd figured it would take them much longer to get around to the real reason for this conversation.

Paul's aura didn't change, but Darlene's pulsed wildly. Ah, she hadn't expected it to go that quickly either.

I noticed Damien watching me closely, this time from the corner of his eye, and I wondered if he knew I was reading him. The other vampire winked at me, and I reminded myself that vampires can't read minds. But they are very good at reading body language. I needed to be more careful.

I realized Paul was speaking, and I forced my attention back to the conversation. As he spoke, Darlene waved her hand, and one of the bartenders brought over two drinks. Whatever was in the glasses gleamed redly in the dim light.

"… had heard something about werewolves. Why do you ask?"

Damien shrugged and took a sip from one of the drinks. He frowned. Evidently something in it wasn't to his taste. "Word gets around, Paul. Everyone knows you mess around with the dogs."

No visible response from Paul, either in body language or in his aura. "They've been useful from time to time."

Darlene snorted. "Useful? Hardly."

Paul raised an eyebrow. "No? They police their own and ensure that the infecteds don't make a mess. A steady supply of dead humans would make your hunting more difficult. But perhaps you enjoy the challenge?"

Her aura did what I could only describe as "stiffened," and I knew Paul had scored something.

Damian's voice was both soothing and patronizing. "That's true, dear. Disposing of that 'tasty morsel' would have been much more difficult if the human police were on alert from other kills. He's right about that."

Paul smiled very slightly, but from the flash in Darlene's eyes, I knew she'd seen it. "Enough of this fencing. What do you want to know, Paulus?"

Paulus?

This time Paul didn't try to hide the smile. "I'd heard that someone had stirred up the infecteds in Chicago. That they were using them for something."

Damien nodded. "We'd heard the same." He frowned. "It's hard to remember. I don't pay that much attention, but word on the street was that some wealthy human was, I don't know, building something and using the dogs as hired muscle." His shrug clearly demonstrated his contempt.

"Did you get a name?" Paul asked.

Darlene answered. "It was something like the name of that eatery the humans like so much."

I stifled a chuckle and said, "You mean McDonalds?"

She nodded. "Yes, that one."

Paul and I exchanged amused glances. Who'd have thought the Golden Arches would be a key to solving this?

"What?" Darlene asked, her voice testy.

"Nothing, dear," Paul said, his voice every bit as soothing and patronizing as Damien's had been earlier.

She huffed but remained silent.

Damien cocked an aristocratic eyebrow at Paul. "We've given you what you wanted. Now, in return?"

I suspected what he wanted, but I remained silent, wondering how Paul would respond.

He shrugged. "What is there to tell? You yourself indicated my reputation earlier. How is this any different?"

"He's cleaner and doesn't smell," Darlene said.

Damien grinned and nodded. "Too true, my dear." He looked at me for a long moment and finally shrugged. "I'll never understand your tastes, Paul. But at least you've given up this ridiculous restraint and are finally feeding properly."

Paul drew himself up, and his aura surged. Alarmed, I put a gentle hand on his arm. I couldn't let Paul ruin everything now.

"Feeding takes many forms," I found myself saying. "I have my needs as well, and Paul satisfies them … quite well." I flared my aura again, and the nasty grin which had been spreading across Damien's face stopped. The considering look in his eye made me smile to myself. There. Let him decide what to make of that!

The cobalt in Paul's aura strengthened, and I knew I'd diffused the situation.

Both Damien and Darlene looked at me appraisingly as they made polite goodbyes and headed back into the crowd.

As soon as they were gone, Paul sighed quietly and relaxed. "Well done. I nearly blew it there. Nice save."

I shrugged. "I was scared stiff, and I have no idea where it came from, but it's what my intuition told me, and I just ran with it."

"Keep listening to that intuition. It seems to know what it's talking about." He looked me over. "You still doing all right? Your aura sight still active?"

I nodded, starting to feel the effects of having it up for so long. Everything around me was starting to blur together, and it was hard for me to separate what was physical and what wasn't. I guess the adrenalin of vampire baiting had kept me going longer than I'd thought possible.

"I'm sorry. I didn't realize this would take so long." Paul paused. "Nor that you'd end up fencing with Lucius."

"Yeah, some warning next time would be helpful." I essayed a weak smile.

He smiled back, his eyes gentle and approving. "I'll do what I can. Think you can read one more before we go?"

I nodded and focused my will. "As long as I can skip the verbal fencing. That's definitely not my strong suit."

He chuckled. "Not that you'd know it from this evening. But, no, you don't need to talk to anyone." He nodded toward the other side of the room. "See that short male vampire, over by the televisions. He's talking to the 'lady' in red."

The scorn as he said "lady" could probably have been heard across the room, and I was surprised she didn't turn.

"Yeah, I see him. What do you want me to look for?"

Paul shrugged. From the way his aura shifted, I knew he was trying to be casual about it, like it didn't mean much. "Nothing in particular. Just, what do you see about him?"

I looked, harder this time. Paul's aura was jigging back and forth. I wondered what was up with the other vampire.

Suddenly Paul's aura smoothed, and it was so sudden that it distracted me from the one I was supposed to be reading. "Sorry. I guess you noticed."

I shrugged, mirroring his earlier gesture. "No big deal. Now let me look at this guy."

"Right."

At first glance the short vampire wasn't much different from anyone else in the room. Lots of black and red.

A bit of dark green, but there wasn't anything special about that either. Most of the room was exhibiting jealousy of some kind or another.

Then I saw it and frowned. I quickly glanced over the rest of the room. Nope, none of the vampires had it. My eyes widened. None of the other vampires, but several of the humans showed an odd mixture of black and orange in their aura.

"What?" Paul's voice was tense in my ear and so quiet I could barely make out what he said.

"There is something strange there."

He grabbed my arm, hard enough to hurt. I'd have a bruise there tomorrow. I blinked and looked away from the other vampire. "Come on." Paul's voice was urgent. "We need to get out of here. Right now."

"But what about—"

He shook his head. "Not here. At the car. Where no one can overhear us."

I nodded my understanding. I wasn't sure exactly what I'd seen, but I had an idea, and I didn't like it. This time Paul was going to level with me.

Paul relaxed his grip on my arm as we left the Lounge. "Sorry about that. I will explain. As much as I can. I promise."

Several vampires, including Damien and Darlene, noted our hasty exit. I didn't see Lucius, but I was sure he'd be told within minutes, if he didn't already know.

As soon as we were outside and hurrying up the stairs to street level, I said, "Hang on. I need a second to shift my sight."

Paul stopped but tapped his foot. I'd never seen him do that before. "Okay, but make it quick."

"I will." I concentrated for a second and sighed in relief when my vision returned to normal. Normal colors returned. The night's darkness surrounded me. Considering what had just happened, that should have been ominous, but for the moment, it felt like a warm blanket. "Okay. Done. Let's go."

Paul removed his hand from my arm, and we hurried to his car. He unlocked it remotely when we were still a half a block away, and I blinked. One second he'd been right beside me. The next he was opening the passenger side door and motioning me into the car.

He didn't use his uncanny speed often. Fear ran down my back and settled uneasily in my stomach. I hurried and as soon as my door was closed, Paul burned rubber out of the parking spot. I hoped there weren't any cops nearby.

After a few blocks, I saw his eyes check the rear view mirror. Reflexively, I glanced in the side mirror. I didn't see anyone that looked suspicious, but then I'm hardly a trained super spy. I looked back at Paul, and the fear eased in my stomach when I saw his shoulders relax.

"I think we're okay. No one's following us."

"You're sure?"

He nodded. "Definitely." A quick grin. "One of the advantages of being a predator. I know what to look for."

I started to relax but stiffened again when he asked, "What did you see?"

"I think you already know."

He looked at me. "Probably. But tell me anyway. I need to be certain."

I frowned, still not completely sure what I had seen. "Okay, mostly his aura was like the rest. Red and black. Some dark green."

"What's that mean?"

I smiled. "Jealousy. Almost everyone in that room had it to some degree or another."

He snorted. "Not a big shock. Jockeying for position and companionship are practically a way of life for my kind."

"But not you."

His eyes widened. "What do you mean by that?"

I shrugged. "Just what I said. There's hardly any of it in your aura."

I watched his face. Even in the deflected light of the passing streetlights, I could see his brow furrow. His fingers tapped the steering wheel. Finally, he said. "I left that behind a long time ago. But that's not all you saw."

"No." I hesitated. "He had some orange mixed in with everything else."

He nodded, as if he'd expected that. His shoulders slumped slightly, and I guessed he'd expected it but hoped he'd been wrong. "And that means?"

"That's hard to say. It's not something I've seen much." I struggled to put something that was pretty subjective into objective terms. "Yellow usually means a connection. If two people are dating, you'll see the yellow in their auras approach the same shade. The closer they are, the closer the colors. The darkness of the shade will tell you how solid the relationship. Darlene and Damien had a lot of dark yellow in theirs. And their shades were practically the same, so I knew they were together."

He nodded. "They've been an item for most of a century. So the other one's aura was yellow?" His voice sounded doubtful.

I shook my head. "No, not yellow. Orange. And I've not really seen that color before."

He frowned. "Orange? But wouldn't that just be yellow and red, like you just said."

"No. Aura colors don't behave like paint. Each color is separate. So red and yellow aura colors don't make orange. It's like green. Yellow is a connection color. Blue is a good color. It generally indicates positive emotions. If auras were like paints, yellow and blue wouldn't combine to make dark green, jealousy."

He nodded. "Okay, but it does make sense that green is a mixture of yellow. It's hard to be jealous if you don't have some connection to someone."

I paused, never having looked at it like that before. "I guess you're right. My aunt never mentioned that."

Right then Paul pulled up in front of his house. "Come in for a bit?"

I nodded, feeling safer right then at his place than I would at mine. I told myself that the vampires I'd met this evening wouldn't have any reason to know where I lived, but still—

We entered his house, and he moved toward the

kitchen. "Want something to drink?"

I was suddenly aware of being incredibly hungry. Long magical workings will do that. I also realized I was a bit light–headed. I needed something to ground myself, and food was the best for that. "Got anything to eat?" I blushed and hastily added. "I mean, something a human could eat."

His deep chuckle floated down the hallway. "I knew what you meant." He paused. "I think I might have some chips or something."

I sat down, finally realizing how shaky I was. He poked his head into the living room. "You okay? You look pale."

I nodded. "I will be if I can get some food. Just suffering a bit of a backlash from having my vision switched for so long."

"Oh," he said. "I didn't realize." His head disappeared, but I could still hear him speaking. "Let me see what I have."

I sat back and closed my eyes. The world spun slowly behind my eyelids. I think I might have started to drift off a bit because I jumped when I heard him ask, "How about a burger? I think I actually have everything."

I blinked. He made hamburgers? I suddenly had the image of him sucking the blood out of a half–raw burger, and I stifled a giggle. "Uh, yeah, sure. That would be good."

"Okay. Give me a few minutes to heat up the grill. How do you like them?"

Was I really having this conversation? "Um, medium,

if that's no problem."

Another chuckle. "A little more done than I like, but if that's what you want."

I rolled my eyes, realizing that my image might have been more accurate than I'd thought. "Yeah, too much blood right now would be bad for my stomach."

I heard another chuckle, but fortunately, he didn't rise to the other straight line I'd just handed him. Hanging out with vampires was never dull.

I stayed limp on the couch, eyes closed, until I heard Paul come in, accompanied by the tantalizing smell of seared beef. I cautiously opened my eyes, glad to see the world remain stable. He put a plate down in my lap and handed me a fancy cloth napkin. I looked at it in alarm. It was way too nice to actually be used.

"Don't worry about it. It's a napkin. Go ahead and use it. Just don't make a mess on the couch."

I glanced at him. "Are you kidding? This napkin looks like it cost more than the couch. And a few of the chairs."

He snorted as he settled himself into the afore–mentioned chair. "Hardly. It's just cloth. The couch is leather, from Argentina. It might have cost more than you made last year."

I restrained the urge to stick my tongue out at him and settled for biting into the burger. It tasted just as good as it had smelled, juicy and perfectly done. There was also some kind of cheese, which was really good but not cheddar, Swiss or anything else I knew.

"How is it?" He had a taken a couple of elegant bites

from his, and I noticed it was considerably less done than mine.

"Really good. What's the cheese?"

He shrugged. "Manchego, from Spain."

"Never heard of that one." I took another bite. "But I like it. A lot." I also figured it was expensive, given Paul's other tastes, but I was afraid to ask, so I just ate it.

I finished my burger, trying to eat it slowly and savor it, but it was finished too soon. However, I felt much better afterward. "Thanks. I needed that."

He nodded and finished his own burger. I stifled a giggle at the sight of him capturing an escaping droplet of blood with his tongue. "I didn't realize it was going to cost you like that."

I carefully wiped my mouth with the napkin, trying not to wince. "Actually, neither did I. I've never kept my vision shifted that long. I should have figured it though. Most of what I do is ritual magic, which takes a lot of focus but not too much actual power."

He cocked an eyebrow. "Sometime you'll have to tell me more. I've picked up bits and pieces over the years, but I still don't know exactly what you can do. And how."

"Sure, but right now, how about we get back to what I saw on that vampire."

He nodded as he wiped his own mouth and settled back in his chair. "Yes. You've told me about yellow, but what's orange?"

I put my feet up on a nearby hassock, and answered. "Well, that's the thing. Since I've never seen orange before, I'm only guessing here."

He waved a hand. "Guess away."

"Okay." I paused. "Umm, any chance I could get a glass of water."

He stood up and gathered up the plates. "Sure." He waved me back down when I started to get up to help. "Stay. After what I put you through, me cleaning up is only fair." He headed off to the kitchen, and I waited until he came back with a large glass of ice water, which he handed me.

I looked at it for a moment. "Seriously? Ice, hamburgers and good cheeses? I thought your kind only went in for blood."

He grinned. "And coffee."

I groaned at the reminder of the first time we met, when, without thinking, I'd invited him out for coffee. Fortunately, he liked coffee, just not hazelnut flavor.

"But seriously," he continued. "We can eat just about anything. It doesn't satisfy our nutritional requirements, but some of us enjoy the taste. Older vampires generally stop eating after their first century, except for the occasional glass of good wine or spirits, but I've never lost the taste."

Ah, another age clue.

"Orange," he prompted.

"Right. Orange. Okay, I know I just said that aura colors don't mix, but they usually run in … families … for lack of a better word. So if yellow indicates a connection, I'd think orange would also imply some kind of connection, just in a different way."

"Different how?"

"Well, here's what's odd. None of the other vampires had orange in their aura, but several of the humans did."

His eyes hardened. "Which humans?"

I swallowed some water before answering. "Umm, the ones who were hanging, well, almost worshipfully, over the vampires."

"You've said aura reading is more of an art than a science. What does your intuition tell you it means?"

"Ownership."

The word hung between us.

He nodded slowly, as if the answer were what he'd expected.

"Tell me about vampires and their humans, exactly." I deserved an answer to this one, and I wasn't going to leave until he explained. "And exactly what this 'Companionship' means."

He sighed. "I'd hoped to avoid this conversation for a time."

"What? Are you telling me you didn't guess where this was going when you asked me to come to the bar?"

The expression in his eyes answered the question for me. "No, I won't tell you that. I weighed the odds when I asked you."

"Okay, then. Talk. You owe me."

It took him a moment to start, but finally, he said, "Dafydd, you must understand first that there are plenty of humans who seek out Companionship with a vampire. We rarely have to take someone who is unwilling."

I didn't doubt that, considering the current media

craze with vampires, zombies and other supernatural creatures.

"Mostly, we recruit from those in the bondage community."

Oh, that made sense. And honestly, I had to admit that changed the nature of "ownership" just a bit for me. I've had several friends who were into the BDSM scene, and while personally, the idea of being dominated by someone else squicked me, I'd learned to accept that plenty of other people felt differently.

I nodded. "That doesn't surprise me. Go on."

His shoulders relaxed marginally. "Rarely are the Companions harmed, directly, by their vampire. True, some of them are mentally ill in some way, and the relationship feeds an already addictive personality."

"In other words, if they didn't get off on being with a vampire, they'd use drugs or something else."

He nodded. "Yes. We are careful whom we choose. Humans who have other issues are safer. Then if something does happen, we can make it look like a drug overdose, suicide, or the like."

I had to ask. "Do you have a Companion?"

He shook his head firmly. "No." He paused. "I won't lie to you and say that I never have, but I gave that up a while ago. I'm strictly on an animal and serial killer diet now."

"So the vampires feed off their Companions?"

"Of course. That's the purpose of the relationship for the vampires. Most of us prefer not to interact so closely with our prey, but the Companionship does give us a way to get our nutritional needs met without leaving a trail of corpses behind."

It did make a sort of twisted sense. I didn't have to like it, but what could I expect, hanging out with a predator higher on the food chain than me.

"So I see what the vampire gets out of it. And the humans?"

He chuckled. "Use your imagination. And understand that being drained by a vampire can be, well frankly, it can be erotic. One of those things your books and movies don't get wrong. It's not an equal relationship by any means, but most of the humans who seek us out aren't looking for that anyway."

The hamburger sat uneasily in my stomach, and I almost wished I hadn't eaten it. "You say you rarely bond with humans against their will?"

He nodded. "Rarely, but it does happen. The elders frown on it, and we strongly encourage vampires to seek willing humans, but there's no consequences as long as a vampire is discreet when disposing of the bodies."

"How long do a human and vampire, umm, stay together?"

Paul shrugged. "Sometimes as long as the human lives. I've probably given you the wrong idea of how much blood we drink. Since I get in fights regularly, I need more to heal. Mostly, we don't need much more than you'd give up if you donated blood regularly. That's why I say the humans aren't hurt directly. Sometimes a vampire goes overboard, and the human dies, but that's a risk most of them are willing to take. They say it adds 'spice' to the relationship."

Ah, our attraction to the bad element. I could see why vampires would be highly desirable.

"Okay, I see then what the aura meant in the humans." A sudden thought occurred to me. "Lucius called it a bond. Is there some sort of psychic connection?"

He nodded. "Yes, and it grows stronger the longer the vampire feeds from the human. After a few years, a vampire can sense the mental, physical and emotional state of his human, even from a distance. And the human can be 'called' to attend her vampire, even if they aren't together."

"From what I saw of the auras tonight, none of them were very strongly bonded."

"Not surprising. Most of the vampires there were very young, probably with their first human. The older the vampire, the stronger the bond and the faster it forms."

"Does Lucius have a Companion?"

Paul shook his head. "Not that I know of. It does make a vampire somewhat vulnerable. If a bonded human is killed, there is a short–term impact on the vampire. Lucius can't afford that vulnerability. He's the oldest vampire in D.C., but among elders, he's still young, and he could be taken down if someone timed killing his Companion properly."

Good information to have. And I could see Paul gave it reluctantly. I didn't want to make a big deal out of it, so I just asked, "But shouldn't the connection go both ways? Especially if it makes a vampire vulnerable.

Wouldn't it show up in the vampire aura as well?"

Paul's voice was chill. "You said the color indicated 'ownership.' While there is a connection, the humans in no way own the vampire."

Oh, right. "Then what did it mean in that vampire? And did I see what you expected?"

"Yes, to the second question. As to what it meant—" he trailed off.

"What?"

Paul waited a long time before answering. I sat on my impatience, sensing that if I said anything, he'd clam up. Finally, he said, "As you've no doubt noticed, I don't like to talk much about my kind in detail."

You think! But I said nothing, just nodded.

"This is one of those things I'd rather not talk about," he continued. "But you are correct. I asked you to help me, and you deserve at least some answers in return. I think I'd said a while ago that vampires used to refer to their progeny as 'slaves.'"

I nodded. "And themselves as masters."

"Correct." His eyes glittered. "Well, those are not just words. There is a … link … for want of a better term between a vampire and his children. That link, if properly set, can allow for a certain degree of control."

My eyes widened. "Meaning that the whole master/slave thing can have teeth behind it." I blushed slightly as I realized what I'd said. "Um, no pun intended."

The dangerous glitter in his eyes softened to an amused sparkle. "None taken, but, essentially you are correct."

"You said 'if properly set.' That implies that not every vampire can or does use the link that way."

He nodded. "Correct. These days most vampires don't bother. The vast majority of new vampires created today are intended to be an immortal companion, lover or friend. Generally the new and older vampire knew each other before the process. It's not done because one wants control over another."

I didn't know if he'd answer, but I had to ask. "Have you ever sired a new vampire?"

He didn't answer right away. "Just once. And it was a long time ago. I don't even know if she is still alive."

His voice held an edge of desolation and something told me he did know, but I didn't press. "Oh. Okay. Umm. Sorry?" I wasn't quite sure what to say.

One shoulder lifted in an elegant shrug. "It's no matter now."

I thought for a moment. "So I think what you're saying is that the vampire I read was being controlled by another, in a true master/slave kind of thing."

Paul nodded. "I think so, yes."

"And you'd already guessed that. Which was why you wanted me to come along?"

He nodded again. "Partially. I suspected some vampire in the city was being controlled by another. I wasn't certain who. Or if he or she would be there tonight. But while you were busy baiting predators, I was scanning the room. Looking for someone who had a certain scent about him."

I grinned faintly. "Glad I could provide you with a distraction."

The corners of his lips twitched. "That was an added bonus, I assure you. Not part of the original plan."

"Good to know."

"But, yes, that vampire—I don't know his name—had something about him that I have sensed before."

"So you know the vampire who sired him."

"Yes." The word hung between us.

I thought carefully before I asked, "Well, then. What do we do about it?"

I was watching carefully or I might have missed the flash of … I think it was gratitude … in his eyes.

All he said, however, was, "Nothing right now."

I finally put some pieces together. "You think that vampire is the rogue you'd mentioned earlier. The one who's going around killing people but making it look like a serial killer."

He nodded fractionally. "Perhaps. He might not be the actual rogue, but I suspect he knows who is."

"Why now?" I asked.

He blinked. "I don't know why the rogue is here now."

I shook my head. "No, that's not what I meant. Why'd you decide to research this rogue thing right now?"

When he answered, his voice was a bit heated. "I know we need to resolve this thing with the werewolves, but rogue vampires in D.C.—"

I cut him off. "No, that's not what I meant. I don't

care if you're investigating both at the same time, and I'm more than willing to help you. What I meant was why did you ask me to come to the Lounge tonight?"

He relaxed. "Oh, that. Sorry. I didn't actually know about rogue activity until last night." He glanced at the expensive watch on his wrist and added, "Well, two nights ago now."

I pulled out my phone. Wow! It was just after midnight. Time flies and all that. "Really? You said the rogue's been here for a while."

The expression on his face would have been embarrassment in anyone else, but that wasn't an expression I'd really seen on him. "It has. But, I don't socialize with the other vampires very often. Saturday night was the first I'd heard of it."

"Okay, so you decide to do some research now. What are you not telling me?"

There was that look again. I thought I got it. "You've had dealings with the rogue before. You know who it is."

He shook his head, his expression returning to the certainty I was used to seeing on him. "No, I don't know who the rogue is. But I do think I know who is behind him or her."

"Ah. The master vampire. You know who he is."

"Correct."

"And you've had a run–in with him before." I wasn't sure how I knew it was a "he," but I did. Chalk it up to intuition.

"Also correct."

I yawned and sighed. "Okay, the whole villain returns in another episode thing. So what do we do about it?"

"As I said earlier, nothing right now. Resolving the werewolf problem comes first. We're the only ones working on that. Other vampires are attempting to track down and deal with the rogue."

"But if you can figure out so easily who it might be, you figure the other vamps probably also know."

He nodded. "Yes, and if they can't, or won't, address it, now I know where to start."

"Give them just enough rope to hang themselves, in other words."

"Exactly."

I shook my head. "I don't know. Leaving something like that to just run around and kill people. That doesn't sit well with me."

His expression softened. "Nor with me. But there are only two of us. And the kid needs justice."

I nodded, agreeing with his point. "Yeah, he does." I yawned again. "Well, if I'm going to be worth anything to anyone tomorrow, I need to get back home and to bed."

"Alone?" His tone was teasing.

I snorted. "Yeah, alone. I'm too tired to do anything even if I had company."

He stood up and grabbed his keys. "Let me drive you."

I got up and swayed. Paul's hand was there, his strong grip steadying me. "Thanks. Not sure I'm up for much walking."

His hand remained on my arm all the way to the car. I was grateful, even though I tried not to need it much.

As he drove, I sat back and closed my eyes. It had been a long day. But then I had a thought, and I sat up.

"What?" Paul asked.

"Paulus? What was with Darlene calling you that?"

He glanced over at me. "Did she?"

I nodded.

Paul shrugged. "It didn't mean much. Vampires can be formal at times, especially Darlene. She's called me that for years." The corner of his mouth quirked. "Especially when she's irritated with me."

"Oh."

"Were you hoping for more?"

I nodded. "Of course. I figure with you guys there must be a meaning to everything. Jockeying for position and all that."

He tapped his fingers on the steering wheel as he drove. "Mostly you wouldn't be wrong. Lucius uses it sometimes, to mock me and my position relative to him. Hardly anyone else calls me that."

Something told me that wasn't the whole story, but I was too tired to question him further.

We made the rest of the drive back to my place in silence, and I was touched to see him wait until I was safely in my building. It was kind of like what my parents used to do when they dropped me off at a friend's house. It made me feel safe. With everything that was going on now, I needed that feeling.

I went into my bedroom and collapsed, too tired to even take off my shoes, much less my clothes.

Chapter 8

Monday, September 7, 2009: early afternoon

J UST AFTER NOON, still in my clothes and shoes, a rhythmic banging woke me up. The sound was coming from the living room so I figured the ferrets were telling me they were out of food.

I groaned and levered myself out of bed. Warlocking is generally a nighttime activity, but I'm still not used to staying up late so many nights in a row. Perhaps it's time to give some serious consideration to adjusting my normal operating hours, to better match Paul's schedule.

Another bang, louder this time. I stumbled into the living room to give Gyre and Gimble some food and open their cage. Naturally, they ignored the food and danced around my feet, nearly tripping me while I tried to walk to the kitchen to make some coffee and grab my own breakfast. I munched cereal and considered my day. I didn't have anything pressing at the moment, which felt strange after the rush of the last few days. I thought about calling Laura to see if she needed help, but I quickly rejected that idea. Since I didn't even have a quarter of her knowledge, I'd just be in the way.

It was a holiday, so even calling prospects didn't make much sense. Finally I decided to run some errands and then call my father. I hadn't told my family about Paul yet, and I decided it was past time. I was pretty sure they'd support me, especially since I had read him and was certain he wasn't a danger to humans.

That decided, I showered quickly and went out to do some grocery shopping, which didn't take long. On my way back from the store, my phone rang. I gladly juggled bags and my phone to take the call from Stephen.

"Hey."

"Hey yourself. You said last night you'd call me today."

Damn! With everything that had happened with the vampires, I'd completely forgotten.

"I'm sorry. You're right. Had kind of a late night last night, and I've been playing catch up today."

His voice grew hard. "Anyone I should know about?"

Again with the Damn! "No, it's nothing like that. Just something I'm working on."

"You mean with that vampire you hang out with?"

Wait a minute. I didn't remember telling him about Paul. I quickly ran back over our conversations, and I was pretty sure I'd never mentioned him. "How do you know about him?"

"Why? Trying to hide something from me?"

I shook my head, even though he couldn't see it. "No, I'm not hiding anything. I figured telling you I'm a warlock was bold enough. I didn't want to overdo it by adding in vampires."

"Oh, I guess that makes sense." His voice sounded

chastened, and I relaxed a bit. "Sorry for being touchy."

"No problem, but how did you know about him?"

"Sonya told me."

That made sense. She knew about him and was completely buying into the media stereotype of vampires as sexy, mysterious bad boys. Before last night, I was still half–way with her on that. Not anymore.

"Dafydd, you still there?" Stephen's voice sounded worried.

"Sorry. Blanked out for a minute. Like I said, long night. So what did you want to tell me last night?"

"I had an idea for Saturday. Want to grab some dinner before we go to Apex? I know this great Indian place, just off the Circle."

By "Circle" he meant Dupont Circle. "Sure, that'd be great. I like Indian. What time?"

We worked out the details and hung up. I was feeling happy. So far I was liking where this relationship was going. The last break–up had left me pretty down on guys, and I was glad I'd found someone okay about who, and what, I am. That was rare. And it gave me a way to start the conversation with my dad, before heading directly into "Hey, Dad. I'm working with a vampire."

I pulled out my phone and dialed my parents' number. They live in California, and I figured they'd both be home, it being lunch time there. Mom has always been big about eating together. As I'd expected, Mom picked up, right away.

"Smith residence."

Would you believe that my parents still use a rotary

phone, which means they don't have Caller ID. It's not because they're anti–technology (my dad has a top–of–the–line MacBook). They just think the rotary phone is retro and cool. Parents. You gotta love 'em.

"Hey mom, it's me."

Her voice, which had been in a typical "don't give anything away in case it's a telemarketer" tone, grew warm. "Dafydd. It's good to hear from you. Anything new to share?" Her voice grew sly at that question, and I knew what she was after.

"Yes, Mom, I am seeing someone."

"Oooh!" she squealed. I'm not kidding. She really did squeal. It's totally embarrassing coming from your mom. "Tell me all about him."

"Not much to tell yet, mom. We've only been out the one time, but it was fun. Seems like we have a lot in common."

"That's good. When do you see him again?"

I rolled my eyes. If I wasn't careful, she was going to start asking for details I was not comfortable sharing with my mother. "Saturday. Dinner and hanging out at Apex."

"That sounds nice."

"I'm sure we'll have a good time. Listen, is Dad around?"

"I think he's working on his computer. Let me check."

I heard her put the handset down, and I went over to my computer desk to fire up my aging Windows XP desktop. Not nearly as nice as what my dad had, but if he was already near the computer, maybe we could Skype. I don't see my parents often, what with us being on opposite coasts, so I liked to Skype with them whenever I could. It's the next–best thing to being there, and Mom can't pinch my cheeks.

Someone picked up the phone on the other end, and my dad's deep, reassuring voice sounded in my ear. "Son? Good to hear from you."

Juggling my cell phone and the mouse, I just barely managed to hold on to both. "Hey Dad. I got some stuff to talk to you about, and I was thinking maybe we could talk by Skype."

"Sure," he said agreeably. "Want me to call you?"

"Yeah. Give me another minute or two to let my dinosaur boot up."

He chuckled. "Okay. Talk to you in a minute."

I spent a couple minutes fighting with the computer and the web–cam, which worked (sort of) and we connected.

Mom was standing behind my dad, waving at me. She was a little overweight for her 5'6" frame, but wore it well. Her long hair, pulled back into a casual ponytail, was still the same dark brown I remembered, with just a hint of gray at the temples. Nope, she didn't dye it. She's just lucky to be graying late. Her skin was still smooth, and she looked at least a decade younger than she really is, which is good since she sells Mary Kay. My mom is a walking advertisement for her own product.

As usual for around the house, she was wearing blue jeans and a t–shirt. Mom never dresses up unless she has to. She does the whole skirt thing when she's working, but the rest of the time, it's pants (usually jeans) all the way. Yeah, it's kind of a weird choice for a successful Mary Kay Director, but it works for her.

Dad, on the other hand, never dresses casually. Even at home, he wears slacks and buttoned–down shirts. (Today was navy and white and blue–striped, respectively.) Sometimes you'll even find him in a tie on Saturday, while sacked out on the couch watching football. It's his second love, after magic. He's only a year older than mom, but his black hair is liberally laced with gray, and his lined face would have looked old, if not for the twinkle in his gray–blue eyes. While my mom is just average height for a woman, Dad is tall, just over six feet. I got her height, not his, but I did inherit his lean build and a metabolism that lets me eat just about anything without gaining weight.

Speaking of which, my mom said, "You look so thin! Aren't you eating?"

I stifled a sigh. She's just being mom. "I'm eating fine. The last couple of days have just been busy, and I think I probably skipped a meal or two."

She wagged her finger and "tutted" at me. "You're coming home for Thanksgiving this year, Dafydd, and I'm going to feed you properly," she said sternly. "No arguments."

"We'll pay for your flight," my dad added.

"Of course we will. He knew that, didn't you Dafydd?"

Reeling at how quickly my holiday travel plans had

been made, I managed to say, "Yeah, sure I knew that. And I'd love to come." Miss my mom's cooking at Thanksgiving? No way. You haven't lived until you've eaten her mashed potatoes. And her pumpkin pie? I dream about that pie.

"Good. Now that's settled, I'll leave you and your dad to it." She waved good-bye and left the camera range.

You see, mom doesn't have any magic in her. It's unusual for a warlock to marry a mundane, but mom and dad met in college. Or rather, mom was in college. Dad was working part–time at a new age shop just off campus (University of California–Berkeley), and my mom stopped in to buy some incense. She's not magical, but she is Wiccan, and the two of them got to talking about magic and spirituality and the like. He offered to show her some real witchcraft, and it was true love after that.

Even so, when dad and I "talk shop," she usually heads off to do something else. She's pretty knowledgea-ble for a mundane, but we still tend to go over her head.

"What's up, son?" my dad asked. "Your mother says you're seeing someone?"

His expression was definitely interested, but not like mom's. Dad wants me to be happy, but he's not ob-sessed about me finding someone and settling down. At least no one is bugging me to have kids. My brothers and sisters have provided plenty of grandkids for them to spoil. And at least one, my oldest brother's first son, was starting to show magical talent, so Dad's happy to have another generation to train.

"Yeah, his name's Stephen, but we've only been on the one date. Bob introduced us."

Dad chuckled, the twinkle in his eyes brightening. "As long as this Stephen has better taste in clothes than Bob."

I laughed. "No worries. He dresses like a normal gay boy."

He nodded. "Ah, ripped jeans and tight t–shirts then."

I glanced down at myself. Almost exactly what I was wearing, except the jeans were tight, and the shirt was old and ripped. "Yeah, pretty much." Dad tried for a couple of years to get me to dress like him, but he finally gave it up as a lost cause. I can dress up nice, though, and I have the suits in the closet to prove it.

He settled back in his chair and reached out to adjust the camera so it remained square on his face. "So what'd you want to talk about?"

How to begin? Probably with Paul and the dream. "You know that dream I've had since I was a little kid? The one about meeting the guy who was haunted by a ghost?"

He leaned forward, forgetting to adjust the camera, so I was left staring at his nose and mouth. "You mean it finally came true?"

"Yeah, it did."

He remembered the camera and sat back a bit so I could see all his face again. "Tell me."

Prophetic dreaming is a rare talent, and I have it

pretty strongly. As with normal dreams, it had been abstract, just an image of a handsome man with a female ghost superimposed over his features. In the dream, I knew I could trust the man, and I knew I had to help him deal with the ghost. Something about the ghost had always left me unsettled, and I'd spent a good bit of time as a teenager studying up on spirits, especially polter-geists. That's why all the reputable psychics in town know me. I'm kind of an expert.

"Well, I sort of ran into him in the alley behind my apartment." I trailed off, still not sure how to tell him that the guy was a vampire.

"And?" I could hear the impatience in his voice and see it on his face. "What about him?"

"Well, dad. He's a vampire."

He blinked and sat back in his chair. I've rarely seen him taken aback by anything. "But from the dream, you always knew you had to help him. That he was in danger from the ghost."

"And that the ghost could be a danger to others as well," I finished. "Yeah, that was all true."

"But a vampire? They prey on people."

"Yeah, but ... well ... Paul's kind of different."

"Paul's the vampire, I assume? Different how?"

"I met him when he was killing a guy, who turned out to be a serial killer he'd hunted down. That's what he does now. He hunts down the bad things in D.C. and keeps them off the street."

The disbelief on my dad's face was obvious, even over the grainy web-cam video. "Are you sure, son?

Vampires can be very convincing when they want to be."

I nodded. "Yes, I'm sure. I read his aura, and the dream told me I could trust him when I finally met him." I paused. "Good thing, too. The dream kind of forgot to tell me I'd meet him with his fangs buried in some guy's neck."

My dad raised an eyebrow. "Better have a word with the Universe about that one. Definitely an oversight."

See where I get my sense of humor?

"I'm still concerned," he continued. "I trust your dreams, son, but this is a vampire. What exactly did you see in his aura?"

I gave him the color run down, and how I'd interpreted it. Basically, Paul's got some good, some evil, all wrapped up in the red I now know all vampires have in their aura. I could see dad wasn't convinced, so I finished by saying, "But there's one color that overshadows all that."

"What's that?"

"Deep blue." I left that for my dad to ponder.

Finally, he said, "That usually indicates a high degree of personal honor."

"Yeah, it does. And everything I've seen since supports that. I don't know much about his history, but I'm guessing that's always been there. It's too interwoven with everything else to be something recent."

He thought for a minute. "What do you know about his background?"

I shrugged. "Not much. He's old, more than a century, maybe as much as two, but I can't say for sure. He's got a Civil War era bayonet in his house, and it resonates strongly. I think he's had it a long time. If I had to guess, I'd say he fought in the War, but I couldn't say if he was a human or a vampire then."

"You've been to his home!" Now my dad sounded worried. And I knew my next piece of information wouldn't make him feel any better.

"Yeah, and he's been to mine."

My dad's eyes widened. "Do you *know* what you've done?"

I nodded firmly. "Yes, I do. I'm telling you, Dad, I trust him. Like I haven't trusted many people."

He snorted. "You're still young." But he also relaxed. "I've always trusted your good sense, son, so if you say you trust him, then I'll accept it. I don't like it, but I'll accept it." He sat back again. "Well, obviously you didn't call to ask my opinion about whether you should hang out with a vampire. So why did you call?"

I filled him in on the resolution with the ghost. When I finished the story, he nodded. "Well done. It sounds like she was heading in a bad direction. Good thing you helped her move on. From the way you said the weather was changing, I think you caught it just in time."

My dad's approval warmed me. This was exactly what he'd trained me for, and I was glad to make him proud. "That's what I'd thought. So, I'd wanted to fill you in on that, but I also wanted to let you know what else has been happening here, magically speaking."

He frowned. "There's more?"

"Yeah." I related the story of the thing near the Washington Monument, making sure to highlight Paul's actions there, and then I told him about the werewolf puppy and everything else that had been happening. I did, however, leave out the part about the trip to the vampire bar. No need to worry him about that.

Dad listened carefully, asking a few good questions here and there but mostly letting me tell it. I knew he wanted to say more about the fight with the werewolves, but he was remarkably restrained, saying little more than, "I'm not sure I want to tell your mom about that part." I completely agreed with him on that. Mom's pretty level–headed, but she reacts like any mother when her kids are in danger. Badly.

When I finished, he looked thoughtful for a minute, then he asked, "Is the level of paranormal activity you're seeing normal for D.C.?"

Pleased that my dad got it, I shook my head. "No, and that's why I called. I've been here for almost five years now, and other than a few ghosts, I've seen nothing like this. I understand from Paul that werewolves have been here and active for a long time, but I'm picking up from him that they aren't usually this bold." I decided to tell him a little bit about what's up with the vampire community. "And he says there's a rogue vampire in D.C. who is killing people, again, more openly than is usual for the vampires."

His eyes widened. "A rogue? Be careful, son, especially if it's known that you are associated with this Paul fellow. I don't know if that makes you safer, or puts you in more danger."

"I'm not sure either. I plan to be very careful after dark until that's all wrapped up. But taken together, it's a lot more activity than I think is normal." I paused for a moment before adding, "But honestly, I can't say if it's actually more activity, or if I'm just more aware of it. Because of the company I'm keeping."

He nodded. "I'd thought about that too." He adjusted the camera again, even though it didn't need it. "I guess you're wondering if this all has something to do with 2012."

That was exactly what I'd been wondering. Sure, I know all of you think there's nothing to 2012 except some weird end–of–the world stories that you don't believe anyway. But the covens have suspected something significant is coming. "Yeah, I was wondering. You told me when I moved out here to keep my ears open and let you know if I was seeing anything. Well, now you know what I'm seeing out here. What about you?"

He shook his head. "Nothing is clear, of course. It never is in times like this." He sighed. "Obviously, the coven is gathering information, but you're still one of the best precogs we have in this generation. Are your dreams telling you anything?"

"Not really. I was having the one about the ghost a couple of times a week right before I met Paul, but my dreams have been pretty quiet since then."

Dad frowned. "That's surprising to me. We're just a few years away. I'd be expecting you to have lots of them."

"Well, I generally only get dreams about stuff I can affect. Maybe what's coming is too big."

"That's not something I want to think too much about, son."

"Me neither, but what else can we do?"

He sighed. "Pretty much what we have been doing." He straightened. "Thanks for filling me in on what's happening out there. The coven meets later this week. I'll fill them in. This gives us something to research. And meditate on. Your grandfather will be thrilled." His voice was resigned, which made me grin. While the rest of the coven was dreading whatever was coming in 2012, my grandfather thought it would be fascinating. Perhaps also dreadful, but since he hadn't had, in his opinion, "any real magical excitement in his entire life," he was eager to experience some soon.

As for me? I'm okay with boring when it comes to magic, but watching my grandfather's eyes light up when he talked about what might be coming was always fun.

"Yeah, I know he will be. Good thing he has you around to keep him grounded."

My dad rolled his eyes. "Like anyone can do that!"

We laughed, said we loved each other and hung up, after my dad gave me one more caution about Paul.

I sat back, pondering our conversation, wondering whether I should tell Paul about it. I don't know what, if any, legends the vampires have about the upcoming 2012 events, but it was worth exploring. It might be useful to get his perspective. He's lived a lot longer, obviously, than I have.

I checked the time. Getting late in the afternoon. I figured I had enough time to grab some food and a quick nap before Paul would pick me up.

Exhausted, I crashed on my couch and slept until frantic pounding, on my front door, jolted me awake. Scrambling off the couch, I ran to the door. I was really groggy, but together enough to look through the peephole. It was Paul, looking ready to break down my door.

Wanting to calm him. I muttered, "It's okay. I was just sleeping. Give me a minute to open the door."

I fumbled with the chain and the deadbolt and finally got the door open.

One second Paul was in the hallway. The next, he was in my apartment, looking around as if he expected trouble.

I sighed. "It's okay. No one's here. Really, I just crashed."

He looked me over, paying special attention to my eyes. "You do look tired. I forget you aren't used to being up so late."

"Yeah, I've been thinking about shifting my hours. When I was a teenager, I mostly slept during the day and stayed up all night. I guess I kind of got out of the habit when I started working."

He shrugged. "It's not a bad habit to be up when normal people are."

"True, except I'm not exactly hanging around with normal people right now."

Paul snorted. "True enough." He glanced at my rumpled jeans. When I'd crashed, all I'd remembered to take off was my shirt. Removing the jeans had seemed too much of a bother.

"Yeah, I guess I should change."

Bang!

We both jumped.

Relieved, we realized it was just Gimble trying to get our attention. Were we stressed or what?

"Right. Any chance you could keep them amused for a minute while I get ready? I'd like to grab a quick shower and a bite to eat."

Paul was already moving to open the cage and waved vaguely my way. "Certainly. You get ready. I'll keep them busy."

I escaped to my room and left my living room to the attentions of a vampire and two ferrets. I hoped it would still be in one piece when I came back. Before hopping into the shower, I sent Laura a quick text to let her know we'd be a bit late.

When I reluctantly left the warm water, I felt more human. Tossing on some clothes, I went into the living room, which I was pleased to see was still intact. Gyre and Gimble were both sacked out on the floor in the position I fondly called "flat ferret." Paul must have tired them out.

I sniffed, suddenly aware of good odors coming from my kitchen. Ginger, garlic, chicken and soy sauce. Curious, I followed the scent and discovered the vampire in front of my stove, stirring something. I went over for a closer look.

"What's that?"

Paul turned, still moving stuff around in my skillet. "Nothing much. I raided your kitchen for some chicken and vegetables. You had enough to make a simple stir–fry."

"Who knew your cooking skills extended beyond burgers?"

He shrugged. "I've been around."

My microwave "dinged."

"Want to get that?"

I opened the microwave and took out a bowl of steamed rice. I didn't even remember having rice in the house.

"I had to dig in the back of your cupboard to find that. Fortunately, rice keeps a long time."

"Right." I was still dazed. It had been a long time since someone had cooked for me in my own house.

Paul turned from the stove to serve up the rice. He shooed me away with his hands. "You sit. This'll be done in a minute. The ferrets should be set for a while. I gave them a few raisins. Hope that was okay."

"That's fine. As if you needed to charm them any-more than you already have."

Paul's chuckle followed me out of the kitchen. I gathered up the two tired ferrets and put them back in their cage. They didn't protest or even give me sad eyes, just curling up in a pile to sleep. I topped off their food and water.

By the time I'd finished with them, Paul had ap-peared with a bowl. "Here. Eat up. Laura's probably wondering where we are."

I took the bowl and tried the stir–fry. "Hey! That's good. Oh, and don't worry about Laura. I sent her a text to tell her we'd be late. I figured Runner would go on up."

"Thanks, and I sent him a text too. I didn't have Laura's number." He frowned. "How can she get texts? Seems like she couldn't use a cell phone."

I took another couple of bites before answering. Now that I had good food in front of me, I realized I was starving. I'd have to tell Mom that his cooking rivaled hers. "She doesn't get them by phone, but you can get texts on a computer too."

"Oh."

I grinned at him. "Don't worry. It must be hard to keep up with all the changes."

He mock–growled at me. "Careful or I won't cook for you again."

I shot him an expression of pretend horror and finished off the stir–fry. "In that case, I shall be on my very best behavior. That was too good to miss."

He smiled at me while I took my bowl into the kitchen. Way cool. He had even cleaned up.

We left and drove to Laura's house. During the drive, I said, "I called my parents this morning."

He raised an eyebrow. "Oh?"

"Yes, I told them about you. And about what was going on."

"What'd he say?" he asked as he smoothly merged onto I395 South toward Crystal City. We were making this trip a lot.

"You mean other than warning me about associating with a vampire?"

He smiled. "Yes, other than that." He glanced at me. "He is your father, after all."

"True. Well, when I came east, he'd asked me to keep an ear open about weird stuff." I thought for a moment. "Might have been nice if he'd been a little more specific. Anyway, do you vampires have any legends about 2012?"

He looked at me and blinked a moment. "You've got to be kidding, right? That's all fear mongery and paranoia."

I shook my head. "Not according to the coven my dad and grandpa belong too. They've been studying it for a long time, and they think there's something coming." I hesitated. I guess Paul's not the only one who doesn't like to talk about everything.

"What?"

"You know when we met that I told you about my dreams?"

He nodded. "Yes. You have dreams that often come true. That's how you knew to trust me."

"Right, well my grandfather thinks that some of my dreams point to what's coming in a few years. Now we could be wrong. We thought the dream about you might be related, and it wasn't, but some of them have been pretty ... well ... dramatic."

He frowned. "Like what?"

I struggled to put one into words. They are so abstract that they're hard to actually talk about and describe.

"Okay, one of them is something like this. I'm walking along and suddenly everything has an overlay. It's like I'm seeing multiple possibilities in the moment. Like if I had made one decision this would happen or another decision and something else would have happened. And I'm seeing all of them at the same time. It's completely disorienting."

Paul shrugged. "Sounds like a normal, if slightly weird, dream."

"Do you dream?"

"Huh?"

"You just made me wonder. Do vampires dream?"

Paul's voice was flat. "No, we don't. Now can we stay on topic?"

Okay, touchy. Duly noted. "Yeah, it does sound like an average dream, but I just know when one is significant. I can't explain how. They have a different—" I trailed off as I tried to come up with the right word. "They have a different resonance about them. And I have them over and over again. I've had that particular dream 216 times."

Paul looked at me. "You count them?"

I nodded. "Yeah, it's part of how I track them. I've trained myself to wake up and record the ones that have that particular resonance. If they change, even subtly, that can be important."

"Important how?"

I shrugged. "Depending on how they change, I can sometimes tell if an event is getting closer, more likely to happen, less likely. Stuff like that."

He paused a long time, and I knew he was trying to decide if he was going to ask me something. I had an idea what he was wanting to ask, and I gave him the time. Eventually, he asked, "How many times did you dream about me?"

I grinned inwardly. I'd known that was what he wanted to ask. "563. With the last one being about a week before I met you."

"And had the dream changed?"

"A little bit. Not too much. I'd had a feeling that it was getting close. Which had been kind of a surprise, actually."

"Why?"

"Because we'd all been convinced that was a 2012 dream. Which means you and I met three years earlier than we'd expected."

"We?" He pulled into a parking space but didn't turn off the car.

"My dad, grandfather and I. It was my grandfather who figured out my dreams had meaning. Kind of scary stuff when you're barely old enough to talk but you're predicting the future."

I thought about describing the first dream I'd had, when I was barely a year old, but that one still shook me. Even after 58 times. We know that one is important, but I'm glad I've had it relatively few times.

"What?" He always knew when I was upset about something.

I shook my head. "Nothing. Just trust me. My

dreams mean something, and my grandfather has been studying the portents about 2012 for a long time. He thinks something's going to happen, and I believe him. The closer we get, the weirder my dreams get. Which brings me back to my original question. What, if anything, do the vampires know about it?"

"Nothing." His voice was firm. "As far as we're concerned, it's a year like any other."

"You're sure?" I hate pressing him, but sometimes there's no choice.

He nodded. "I'm certain."

I wasn't sure I believed him, but now wasn't the time. We still had a couple of years to worry about it anyway. "Okay then. Let's head inside. Werewolves are more pressing. Dad agreed we needed to do something about them. He didn't like hearing about them being so active."

Paul opened his door. "Your father sounds very sensible. He and I agree on that."

I caught something in his voice that I couldn't quite identify, but I'd already pushed the vampire about as far as I thought I could get away with today. So I just got out, and we rode up to Laura's apartment in silence.

When we entered her apartment, we heard laughter and soft "yipping." Curious, I glanced around and saw Billy and a puppy playing in the living room. Laura and Runner were both watching and smiling at the antics.

"Is that—" I started to ask.

Runner answered before I had a chance to finish. "Yes, it's the kid. We still don't know his real name, so his new family decided to call him Jimmy."

The puppy glanced up at the sound of the name but then charged Billy, nipping at the black lab with his tiny teeth.

"Why did you bring him?" Paul asked.

Runner shrugged. "He's the reason we're doing this right? He's a part of this, and I thought he deserved to be involved, in a small way."

"He's safe?" Paul's tone implied there would be trouble if the answer was "no."

Runner scowled at the vampire. "Of course, man. You don't think I'd put anyone in danger, do you?"

Paul's voice softened. "No, you wouldn't. I apologize."

I was barely paying attention to them as I did some quick math. "Hey! Wait a minute. The full moon's past. He shouldn't be able to change."

Runner grinned. "Wondered how long it'd take you to figure that out. We're not sure why actually. I was visiting him, just to see how he was settling in, and was about to leave. As I was walking out the door, he started growling, dropped to the floor and changed."

Paul frowned. "No infected were should be able to change now. Last night was the end of the cycle."

"I know. That's the other reason I brought him along. I'm keeping an eye on him to see if I can figure it out."

"If he can change when he shouldn't be able to, how can you know that he's safe?"

Runner motioned to the floor. Billy and Jimmy had

stopped playing. Jimmy was lying on his side, flat on the floor, and Billy was settled next to him, licking his head and ears. "Look at him. That's not a threat."

I was only half paying attention to them. Finally, I said, "We missed it. They were killed too early."

Suddenly everyone's attention was on me. "What do you mean?" Paul asked.

"Look at the dates, okay? The actual full moon was Saturday." I glanced at the vampire. "You said werewolves could change on the full moon and one night before and after, right?"

I could see Paul starting to do the math I'd just done. And coming to the same conclusion.

Runner answered. "That's right. Which is why the kid changing is so weird. But what do you mean 'they were killed too early?'"

Before I could say anything, Paul's eyes snapped to mine, and I saw he'd gotten it too. "His parents were killed Thursday night. By werewolves. One night too soon. They shouldn't have been able to change that night."

Laura looked confused and a bit scared.

Runner's eyes widened. "Oh my God! You're right. I never should have missed that."

Paul shook his head. "Not your fault. I'm not sure I ever told you when the parents died. You probably assumed they were killed Friday night. But I should have seen it."

"What does it mean?" Laura asked.

"I don't know," I said. I glanced at Paul, who was

still frowning. "Don't worry right now about missing it. That's not important. What is important is that these werewolves obviously don't follow the rules."

I thought for a minute. "Are you sure they are infected wolves?" I asked Runner. "Not naturals like you?"

The werewolf nodded. "No, they are definitely infected. Remember that they were too clumsy. If they were naturals, there'd be none of that."

"Then what are they?" I asked.

Laura spoke up. "I don't know if this answers it, but I did run across something really weird when I was researching McDonald and the other stuff."

All our attention shifted to her. "What did you find?" Paul asked.

She rolled over to her computer. "It might be easier to show you than try to describe it. Dafydd, I definitely wanted you to take a look at this. You might understand it and be able to tell me if it's real or a typical online hoax kind of thing."

She definitely had me at that. I followed her, and we all hovered while she gave her computer a series of commands. A few moments later, we were looking at an online forum, not very helpfully named "WeirdNet."

"What's this?" I asked as I scrolled through the entries, ranging from alien abductions to sparkly vampire sightings (Paul snorted at that one). There also appeared to be a few discussions of magic.

"It seems to be pretty much what it looks like," Laura answered. "A place for people to post all the weird things they've found or seen."

Runner pointed to an entry. "Hey, Bigfoot's been seen in downtown Chicago. I told you there's odd stuff there."

Paul shook his head. "That can't be Bigfoot. The vampires killed him a few years ago."

I shot the vampire a look. "You're kidding, right?"

Paul's eyes gleamed. "Of course. But they really do exist, you know."

"Bigfoot exists?"

Runner nodded. "Actually, it's more like Bigfoots or Bigfeet." He frowned. "I never was sure how to say the plural of that one."

Laura and I glanced back and forth between the two of them. Paul raised his hands. "Honest. They do. As far as we can tell, they've been around for centuries. I'm not sure exactly what they are. I don't know much about wilderness supernatural creatures, but the werewolves have communicated with them."

Runner nodded. "Assuming you call grunts communication, yeah. They don't seem to have a spoken language, but some packs say they use some sort of sign language. There's a large pack near Vancouver that lives near a Bigfoot tribe." He shrugged. "I've never been there, so I haven't seen them, but stories come this way sometime. It's no big deal."

Not to him maybe, but I'd never heard of them. "Okay, enough about Bigfoot. Back to this forum. Laura, what did you find that you wanted me to look at?"

She gave the computer a few more commands, and opened up a forum topic. I leaned forward to look at it closely.

As I read it, Laura said, "This forum isn't just out there for anyone to find. It's hidden behind several layers of online misdirection. I can go into more detail if you'd like."

Runner and Paul both shook their heads. "That's okay." Paul said. "I doubt I'd understand it anyway. My use of the Internet is pretty much limited to Wikipedia, Netflix and email."

"Mine too," Runner said.

Laura nodded. "Okay then. Just remember that you have to know what you're looking for and go through several levels of authentication to even get here."

"How'd you find it?" Paul asked.

"I've got scripts that search out any keywords I give them. And I've got ways to have them search places most people can't get to. When I searched for 'were-wolf,' this came up."

"What do you think, Dafydd?" Paul asked me.

I waved him to silence. I wasn't quite finished reading, and I wanted to get through it all before I started explaining. If this was real, it was scary stuff.

Everyone fell silent for a few minutes until I had a chance to finish. I straightened up and turned to look at them.

"Is it real?" Laura asked.

I shrugged. "It could be. Or not. If you'd asked me a couple of days ago, I would have said it was definitely a fake. After what we've seen, though, who knows?"

"So what does it say?" The impatience in Runner's

voice was obvious.

I took a moment to gather my thoughts. I knew Paul had a decent amount of magical theory, but I didn't know about Runner. And Laura only knew what I'd told her, which wasn't much.

"Okay, this is kind of technical, but I'll try to keep it simple. Most people think magic can do a lot more than it really can, but really, there are no fireballs or major transformation spells."

"You were able to create a potion to shrink me." Paul said.

I nodded. "True, but it had limits. It didn't last very long, and I couldn't reduce your mass all the way." I rubbed my shoulders. "Believe me, you were still damn heavy."

We all chuckled, and I continued. "All I did was shrink you. I didn't change you into a frog or anything. I can enhance what you already have, like I've done with other potions, but I can't give you what you don't have. So no potions or spells to give me night vision or allow me to change into a wolf. My shrinking potion is about the limit of what magic could do to change someone."

I nodded at the screen. "At least that's what I thought. This forum thread seems to imply someone has learned to go a bit farther."

"You mean change someone into a wolf without them being an actual werewolf?" Runner asked.

I shook my head. "No, nothing quite like that." I glanced at the screen to refresh my memory. Not that I really needed to. If this were true, it changed a lot of what I thought I knew. "They talk about changing werewolves. Not changing people into wolves. What they hint at in the forum is a way to change the nature of lycanthropy, allowing a werewolf to change at times he or she would ordinarily not be able to."

"So they are still lycanthropes, but someone has found a magical way to change the rules somewhat," Paul said. "Kind of like I was still a vampire, just smaller."

"Kind of," I agreed. "But this goes beyond that. I admit I don't understand exactly how lycanthropy works, but it has rules, right? Getting bitten leads to an infection that changes the body and allows the transformation into an animal under certain conditions. Do I basically have that right?"

Runner nodded. "Pretty much, yeah."

"Okay," I continued. "They say they've found a way to change the trigger for a lycanthropic transformation."

Runner's eyes widened. "Are you sure? That's big."

"That's what they say."

"I don't think I understand, Dafydd," Laura said. "Why's that a big deal?"

"Let me try and see if I understand," Paul said, looking at me.

I nodded and motioned him to continue.

"It would be like Dafydd coming up with a spell to, I don't know, allow me to go out in the sun without burning."

"Pretty much," I agreed.

Laura thought for a moment and then nodded. "I

think I get it. As far as you've understood until now, magic could make subtle alterations, like shrinking someone or making them a bit faster or stronger, but it can't change the essential nature of someone."

"Exactly. If I wanted to, I could probably create a potion to turn a man into a woman. It's a huge change, yes, but the subject would still be human. Each of us has parts that are the analogue of the other sex."

"That'd still be a pretty big change," Runner said.

"Sure, and I'm not completely certain I could do it, but you'd still be human and operating under the same rules and natural laws as a human. Up until now, that's about as far as I thought magic could go. From what I just read, they've figured out how to modify the trigger for changing from human to animal. That goes way beyond magic as I know it. It's changing the natural, or in this case, supernatural laws under which the creature operates."

Paul frowned. "But lycanthropes are supernatural, by their nature, not natural. So why not change their nature by magic?"

I nodded, pleased he'd seen it. "That's why I'm willing to tentatively believe what they are saying. My training was kind of light on supernatural creatures. I knew some of what existed, but I paid the most attention to ghosts and the minor demons. However, my guess is that using magic to change supernatural rules would be easier than using magic to change natural laws. I'd want to run some of this by my dad. He's more of a theorist than I am. He'd see more of the implications than I can."

Paul nodded and asked, "So what did they change the trigger to?"

"Sunrise and sunset."

Runner leaned forward. "During any time of the month?"

I nodded. "Yes. It makes sense. Lycanthropes already change at those times during the full moon. All they did was remove 'full moon cycle' from the trigger."

"That's all?" Runner said, his voice tense. "That's huge."

"Yes, but from a magical sense, it's straightforward. Much easier than removing times of day entirely. Sunrise and sunset are already magically powerful times. I'm guessing the transformation requires a lot of magical power. Moon cycles are potent, so it makes sense that moon cycle plus sunrise/sunset could power that big a transformation. These folks have just found a way to take out the moon cycle."

"But Dafydd," Laura said. "You've told me that magic requires energy and kind of follows physics that way. You can't create energy by magic. It has to come from somewhere."

Paul nodded. "Right. So if the power of the moon cycle isn't powering the transformation, what is?"

"That's why this is so scary," I said. "Yes, the power has to come from somewhere. In this case, it looks like the extra power comes from the person. Each time they transform, they are using up a lot of life energy. I'd be surprised if any of these lycanthropes live more than a few years."

We all looked at Jimmy, curled up sound asleep by Billy. The black Lab lay with his head protectively on the puppy's body.

"You mean—" Laura started.

I nodded. "Yeah, my best guess is that his lifespan now isn't much longer than Billy's. And maybe not even that long."

That stopped everyone for a moment, and we watched the two canines curled up together, so content and completely trusting of each other and the people in the room. It was a shame to do anything to ruin that trust, and I felt hatred growing in me toward the people who would ruin a kid's life.

After a moment, Paul asked, "Is there any way to put his trigger back the way it was? He'd still be a werewolf, but at least he'd have a relatively longer life."

Both Laura and Runner looked at me, hope in their eyes. I had to be honest. "I don't know." I motioned to the computer. "They talk about what they did, and there's some general discussion of how, but it's not specific enough. Based on what's there, I'm not sure where to even start."

Hope died in three sets of eyes. "But," I added. "If you copy the entry and email it to me, I'll forward it on to my dad. He and my grandfather are better grounded in theory than I am. No promises, but if anyone can reverse engineer the spell, it's them."

Laura immediately began speaking commands to her computer, and a moment later, she said, "Done. You've got it."

Paul stood up and paced back and forth. "Well, we know more now. Whoever is creating the werewolves is obviously using the same magic Laura found, so it's all related." He turned to Laura. "Were you able to find anything about who and why?"

She nodded. "I think so." She spoke a few commands, and several video screens popped up and began playing. We all leaned forward to look and saw three videos playing. One I recognized as the fight between Paul. me and the werewolves a few nights ago. I had to admit that we looked pretty good, especially me macing the wolf.

Runner grunted, and it sounded approving. "Nice move there, Dafydd. But you do know not to try that on a vampire, right?"

I nodded. "Paul already mentioned that."

The other two videos showed a man, whom I didn't recognize, with a large wolf. One appeared to be at a political rally. He must have had serious pull to get an animal past security. The other was probably a private event. The man was by a pool, and other people milled around, in various states of dress and undress. There was no sound, but it was obvious most of the people were having fun.

Both videos were shot in daytime, which had some disturbing implications. The large animal lay beside the man, watching the crowd with uncanny alertness. Anytime someone approached the man, it stiffened. The man also watched the crowd. He did look amused, but his amusement seemed to have an edge to it—almost as if he were throwing a party to watch for opportunities to pull strings.

Runner closely examined the two videos with the wolf. After a moment, he said, "That's definitely not a natural wolf. It's one of my kind."

"One of your kind as in a werewolf, or one of your kind as in specifically a natural werewolf?" Paul asked.

Runner shook his head. "I can't be certain. Before I learned that someone can change an infected's trigger, I would have said definitely a natural werewolf. I wouldn't have thought an infected could be in animal form during the day. Now?" He shrugged. "It's hard to say. He moves like he's comfortable with the form." He pointed at the political rally video. "See how he moves? There's no hesitation there. He's changed often."

"Let's not create trouble," I said.

"What do you mean?" Laura asked.

"The forum talks about changing the trigger, but they still only take animal form at night," I said. "No mention there of changing during the daytime."

Paul nodded. "Meaning you think the wolf in the video is a natural werewolf."

"Exactly." I turned to Runner. "Make sense?"

"It makes sense," the big werewolf agreed. "Doesn't mean it's right, and I don't like the thought of one of my kind working to infect people. We try to stop that sort of thing, not make it happen more often."

"It is disturbing," Paul said. "But we can't ignore the evidence."

"Anything else for us, Laura?" I sensed Runner getting worked up over the issue, and I wanted to change the subject.

"Yes," she motioned to the video. "Both of those are from Chicago. From what I could learn, McDonald was very influential in state and local politics, but always behind the scenes. He gave money to people he wanted to win, but he never ran for office."

"That explains how he could get a wolf into a political rally," I said.

"Right. The other video is from a private party he held at his house."

I decided I probably didn't want to know how she'd gotten the video.

"So we know he was powerful in Chicago," Paul said. "That matches what I'd learned from the vampires. So why did he leave Chicago and come here?"

Laura shook her head. "I don't know the exact reason. If it's out there, it's buried deeper than I can get at."

Which meant it was buried very deep.

"But from piecing together information," she continued, "I think McDonald got into trouble with some of the buildings he put up. While they passed inspections and code during and after construction, a couple developed some serious defects a few years later. One collapsed and killed a lot of people. The city tried to sue, but the case mysteriously disappeared. There were news articles about the collapse and its impact on the businesses and the families of the people who died. I found several article about the formation of a grand jury. And then nothing."

I blinked. "Nothing? Really? How do you make a grand jury case go away?"

She gave the eyebrow lift that served as a shrug for her. "I don't know. That's what I couldn't find out. But the case went away. There are no court records that I can find anywhere. And a few months later, he arrived in D.C. and started buying up land near 14th Street. And—" she paused significantly.

"And?" I asked.

"And he bought some land near the warehouse district where you found the bodies."

I nodded. I'd been expecting it. "That might explain why we were attacked."

"And why the bodies hadn't been found yet," Laura said.

I cocked my head. "What do you mean by that?"

She frowned. "Well, I checked out the police patrol records, and it's funny how no one ever patrols that area."

Runner whistled. "You mean he's got the cops in his pockets? How long did you say he's been in town?"

"Just over a year," she answered.

"That is fast," Paul said. "He's had to pay some significant bribes to get that."

"Okay," I agreed. "But then why leave the bodies? Sure, the cops won't find them on routine patrol, but someone might call it in. Surely he doesn't have enough pull to stop an investigation then?"

Paul motioned to the video of the political rally. "I wouldn't count on that."

I nodded in acknowledgment. "Okay, but still. Why leave them out at all? Why not dump them where they won't be found?"

Runner answered. "Two reasons. One, to send a message. Don't mess with me or this could happen to you. Two, he's marking his territory."

Paul nodded slowly. "I agree. Both of those make sense."

"And it implies he's picked up behavior from the werewolves he employs," Laura added. "Do you think he's a lycanthrope himself?"

Runner shrugged. "Possible. I don't think so from watching the videos, but they are too short for me to get a good feel for him."

Time for a recap. "Okay," I said. "We know McDonald is dirty, and he's got something going on here. He's probably using werewolves as muscle, and he has some link to the forum mages, who may have created the spell to modify his muscle, making them more useful. He wants to develop the 14th Street area, and he's got something going on in the warehouse district. Anything else? Did you find out anything about gangs in the area? That might be where he's recruiting his muscle."

"Plus we still don't know where the kid fits into this," Paul added.

"I'm guessing he was in the wrong place at the wrong time," I said.

"I do have some information about the gangs," Laura said. "As you may know, most of the D.C. gangs are local. Not too much influence from the national gangs here. The ones working that area are the Smoking Ice Scorpions and D.C. Knights. They don't have much influence around 14th Street, though. Northside Angels rule there."

"So he's got influence in three separate gangs?" I asked. "That's impressive."

Paul shook his head. "Not as much as you might think. Remember they are fragmented here. Pay each of them enough, don't pick any who are out–and–out rivals, and it's possible."

"You're saying that potentially we might have to deal with three gangs to stop this guy?" Runner asked. "That's going to be tough."

Paul shook his head. "I doubt it. My guess is that he's not told them much about what he's doing. Maybe he's paying them for some low level work and using that to target the ones he wants to infect. We don't know how many wolves he has, but I think they'll be all we need to deal with. He wouldn't involve the gangs too deeply in his work. Too dangerous to let too many people know about the infection."

I'd been thinking while Paul talked. I agreed basically with what he was saying, but a bigger question was nagging at me.

Laura must have noticed my distraction. "What's up, Dafydd?"

Runner and Paul both looked at me, and I colored slightly. "I was just thinking. I think we've missed an important point."

"What's that?" Paul asked.

I hesitated, not sure how this was going to be received. Hell, I wasn't sure what I thought about it myself. "Well, it's kind of like this. What do we want to accomplish here? I don't think the four of us can take down McDonald. He's clearly got power. He might not be as well–established here as he was in Chicago, but he's still going to be hard to take down. And three gangs is way beyond us, even if they are only peripherally involved. So what can we do that's going to make a difference?"

Runner nodded. "Good points, but I think I have an answer."

"Yeah?" I couldn't help the skepticism in my voice, but Runner simply gave me a quick wink.

"Yeah." He turned to Laura. "Have you been able to find evidence that the big wolf is still with him here?"

Laura nodded and talked to her computer. A moment later, a Washington Post article came up on the screen. It showed McDonald at some event, maybe a golf tournament. The wolf was beside him. "This is just a couple of months old. Some sort of charity golf tournament he sponsored."

Runner said, "Okay, that tells us what to do."

Paul nodded, but I was still lost. From Laura's expression, I could tell she didn't know what they were getting at either.

Runner continued. "We take down the wolf."

Ah! Now I got it. "You're saying the wolf is what keeps him in control of all the infected lycanthropes?"

Paul answered. "I think so." He turned to Runner.

"Correct me if I'm wrong, but most werewolves won't easily take orders from a human. Political power doesn't mean much to them."

"Yep. From what I've seen on the video, that wolf is a tough customer. McDonald may be coming up with the plans and the orders, but he's passing them on to the wolf to enforce. Even infected werewolves respond to a pack hierarchy. The big wolf looks pretty bad–ass. He'd be able to keep the lesser wolves in line."

I thought it through. It made sense. "So we need to get the wolf off by himself somehow. Obviously we don't want to go after him in public."

"My guess is he's meeting with the pack somewhere alone, at night," Runner said. "McDonald probably passes on the orders for each night, and the wolf delivers them. That's how I'd do it if it were me."

"Do you think they use the same meeting place?" I asked. "Or would they change it around?"

Runner and Paul looked at each other. "I'd think they'd use the same place," Paul said. "No one knows what they are up to. Why make it more complicated by changing it around each night?"

Runner nodded. "I agree. Now we just have to find the place. My people can help with that. Now that we know what we're looking for, it should be fairly simple for us to track down the wolves."

"I'll help as much as I can," Paul said.

"All right," I said. "Laura, any research you can do on your end?"

"I think so," she said. "I'll check video feed from the

areas we think they are targeting. I might catch them in action."

"Excellent," I said.

"What about you, Dafydd?" Paul asked. "Hunting down werewolves isn't exactly your strong suit."

"True," I agreed. "Unless you can get me some fur to ritually trace, but I think that'll take longer than what you all are planning. However, there's something I can do that's useful and plays to my strengths."

"What's that?" Laura asked.

"I'm going to figure out how to make the kid a normal werewolf. I don't think I can change him back to human, but if those guys can change the trigger, maybe I can put it back to the way it should be."

WE TALKED FOR a few more minutes, but it was obvious we all knew what to do next. Paul drove me home so I could get some sleep. I planned to call my dad in the morning and run the problem past him. With his theoretical knowledge, I thought he had a good chance of cracking the spell and coming up with a way to reverse it.

Runner was going to talk to his people and mobilize them to scour the city for the scent of werewolves. He hoped they'd be able to narrow down locations to scout out tomorrow night. Paul was ready to assist them. Laura was going to look at video feeds and see what she could learn that way.

"Do you really think you can do it? Change him back?" Paul asked as he pulled up in front of my house.

I shrugged. "I don't know for sure. But if those guys in the online forum are right, it should be possible. My dad will sure give it a try. He's good at this."

Paul smiled at me. "I can tell. He trained you well."

I looked back at him, a slow smile spreading across my face. "Thanks. I'll tell him you said that."

He laughed heartily, something he didn't do often. "You do that."

I waved back and headed into my apartment. I needed some sleep to prepare for what was coming.

Chapter 9

Tuesday, September 8, 2009: mid-morning

THE NEXT MORNING I awoke to the sun shining in my eyes. That didn't make sense. The curtains in my bedroom usually blocked the sun. I sat up and blearily looked around. As my eyes gradually focused, I saw my living room. I was on the couch with a dim memory of stumbling into my apartment last night, topping off the ferrets' food and water and collapsing on the couch for a moment to find the energy to get ready for bed. I guess I fell asleep.

Gimble was looking at me through the bars of her cage. "Yeah, little one. I really do feel as bad as I look. Thanks for asking."

She blinked at me, curled back up next to Gyre and closed her eyes. I wished I could do the same and vowed that once this was over I'd sleep for at least a week.

Staggering through my morning routine of shower and breakfast made me feel almost human. I checked the time. 10:00. Early for California, but my parents were usually up. Crazy aren't they? I opened the ferret cage, and they woke up to dash around the living room while I called my parents.

This time Dad answered. "Hello?"

"Dad, it's me."

He chuckled. "Considering how many sons I have and how alike you all sound, a bit more specificity might be in order."

I snorted. "Okay. Me as in Dafydd me."

"I knew that."

I rolled my eyes.

He continued. "I'm just so shocked to receive two calls from you in the same number of days. That makes me wonder who you are and what have you done with my son."

Yeah, I probably deserved that, but all I said was, "This is serious, Dad. Can we Skype?"

The light tone in his voice vanished. "Certainly. Give me a few minutes for the computer to boot up. I haven't turned it on yet." He paused and then added, "Does your mother need to be on for this?"

"No. It's magical stuff. I'm okay. I just need your help with something."

"All right. I'll call you back as soon as my computer is up."

"Thanks."

I hung up and paced the apartment until the "ding" of an incoming Skype call sounded on my computer. I sat down and accepted the call.

As always, the calm, reassuring face of my father steadied me. He smiled and sat back. The wrinkled face of my grandfather appeared on the screen. "Good morning, Dafydd."

"PopPop!" I greeted him in delight. "What are you

doing there?"

He shrugged. "I woke early this morning with the strong sense that I needed to be at my son's house. And then you call just moments after I arrive."

A bit of weight lifted off me. PopPop (as we all called him) had a touch of my prophetic gift. But his didn't come in dreams. It came in feelings like he'd just mentioned. If he'd felt that he needed to be here, that was a good sign that we'd be able to do what I wanted.

I grinned. "Almost makes one believe in magic, doesn't it?"

They both grinned at me for a moment while my dad arranged chairs and camera so I could see both of them. That done, my dad asked, "What's up, son?"

I filled them in, bringing my grandfather up to speed and then telling them what we'd discovered last night. When I was done, I sat back and waited for their reaction.

PopPop spoke first. "This is bad, Dafydd, though not completely unexpected."

I frowned. "What do you mean?"

"I've been receiving some strange omens, but I wasn't certain how to interpret them. This gives me new information to work with. I knew something was happening far away, and I sensed you might be involved, but I hadn't expected this."

Well, nice to know he's still looking out for me, metaphorically speaking.

Dad's turn. "I think your grandfather is referring to the increase in supernatural activity that you and I spoke about yesterday."

PopPop nodded, his gesture clearly communicating, "Of course. What else?"

Dad continued. "While I am concerned about that too, I'm very troubled by what you've said about the werewolves and that online forum. Do you remember the URL?"

It was always weird to hear my father talk computer terms. He's become quite the modern warlock. I shook my head in answer. "No, it's not that kind of forum. You need special passwords and access. But Laura copied it all onto a flash drive before I left." I picked up the flash drive in question and showed it to them. "I've already uploaded it to our shared Dropbox folder, and you can take a look."

I loved shared folders and cloud computing. It made things so much easier. Laura had turned me on to Dropbox, a Web–based file sharing service earlier this year, and my dad immediately latched on to it. We hardly ever emailed anymore. If we wanted to share stuff, we just uploaded it.

My father sat back and pulled out his iPhone to check the folder. PopPop looked at him and sighed. My grandfather recognizes the advantages of technology but tells us he's too old to change his ways.

My dad read quickly, nodding as he went. My grandfather moved so he could read over his shoulder, and soon he was frowning. I waited, aiming for patience and probably managing tolerance. Just as I was about to succumb to the temptation to tap my foot, my dad looked up.

"This is significant, if it's true."

I nodded. "That's what I thought. It changed most of what I thought could be done with magic."

My grandfather scoffed. "Youngsters, both of you!"

My dad looked at the older man appraisingly. "You knew about this?"

PopPop nodded. "Of course. It's not something to do lightly, and it requires skill and talent, which, by the way," he said, gesturing at the iPhone, "those young pups do not have. They are correct that it can be done, but they are completely wrong about how."

I frowned. "Then McDonald didn't learn about it from that site."

"No," my father agreed. "Not if he's managed to do it. I concur, by the way, with your grandfather. What they talk about here would not work."

"Ah, you agree with me now!"

My dad grinned at his father. "I usually agree with you. When you are right."

My grandfather smiled back. The two of them have needled each other for as long as I can remember, and it was good to hear the familiar banter.

"So what you're saying is that I could use magic to fix what was done to the boy?"

My father nodded, although the gesture was cautious. "You can fix the trigger that changes him into a wolf. You can't change him back to a normal human though. As far as I know, that can't be done." He glanced at PopPop, who was nodding in confirmation.

I sat back, relieved. "That's what I'd thought. It'd be nice to change him back to human, but we'll settle for making him a 'normal' werewolf. Runner has found a family to raise him. They'll teach him how to make sure he doesn't hurt anyone by his change."

"I'll work with PopPop to write up the spell and get it to you."

"Thanks."

We talked a few minutes more, both of them cautioning me to be careful. PopPop was very interested in hearing about Paul, and he asked me a few questions about him in specific and vampires in general. I answered as best I could, without revealing anything I thought Paul would want to remain between us. I think PopPop knew I was holding back, but he didn't press.

We ended the conversation with PopPop giving me a quick list of things to pick up for the spell. From the easy way he listed off components, I suspected he'd done a similar spell in the past. From the sharp looks my father gave him, I knew he suspected it as well. I wished I could be a fly on the wall during the conversation I knew would follow when we hung up.

We disconnected, and I sat back to think. I'd learned that more could be done with magic than I'd thought. That, of course, made me wonder. What else didn't I know?

I took the chance that Paul was still awake and called him. He picked up after only two rings.

"Did you talk to your father?"

I smiled and said, "And good morning to you, Paul."

A brief silence. "Sorry. Good morning, Dafydd."

I didn't make him wait long. "Yes, I talked to my father and grandfather. Turns out grandfather already knew it could be done."

"Then you can help Jimmy?"

"Yes."

I heard the relieved sigh on the other end. "Good. I'll call Runner and let him know. He'll be glad to hear that."

"I'm sure, but there's something else."

"What?" His voice went from relieved to guarded.

"Grandfather says that what we found on the web forum won't work. They were correct in theory, but wrong in application."

"That's good, right?" His voice was hesitant.

"No, it's bad. The 'kids,' as my grandfather put it, on the forum are probably inexperienced. Maybe not even all of them are magically capable. I think they just stumbled onto something. You know how you can sometimes discover something because you don't know enough to know what is possible?"

"Yes." A pause. "You're saying there's an experienced warlock out there?"

"Not just 'out there.' Actually in D.C. You've got your rogue. We've got ours. We might be able to stop the werewolves, but we've got no lead on him." I thought of something. "Or maybe her. This type of transformational magic is generally the work of witches."

Paul chuckled on the other end of the line. "So, women are better at aura reading and transformational magic. Are warlocks good at anything?"

I scowled, even though the expression was wasted on him. "Divinations are our strength. Well, and communication with other beings. But I never learned much of that. Dad never wanted me to mess with demons, and angels generally take offense at being bothered too often."

"I'd imagine." I could hear the humor in Paul's voice. "So what's next?"

I smiled. "Shopping."

I could almost see him blinking on the other end. "Shopping? Is it really the right time for that?"

"Hey, what else does a good gay boy warlock do when things get tough?" I paused for a moment before adding. "We shop for ritual components. Dad's going to send me the details of the spell later, but grandfather gave me a quick run–down of the major things I'd need."

"Right." His tone was very dry.

"What about you?"

"Not much I can do until the sun goes down. Runner called at dawn to tell me he's organized his people to start their search from the warehouse district. Depending on what they find, I'll scout them out this evening."

"Sounds like a plan. I'll call Laura after I finish shopping. Maybe I can help her look at videos. Narrow stuff down if we're lucky."

"That would be a help."

"Think we'll find that they meet at the warehouses?"

"I doubt it." Paul's voice was firm.

"Why?"

"Because McDonald and the big wolf will want deni-ability. If someone, like the police, finds the werewolves near the warehouses, they will find whatever McDonald is protecting. And they could take down the werewolf gang."

"Assuming they know what they are up against and don't get themselves killed."

Another pause. I recognized that one as the "Paul doesn't know if he wants to tell me something" pause. "What? Just tell me already."

He sighed. "There are selected people in both the police department and the city council who know about supernatural activity. They'll know what they are up against and take appropriate precautions."

Okay, that was news. And the more I thought about it, the more sense it made. Yes, while humans are good at explaining stuff away, relying on that trait can be risky. The easiest way to keep supernatural stuff quiet is to let only a few select humans know what's really going on, and then have those people hide it with quick action and a good cover story.

I made another connection. "And the vampires know the select group and pay them handsomely to cover it up, right?"

Paul's voice was hesitant. "Yes. It does make things easier."

"Easier, maybe, but it also allows your people to have a free rein." I couldn't keep the anger out of my voice.

"Not free. Easier, yes, but not free. Our side of the

bargain is that we police our own. Our contacts in the city just buy us some time when someone moves into town who doesn't want to follow the rules."

"Like the rogue."

"Like the rogue."

I didn't like it, but I couldn't wipe out all the vampires, werewolves or other stuff by myself. I'm only one guy. I'm good, but I'm not in that league. And Paul was one of the good guys, vampiric nature aside. I could hear in his voice how much it bothered him.

"Okay. I don't like it, but it makes sense. And it probably does keep people safer."

"I think so."

"Right then. So the police can handle werewolves without getting themselves slaughtered. That's a good thing. And I see now why McDonald would have his wolf give orders elsewhere."

"It still probably isn't too far away. Most likely somewhere in North or South East."

"Well, when we know something, we can take care of them. Until then—"

"Yes. We wait."

I hated that part. But what else could I do?

"Go get the stuff. Helping the kid is a worthwhile thing."

Yeah, it was. "Will do. I'll text you later if Laura and I find anything that might help."

"Thanks. Don't be surprised if I don't respond right away."

I chuckled. "I won't be. Keep that phone on silent

mode. Nothing will ruin your day faster than having it beep while you're tracking the bad guys."

"I'll remember."

We said goodbye, and I hung up, sitting for a moment before getting up to go get magical supplies.

THE SUPPLIES WERE straightforward, and I was able to find them all easily. Just as I finished paying, my phone beeped with a text message from my dad:

Spell uploaded. Add marjoram and rosemary to the list PopPop gave you. Love you!

Lucky timing. I quickly added the new supplies to the list, paid Mr. Lin and started to leave.

"You ever find out what was going on with the threats?" Mr. Lin asked.

I turned back and smiled. "I think so. Give me a few days, and I don't think you or the other local shop owners will be bothered again.

He nodded. "Good. Thank you."

I waved. "No problem. It's what I do."

I left the store, feeling much like a comic book superhero must feel. I've got powers and the knowledge to use them. I can do things to keep other people safe. I liked that.

I started for the Metro. On my way, I juggled the bag of supplies and my phone to call Laura. She picked up right away.

"Good morning, Dafydd."

"Good morning. Want me to come over and help you look at video?"

"Sure. The help, and company, would be nice."

"Great." I trotted down the stairs into the Metro. "Let me drop off some stuff at home, and I'll be right over." I remembered that she didn't know about the call to my dad yet. "Oh, good news," I added. "I talked to my dad and grandfather. I think we'll be able to help Jimmy."

"Great!"

"Okay, see you in a bit." I hung up and was happy to see my train just pulling into the station. I took it as a good omen for the rest of the day.

It didn't take me long to drop off my stuff and get back on the Metro to Laura's. On the train, I quickly pulled up the spell file and looked it over. I frowned as I read. In hindsight, most of it should have been obvious. I'd just never been taught to use magic this way. I sat back in my seat and thought about my training. Then I looked back at the spell. Finally, I got it. It wasn't that I hadn't been taught some of this. My grandfather had purposely misled me into thinking it *couldn't* be done. He'd deliberately directed my education away from this sort of spell.

I pulled out my phone and texted my dad.

I looked at the spell. PopPop deliberately taught me this stuff couldn't be done. Guessing he didn't want me experimenting. What about you?

A few minutes later my phone beeped.

Me too. He and I are talking about it. If we don't know it CAN be done, we can't look for it or protect against it.

I smiled. It didn't take much to make my dad angry. The top of this list was deliberately withholding knowledge, or worse, misdirecting him.

Giving him the what for?

A moment later

You could say that. ;)

PopPop was in trouble. I hadn't seen it happen often, and I wished I could be there.

Give him hell, Dad! Love you.

No answer, but I hadn't expected one. I wondered what else PopPop had taught me that was less than true. I suspected my dad was learning that right now, and I'd be getting some new instruction in the next few months.

Arriving at Crystal City, I hurried out of the station to Laura's apartment. The door opened just before I could knock. I walked in, and Laura was behind her computer.

"Come on in. I just found something interesting."

I walked over, glancing around the room.

"He's not here right now."

I nodded. I had been wondering where her assistant was. "Sent him out shopping?"

She nodded. "Yeah. After Mary, I'm not in too much of a hurry to fill Jim in on the weird stuff."

Billy came out of the bedroom, wagging his tail. I gave him a good ear scratching and said, "Guess he's happy to see me without a vampire in tow for once."

She chuckled. "Yeah. I'm not sure he's ever going to warm to Paul. He likes Runner, though."

"Similar species, I guess."

We shared a grin before Laura motioned to the computer screen. "Take a look at this."

I stared at the screen as she started a video. It showed a parking lot next to a street. Nothing at first but after a moment, across the street, several creatures came on the screen, glanced around and then disappeared around a corner. They were very small on the screen. The camera was obviously placed to monitor the parking lot, not the nearby street.

"Can you blow it up?"

She spoke a few commands. The video paused, backed up and zoomed in. For a moment, the creatures were no more than blurs, but seconds later the focus sharpened. The video started again, and I watched the creatures move. Even blurry and out of focus, I could identify them as werewolves.

"When was this taken?"

"Several days ago. Look at the time and date stamp."

"Oh right." I glanced down. 19:46 09/05/2009. "Just after sunset on Saturday."

"Exactly." She spoke a few commands and two other video screens opened. They showed a similar group of wolves going in and out of the building. I checked the stamps. Sunday and Monday nights.

"Guessing that's it."

She nodded. "That's what I thought. That looks like the meeting place. It was only luck that I found it, though."

I pulled up a chair and sat down. "Why's that?"

"Well, I checked other cameras in the area to see if I could track them, either where they're coming from or where they are going. Nothing. I can only see the creatures on this camera's video. It's a new installation. Only a week old." She motioned with her chin at the screen. "Just across the street is a new moving and storage facility. The camera is theirs."

I thought I saw where she was going with this. "You're thinking that McDonald knows where all the cameras are in the area, and he's instructed the were-wolves to avoid them."

"I think so. Either that or he knows someone like me who's erasing the video of the wolves. I found a couple of feeds that looked altered. I can't be certain, but there were suspicious markers."

I nodded. "That makes sense. He wouldn't want vid-eo evidence of his wolves around town." I grinned at her. "Good thing his hacker isn't as good as you."

She smiled. "Yeah, we were lucky there. I've saved the video feeds, so we've got evidence if we ever need it. If I'm right about the other hacker, these will vanish in a day or so, as soon as he or she discovers the new camera."

I thought of something. "If he's got a hacker modifying video images then how were you able to find the feed of the fight a few nights ago?"

She shrugged with her eyebrows. "Not sure. I'm guessing he's lazy and I beat him to them. After I saw these videos, I went back to check that camera. The feed is changed. It's just a view of the building with nothing happening. I'm guessing he spliced in coverage from a few minutes before or after. He's pretty good. If you're just looking at it casually, you'd never notice."

"So McDonald definitely has a hacker working for him, but he doesn't erase stuff every day."

"Probably. Also that camera may not be one he monitors regularly."

I nodded. "So McDonald would have had to know a fight had happened there and contacted his hacker to make the changes."

"Which he might not have done right away, giving me time to get there first."

"Lucky break for us."

"Definitely."

"Got an address for this place?"

"Sure thing." She read me off an address near the Arboretum in South East.

"Nasty part of town. Good choice for McDonald. No one's going to hang around there after dark if they can help it. I'd better give Paul a buzz and let him know what you found. That'll definitely give him someplace to check out tonight."

I pulled out my phone.

"Tell him to be careful," Laura said as I dialed.

"Will do." He didn't answer, but I did get voice mail. Huh? Guess he decided to set it up. The message was just a standard "The party you are trying to reach is unavailable" message. Need to work with him on that. I left him all the particulars, including Laura's admonition to be careful. He'd like that.

Laura and I checked out a few more things online, but we didn't really find anything new, so we just hung out for a while. With everything that had been going on, we hadn't just chatted in a long time. I told her about the conversations with my dad and how I thought I could help Jimmy. She asked me a few questions about the spell and how it worked. I explained it as best I could, but it was obvious she didn't really get it.

She also asked me about Stephen and how that was going. That conversation was much easier, and she was happy for me. Soon, Jim came back. We exchanged pleasantries, and I left.

I walked back to the Metro, feeling kind of at loose ends. I checked my phone. Three o'clock. Paul wouldn't be up. Laura had her stuff to investigate. I almost wished for a call from one of my downline, but it was still too early in the week for anyone to be panicking.

I shrugged and pulled my phone out of my pocket. It was a long shot, but maybe Stephen was available for a coffee or an early dinner. I dialed his number, but it went to voice mail. Disappointed, I got on my train and decided to head back home to do some much–belated business follow up. I still needed to make some money, even if the magical stuff was more exciting.

I MADE A bunch of calls and scheduled some appointments for next week, figuring I needed to keep the rest of this week open, not sure exactly when Paul and Runner were going to want to make their move. The ferrets gave me looks the entire time, but I knew I'd never get anything done if they were racing around, so I ignored them.

As I left a voice mail on the last number, a text popped up. Stephen!

Sorry I missed your call. Is now a good time?

I texted back *Sure!* A moment later the phone rang.

"Hey."

"Hey," he said. "Sorry about earlier. I was in the middle of a business presentation to a potential distributor."

"Cool! Did they sign up?"

"Not yet, but I'm feeling pretty good about it."

Customers are good in our business, but our real money comes from signing up other distributors. "Good job. I hope you get them."

"Thanks. What's up?"

"Just kind of at loose ends and wondering if you wanted to get together for a bit." I checked the time.

About 5:30. "I haven't had dinner yet. You free?"

He paused a moment, and I figured he was also checking the time. A moment later, he said, "Sure. I've got another meeting at eight, but I do need to grab some food. Annie's again?"

"Works for me. When can you get there?"

"Give me about 45 minutes. I'm in Silver Spring, and I think it'll take me that long to Metro there."

"Okay. Meet you at Annie's then. I'll get there a bit early and grab a seat."

"Great. See you in a bit."

I felt much better. Setting two business appointments and meeting my new boyfriend. Not bad juggling of priorities.

When I got to Annie's, Sonya wasn't working, but Mick, another waiter who knew me, sat me by the window. I ordered iced tea and settled in to wait, watching for Stephen out the window. It was just a few minutes before I saw him hurrying up the sidewalk. He saw me in the window and waved.

He looked good, dressed in khaki slacks and a red polo shirt. His well–muscled shoulders stretched his shirt pleasantly.

As he slid into the seat opposite me, I motioned at the menu. "My treat."

He smiled. "Thanks, but are you sure?"

I nodded. "Yeah. Gotta celebrate your meeting, right?"

He picked up the menu. "Better let me close him first before we do too much celebrating, but I appreciate the sentiment."

We quickly decided, and Mick took our order. We didn't talk about anything too important. For right now, I just wanted to be a regular person, eating dinner with a new and very potential love interest.

We ended with a shared dessert. It had been a toss—up between the Ultimate Chocolate Cake (me) and the Peach Bread Pudding (him), but I'd let him convince me to go with the pudding, and I wasn't regretting it a bit. I was diving for the last bite when my phone rang. Stephen used my momentary distraction to grab it out from under my spoon, and I shook my fist at him while I answered.

"Dafydd?"

It was Paul. I glanced at the time. Just a little after seven. The sun would be setting soon. I suddenly kicked myself for forgetting. Paul needed to get a message to Runner in time so the werewolves could be in place to follow the other wolves.

"Dafydd?"

I realized I must have waited too long to answer. Even Stephen was looking at me oddly. I needed to be alone. I hated to get rid of Stephen so soon, but now wasn't the time to explain all this to my new boyfriend.

"Sorry. I just realized the time. I'm with someone. Can I call you back in five?"

Stephen's expression had changed. Now curiosity was all over his face.

"Sure." He hung up.

"Who was that?" Stephen asked.

I'd had just enough time to create my cover story. "Just a customer. We'd agreed to meet this evening to go over his first order. I guess I lost track of time." I gave Stephen my best, most distracting smile. I wasn't really sure why I lied, but some instinct told me now was not the time to talk about Paul with Stephen. If nothing else, I didn't want Stephen to think Paul was a rival. But my gut told me there was more than that. I'd have to figure that out later.

I signaled Mick for the check, and we argued good–naturedly over it. I won, of course, and left money to cover it with enough for a very nice tip.

We walked outside. Stephen glanced at his watch. "Wow! 7:15 already. I'm going to be late if I don't leave now."

"Sorry about that."

He grinned. "No problem. I've got just enough time."

We stood awkwardly for a moment. Finally, Stephen leaned forward and kissed my lips. It was just a brief kiss, but it was good and it broke the awkward moment.

I smiled as he pulled back. "I'm really looking forward to Saturday."

His brown eyes gleamed, looking almost amber in the setting sun. "Yeah, me too."

And with that, he turned and left. I sighed and picked up my phone to call Paul.

Paul picked up right away. "Sorry about that," I said. "I was with Stephen, and I lost track of time. Did you get my message?"

"Yes, I did. I called Runner and passed it on. He's gathering his people, and they are going to check out the site."

I glanced at the skyline. The sun hung low in the sky. It hadn't set yet, but it was getting close. Maybe another ten minutes. "Will they get there in time?"

"I think so. It was a near thing, though. You weren't the only one who overslept. I'd intended to be up an hour ago, to have time to shower and eat."

"Guess you'll just have to chase down the vampires while you're dirty."

He chuckled. "Guess so. Good thing vampires don't have body odor."

I frowned, just realizing now that I had never smelled anything on Paul, not even the scent of laundry soap. I'd never thought about vampires not smelling like anything, and I guessed Paul used unscented products to maintain it.

"Uh, right. Yeah, good thing that. What do you want me to do?"

I could hear him walking in the background, followed by the sound of the fridge opening and closing. "Not sure there's much for you to do right now. Runner's people will check out the area and try to figure out how many wolves there are. Then we'll plan our next step." He paused, and I thought I heard swallowing sounds. "I'm going to guess we'll know what we need by, say, ten o'clock or so. Want me to come by and pick you up? Then we can plan how we're going to take them."

Another long night. Good thing I slept in. "Sure.

That works. Want me to call Laura? She'll want to be in on the planning, even if she can't be there for the actual dust–up."

"Good idea. She might see something we're missing. She's good."

"Thanks. I've got a better idea. Why don't I call Laura now? If she's okay with it, I'll wait there. That way you can come straight to her place."

"That works. Text me either way."

"Will do." A grin spread across my face. "Don't forget to put your phone in silent mode."

He laughed. "Yes, I'll do that. Now off with you."

I hung up, still chuckling and called Laura.

"He get our message?" she asked as soon as she picked up.

"Yeah. He's heading over to hook up with Runner's people and scope out the area. He figures they'll have what they need by ten or so. Then he wants us all to get together to plan the attack."

"Us all? I hope that includes me." Her voice was firm, with a hint of excitement.

"You bet. He says you might catch something the rest of us might miss. He likes you."

She laughed. "That's nice, but tell him I'm not going to fight you for him."

I rolled my eyes. "It's not like that, Laura. You know that."

"Sure. You just keep telling yourself that."

I let it go. There was no convincing her. "Okay if I come over now?"

She paused for a moment. "Yeah, but don't hurry. Jim and I still have a few house–keeping items to take care of."

That was what Laura said when she meant "time to take care of crip stuff." Her term, not mine. She didn't talk much about her condition, but when she did, she didn't pull many punches.

"No problem. I need to stop by home for a few things anyway." I didn't, but no need for her to know that.

"Okay. See you soon."

I hung up and decided to go for a bit of a walk and stretch my legs. I'd give her about half an hour before heading to the Metro. That should be plenty of time.

As I walked, I texted Paul.

Meet me at Laura's. We're a go.

I started walking, figuring the next few hours were going to feel very long.

I WASN'T DISAPPOINTED. I killed some time and got to Laura's around nine. Jim was gone, and Laura said she'd asked him to come back around midnight.

"I hope you pay him well for those odd hours."

She nodded. "He knew the deal when he started. Supernatural stuff aside, hacking has always meant I kept weird hours." She motioned to her computer. "Which reminds me. I'm doing some work for a client in London. Okay if I take care of that while we wait?"

"Sure. Can I watch?" I loved watching her work. Screens flashed by so fast. I never knew what she was doing, but she made it look so easy.

She thought for a moment. "Not this time. Confidentiality."

"Got it. I'll just read a book." I took out my iPod Touch and opened up an e–book. I love e–books almost as much as I love cloud storage. I settled back into one of her comfortable arm chairs and managed to lose myself in the latest Harry Dresden book. It had been out for several months, but I'd just gotten around to reading it.

Chapter 10

Tuesday, September 8, 2009: late evening

I WAS SO absorbed that I jumped when a knock came at the door. I glanced up to see Runner, Paul and a strange man enter the apartment.

Runner nodded at the stranger. "This is Mack. He's the one who adopted the kid."

I looked Mack over. He was a bit shorter than Runner but every bit as well muscled. His long, black hair was pulled into a neat ponytail that hung halfway down his back. He dressed similarly to Runner. I guessed that t–shirts, blue jeans and Western boots were what all fashionable werewolves were wearing this year.

His brown eyes reflected a mixture of emotions. Gratitude blended uneasily with anger. "Thank you, Dafydd. Runner has told me what you did for the boy. We love him already. We'll take care of him, even if you can't help him any further. But as for the one who did this to him—"

I glanced at Paul. "You didn't tell them?"

Runner and Mack's eyes flicked to Paul and then back to me. "Tell us what?" Runner asked.

Paul blinked. "I'm sorry. With all the excitement, I forgot. Go ahead, Dafydd."

I smiled. "I spoke this morning with my father and grandfather. They are far more experienced in magic than I am, and they are certain what was done to Jimmy can be reversed. Not the infection part," I hastened to add. "But they sent me the details of a spell to put back the usual trigger."

Both Runner and Mack sighed deeply. "That is good," Mack said. "Runner said his lifespan would be … very short … if something couldn't be done."

I nodded. "That's right. But if I put the trigger back, that should fix that as well. He'll still change into a wolf during the full moon, but I think his life will be normal the rest of the time."

"Excellent." The relief in his voice shifted to a low growl. "Then let us decide what to do with the ones who did this."

Laura directed everyone to the kitchen for refreshments, and we all settled down to make our plans.

"What did you learn tonight?" I asked. "Were we right about where they are meeting?"

Paul nodded. "You were right on. When I got there—"

"Late, I might add," Runner interjected.

Paul lowered his eyes. "Yes, even vampires can oversleep."

"No problem, blood sucker. The wolves covered for you."

The three of them shared a grin before Paul continued. "As I was saying, Runner's people were in place just before sunset."

"It had been one of the places we'd located during our daylight investigations. We staked out the other possibilities as well, but Mack and I were at that one." He nodded to Laura. "Thank you for finding it on video."

She smiled back. "Anytime."

Runner picked up the story. "There were at least six infected werewolves in the building, which looks to be an old drugstore, by the way. I also smelled one of my kind."

I leaned forward. "You're certain?"

He nodded firmly. "To us, there's a definite difference. I've no doubts."

"So this is the place," I said.

"Yes," Paul answered. "Now we need to decide when and how we want to attack."

"Do we have to attack?" I asked.

Runner and Mack both frowned. "What do you mean?" Runner said, his voice a growl. "How can you even ask that with everything they've done?"

Paul waved a calming hand. "Hold on. I think I know what Dafydd is getting at."

Runner's shoulders relaxed slightly, but Mack remained tense. "Go on," Runner said.

I gave Paul a grateful look. Becoming Wolf Chow hadn't been part of the plan this evening. "I'm just checking. While I've used violence in the past when there was no other choice, it's not my first impulse." I glanced over at Paul and, from his grin, I knew he was also remembering the shuggoleth from earlier. "I want these guys to pay for what they did," I continued. "But I want to be sure that a fight is the best, or only, way to get that done."

Runner and Mack both slowly relaxed as I spoke. Mack nodded. "I see. It's a good question. You're right. Someone needed to ask it." His face flushed slightly. "And I admit I was too close to the situation to be the one."

I smiled at him. "No problem, I get where you are coming from. It's just I kept hearing my dad's voice in my head reminding me to always look at options. When I saw they'd modified the kid, well, I pretty much wanted to kill them all right then."

Paul reached over and put a hand on my shoulder, squeezing firmly. "I almost forgot my vows as well. Thank you for reminding me."

Everyone sat back and thought for a moment. I admit that I didn't see any other options, but with five of us working on it, maybe someone would come up with something.

Laura surprised me by being the first to speak. "I know this isn't exactly my area, and I don't like to admit it, but honestly, I don't see other options."

"Go on," Paul said.

"Well, it's like this. I've seen what these guys can do, on the video, and it doesn't look like they hesitate to takes lives. You think this other wolf is leading or controlling them. I suppose maybe if you just take him out, the others might stop killing, but I kind of doubt it."

Runner nodded. "I agree. From what we know of

infected wolves, if they learn to enjoy killing, and it looks like these have, there's not much that can be done."

"And it's not like we can turn them over to the police," I added. I glanced at Paul. "I know you said that there are people in authority who know about supernatural stuff, but I'm guessing there aren't jails that can handle werewolves."

Laura looked surprised to hear that some cops know about the weird stuff, and I saw the look on her face that said she was going to research that as soon as we were done here.

"No, even the authorities tend to kill creatures and dispose of the bodies." He shrugged. "That's part of why I don't worry too much about taking out and feeding off serial killers. They are as much monsters as rogue werewolves."

"We try to reason with infected werewolves." Runner said. "But most of the time we have to execute them too."

"All right then," I said. "We're agreed that violence is the only option?"

Everyone nodded.

"Then how do we deal with them?" I asked.

"Runner and I discussed that on the way over," Paul said. "When his people checked out the area during the day, it looked like the wolves meet there both morning and evening."

"Really?" I asked. "Doesn't that increase their chance of being discovered?"

Runner nodded. "It does. But we don't know that

they have much choice. The infected ones will get harder to control over time. The older ones will start to jockey for position in their own ranks, and one of them will eventually decide to challenge the natural wolf for leadership."

"It's probably already happened," Mack added.

"Agreed. So if he meets with them morning and evening to reinforce his position, it will keep them in line longer." Runner took a quick swallow of beer. "They are weaker in the morning, close to sunrise. Reinforcing his authority in the morning keeps the memory fresher in the evening when they change and are more likely to feel their oats."

"So to speak," I said, chuckling. "Guess werewolves don't much go for grains."

Runner laughed and raised his bottle. "Not unless the grains are used for brewing."

"So you were thinking about hitting them in the morning?" I asked. "When they are weaker?"

Paul nodded. "Yes. Like you, I hadn't thought they'd be foolish enough to meet both times, but Runner's people assure me the scent trails support it."

"What did your nose tell you?" I trust Runner and his people, but, okay, I admit it. I still trust Paul more.

He shook his head. "This is their strength, not mine. My sense of smell is good, but theirs is better. I can track a days—old blood trail, but they are better at tracking without blood."

I nodded. "Okay, then. Any reason not to go this morning?"

"So soon?" Laura said.

Paul and Runner nodded and the big werewolf said. "That's what we were thinking. The sooner the better. Before they've had a chance to change their routines. They might figure out we're investigating. We think they haven't caught our scent yet, but we can't guarantee they won't. I had a lot of my people out looking. Someone might have been seen."

"I agree," Paul said. "It looks like they met as usual this evening, so we can expect they will do the same in the morning. Beyond that?" He gave an elegant shrug. "We can't guarantee it."

I hated to admit it, but it made sense. I'd have liked some more time to brew a few potions, but not at the expense of making the whole thing fall apart. "I can see the sense there." I turned to Laura. "Any good reasons you can come up with to rethink it?"

She slowly shook her head. "No. It's going to be dangerous whenever you do it. I guess I can't come up with any reasons to delay."

"Runner, you said there were six plus the leader?" I asked.

"That's what we smelled," he answered. "I can recruit some of my people to help."

"How many can we count on?" Paul asked.

Runner pointed to himself and nodded at Mack. "The two of us certainly, and I think maybe three more." He looked at me, his expression apologetic. "It's not like all of us wouldn't like to help, but not all of us are trained in fighting. Werewolves are a lot like you people that way. Most of us in the urban packs just go through life, holding down some sort of job. The real tough wolves are in the rural packs and the ones that live in the forest. But I don't think we can gather up any of them by morning."

I smiled. "Don't be embarrassed. It's not like I could rustle up a ton of warlocks on short notice." Come to think of it, I'm not sure I could rustle up any on short notice. "So that makes seven, counting you, Paul and me."

"You're sure you want to be a part of this, Dafydd?" Paul asked. "It's going to be dangerous."

"I'm already a part of it. And it's not like I haven't already fought werewolves." I was nervous, sure. Maybe even scared, if I was honest with myself, but I wasn't going to be left behind. "I've got a few potions that might be helpful," I continued. "But I wasn't really stocked to boost a small army."

Runner raised an eyebrow. "Potions? What kind of potions?" His voice was skeptical.

Paul grinned at him. "Dafydd's quite good with them. His potions were a big help a couple of nights ago when we faced the three werewolves. What do you have on hand?"

I counted quickly in my head, visualizing my potion shelf. "I think I have three of the strength/speed boost ones. Only two of the reflex enhancing ones like I used a couple of night ago. And one I've been experimenting with that lets you ignore pain."

Runner frowned. "Not sure we want to mess with

something experimental on this."

I shook my head. "Oh, it works. No question about that. What I've been working on is making it last longer. Right now, it can block pain for just a couple of minutes. Then when it wears off, you get it all back, right at once."

Paul shot me a look. "And exactly how are you testing this one?"

I grinned. "The ferrets have been helping. I take the potion and then let them attempt to beat the crap out of me. They have a blast playing rougher than usual, and I get to test it without serious consequences." I rolled up my sleeves to reveal long scratches on my arms.

Laura whistled. "Some of those look pretty bad."

I shrugged. "I'm kind of used to the sting by now. It's for a good cause."

Runner was shaking his head. "Still not sure I want to mess with something like that."

"They'll help. Trust me," Paul said. "Dafydd, you'd better keep a reaction potion. Give me a strength/speed boost. I know how to work with that one." He turned to Runner. "You're the toughest of your pack. You get the pain block. Take it if we need to send you into the middle of something. Hand the rest out as you think best."

"I'll take something to increase my reaction time," Mack said, his voice calm. "I'm already fast and strong. With boosted reactions, I think I can kick some serious butt."

Runner turned to him. "You sure, man? I mean, our

own abilities have always been all we needed. How do we even know these will work on our kind?"

I started to answer, but Mack beat me to it. "I trust him. He's going to help Jimmy." His gaze on me was steady. "That's all I need to know. He's human. He doesn't have to help our kind, but he is. And he's not asking for anything in return."

My throat choked up slightly at his quiet confidence. I'd do my best to be worthy of it.

Runner frowned but then shrugged. "Okay, then. If it's what you want, then I'll take one too." He turned to Paul. "How early do you want to get in position?"

Paul looked at me. "What time is sunrise this morning?"

I didn't hesitate. "6:44."

Runner and Mack looked at me, surprise on their faces. Paul grinned. "Yes, someone who knows the times as well, or maybe better, than I do."

Runner nodded. "That's right. You did say that sunrise and sunset were important times for magic. Guess you'd know the time, then."

"Yeah, pretty much." I grinned. "Plus it makes an awesome parlor trick."

We all laughed for a moment before Paul said, "We'd better be in place no later than five. We got there too late this morning to see if they do any scouting before the meeting."

"I'd be surprised if they didn't," Runner said. "I agree. We'll be in position and to deal with anyone who shows up early."

"What if taking out a scout gives them warning?" I asked.

"It's a risk," Paul said. "But I think it's worth it. Ideally we'd jump them during the meeting, when they are focused on each other, but if they notice someone is gone, we'll deal with it."

"It also means one or two fewer to face as a group," Mack said.

"Good point." Paul turned to Laura. "Got some paper?"

She nodded in the direction of a roll–top desk off to the side of the room. Paul moved quickly, opened the desk and pulled out a pad of paper and a pencil. He came back to the group and rapidly drew a sketch of the buildings. Runner and Mack leaned over, the lead werewolf nodding as Paul drew.

Finished, the vampire leaned back and made room for Laura to wheel her chair in to see. I moved to stand behind her.

Paul had drawn three buildings, fairly close to each other. They formed a rough "U" shape. He'd also noted a large area off to the side which he'd labeled "parking lot." Finally, he'd added a long squiggly line that I assumed was a road.

He tapped the building in the center of the "U." "They were meeting just behind here."

"Not inside?" I asked.

He shook his head. "No. I'm not sure what they are, but I'm guessing they don't have access."

"It's just some buildings maintained by the Park Service," Laura said. "All the land to the east of that is Anacostia Park."

I nodded. "Okay, I know the area. Some decent trails there."

"We think they're getting there by way of the park. That's where the scent trail led." Runner said, pointing to the side of the rough map. "A little less obvious than strolling down East Capital Street."

I couldn't help the sudden image of a group of werewolves trotting down the street in kind of a weird parade. "Can you take them as they come out of the woods?"

Runner shook his head. "No, they seem to come from different directions. If we had enough help to blanket the area and take them individually, that might work. But not with only seven of us. Their leader is going to be cautious, expecting trouble from his troops. If he gets a sniff of trouble, he'll be gone."

"And be a devil to track down," Paul said. "I agree with Runner. We've got to let them come together as a group and then attack."

It made sense to me. "Where should we be then?"

Runner took the pencil and made some "X's" on the map, indicating positions. "Here's where I'll place my people." He added a "P" on the roof of the middle building. "Paul, I trust you'll be able to get down from there with little trouble."

Paul nodded. "Yes. It's a good idea. Most people, or wolves, don't expect an attack from that direction."

"What about me?" I asked.

Runner frowned. "I'm not sure. Other than potions, I'm not sure exactly what you can do."

Good point. What could I do effectively to help out? I noticed an odd look on Paul's face, and I asked, "What?"

Everyone turned to him as he said, "Well, I did have an idea, but I don't know if you'll go for it."

I shrugged. "Tell me and let me decide."

"Are you willing to be bait?"

I wasn't quite sure what to say to that, so I simply repeated, "Bait?"

He nodded. "Yes. If you can draw them out in the open, it will make it easier for the rest of us. It would be dangerous, though."

I considered for a moment. "It might not have to be," I said, my voice slow as I thought through the details of the spell I might try.

"How do you mean?" Paul asked.

I smiled as I figured out how to work it. "I've got a type of spell you've never seen me cast. If Runner or Mack are willing to give up a bit of blood and if someone can get a sample from Jimmy, I think I can make it work."

"Make what work?" Runner asked. "Before I give up some blood, you're going to have to be a lot clearer."

Paul was nodding, and I thought maybe he'd seen where I was going with this. "You're going to put up a protective circle."

"Yep. With the blood samples, I can key it to affect just werewolves, both infected and natural. And I think I can add a veil to it as well."

"A veil?" Laura asked.

"Pretty much what it sounds like. It would conceal me from their senses until I was ready for them to notice me. That would allow me to get everything in place and be standing basically in plain sight until you wanted them to see me."

Laura frowned. "If you're protected, why can't you just be under cover?"

"Because it's a fixed circle. It'll take me a while to cast it, and once it's cast, it's fixed. I won't be able to move from the circle without losing the protection."

She nodded. "Okay, I get it now."

I looked at Paul and Runner. "Well, will that work?"

Paul and Runner were both looking at the map. Paul pointed to a spot just north of the buildings, about halfway to where he'd indicated several parked trucks. "Right there, I think." He glanced at Runner, who nodded.

"Yeah, I can have my pack hidden among the trucks. Diesel stench will hide our scent pretty well. Then if you are on the roof, you can jump down behind them. We'll have them surrounded."

"No reason my pepper spray won't cross the circle. If any get close enough, I'll use it on them."

"Agreed," Paul said. "But we won't count on them getting close enough for it to work. I'm betting on surprise. Keep them focused on you while we get in position and attack."

I grinned. "Don't worry. I can be pretty distracting when I need to be. I bet I can lure at least one into range of macing."

Paul looked at Runner and Mack. "Are we agreed on the plan?"

Both werewolves nodded. "It sounds like it will work," Runner said.

"What about me?" Laura asked. "Is there anything I can do from here?"

I nodded. "Actually, there is. It's not likely to be a high–traffic area, but can you manufacture a diversion? Street lights failing nearby or something? Keep the cops and other innocents distracted enough that they don't come our way?"

She smiled. "I can. A few messed up street lights and false alarms should keep people well tied up."

"Good. That's it then?"

Paul nodded. "Yes. I'll take you home to grab a few hours of sleep. Mack, you'll get the sample for Dafydd?"

The werewolf nodded. "I'll do that."

"If the rest of us are going to be in position by five, and you need time to work the spell, how about the four of us meet a bit earlier?" Runner suggested.

I nodded. "Works for me. I've got everything I need at home to do the circle."

"I'll pick you up at three then," Paul said.

We had the timing down and our roles. Paul and Laura took a moment to exchange phone numbers. We'd agreed he'd be the one to keep her informed on timing since I'd be busy casting while Runner and Mack would be in wolf form and unable to take calls.

We said goodbye and went our separate ways. Paul took me home, and I put everything I'd need in a day–pack. Then I settled down to try to get some sleep.

Chapter 11

Wednesday, September 9, 2009:
too damned early

I'D SET MY alarm for 2:15, and it felt like I'd hardly slept when it went off. I groaned and levered myself out of bed, stumbling to the kitchen to put on some coffee. While it brewed, I grabbed a quick shower. Protective circles didn't require the same level of purification as ritual magic, but being clean never hurt. Besides, turning on the cold water full blast woke me up fast.

I dressed in simple clothes, a dark gray long–sleeve t–shirt and faded black jeans. I figured if I needed to hide in early morning light, they'd help me fade pretty well. Gulping down a mug of hot, black coffee, I reviewed my backpack. Everything I needed was in there. All the materials for the circle were in a wooden box. The potions, in their little sport bottles, were clearly labeled and tightly sealed. I wondered for a moment how the wolves were going to swallow them, but they seemed pretty capable, and I thought they'd figure something out. If nothing else, I guessed they could bite through the plastic and suck them down the way Paul usually did it.

I was waiting by the door, sipping a second cup of

coffee from my travel mug when Paul arrived. I opened the door and quietly slipped out, not wanting to wake any of my neighbors. The air was still, heavy with humidity and a recent light rain, enough to dampen the sidewalk without soaking the ground.

"Hey," I said.

"Good morning," Paul said.

We walked to his car, and I said, "I thought of something just as I was drifting off to sleep."

He cocked an eyebrow at me as he unlocked the passenger door.

"Well, the timing. If we attack them just at dawn, won't that cause you problems?"

He shook his head and started the car. "The sun will be low enough that I'll be able to keep to the shadows during the fight."

"Okay." He seemed confident, so I figured I could trust him on this.

"However, I'll probably need you to drive me home." He nodded toward the back seat, and I glanced back to see a blanked neatly folded in the seat. I got it. "You'll get under that to protect you while I drive."

"Right. It won't be the first time I've made a mad dash from my car to the house under the blanket."

"As long as you're okay with it." I drank my coffee, and we made the rest of the drive in silence. With the streets so quiet and deserted, we made good time, and pulled into the area with a few minutes to spare. Paul parked his Prius in the shadow of one of the big trucks, and we got out.

I rummaged in my pack and handed him a potion. He took it and examined the label. "Any changes from last time?"

I shook my head. "No, I'm trying to get them to last longer, but no luck so far. You can count on maybe two minutes, but no longer."

He nodded. "It's what I expected."

His head shot up, and I glanced over to see two large wolves loping out from the nearby trees. Paul sniffed the air once and then relaxed. "It's them."

I sighed and greeted them as they approached. "Hey Runner and Mack." I wasn't sure which was which, and I looked at them, trying to figure it out.

Paul pointed. "The one on the left is Runner."

The wolf he pointed at sat down and gave me a canine grin. Runner was a bit larger and his color was darker. Mack had a streak of light gray running down his back where Runner was a solid dark gray all over.

Mack had something in his mouth, and he dropped it at my feet. I picked it up. It was a small bag. I opened it and saw two small vials, filled with what I assumed was blood. I could just make out the writing in the dim light provided by the security lights on the buildings. "Runner" was on one while the other said "Jimmy."

"Will that do it?" Paul asked.

I nodded. "That should. I only needed about half that, so we're good." I glanced around. "Guess I'd better get on it. Where exactly did you want me to be?"

Runner paced over to a spot and glanced back at us, his attitude questioning.

Paul looked from Runner to the buildings and motioned him a bit closer. "I think this'll be better. I'm fast, but it will still take me a few seconds to cover the ground."

Runner nodded and stepped a few paces closer. I looked over the indicated spot. It was level and paved. I felt the ground. Like the sidewalk near my apartment, the asphalt was slightly damp, but I thought I could still draw on it. I nodded. "That should work. I can draw a circle on that with chalk." I put my bag down and pulled out the box of magical supplies.

"Anything I can do to help?" Paul asked.

I nodded. "Yeah. Can you draw the circle? It doesn't need to be perfect, but the better it is, the better the spell."

"I can."

"Good. You get on that, and I'll get everything else ready."

Paul spoke to the wolves. "Guard the perimeter? The rest of your people will be here in about an hour, right?"

Runner nodded and both wolves faded into the darkness.

"I've never seen you work magic before," Paul said as he began to draw.

"No, I guess you haven't. I'll be curious what you think." I pulled out incense and an incense holder/burner and set them aside. Next came what I still had left of the wolfsbane I'd bought for the finding spell. Then I took out my portable cauldron and white–handled knife. This was a fairly simple spell and didn't require as many ingredients as the one I'd cast to find Jimmy's parents. I stepped carefully into the center of the circle Paul was drawing.

Looking over his work, I was pleased. He was draw-ing free–hand, but it was very close to perfectly round. I nodded and began organizing my materials. Using a lighter from my backpack, I lit the incense and started it burning.

Paul sneezed once and looked up in surprise. "I don't think I've done that in over a century. What's in the incense?"

"Nothing too weird. Just a mixture of rosemary and mint."

"Odd combination."

I shrugged. "Yeah, that's what my dad said when I first mixed it up, but it's one of my favorites."

He sneezed again and quickly closed the circle. Step-ping back quickly, he said, "I don't think it's going to be one of mine."

"Probably not." I aimed the burning incense so the slight breeze would carry it away from him.

"Thanks."

"No problem. The circle looks good. I appreciate you drawing it." While I spoke, I mixed the wolfsbane and blood samples together in the cauldron, stirring them with a disposable wooden coffee stirrer. I filched them regularly from a Starbucks near my house. They came in handy for all sorts of things, in addition to stirring coffee.

Paul came closer, careful to avoid the drifting smoke.

"How's this going to work?" He paused and then added, "Or should I not distract you?"

I shook my head. "I can both talk and work up until the point of actually casting the circle. This is a pretty easy spell. Right now I'm mixing wolfsbane and the blood samples together. I'll place those at the cardinal points of the circle. That will form the basis of the protective spell. If I cast it right, they won't be able to cross the barrier to get at me."

He nodded. "That makes sense. But what about the magical veil?"

I grinned and put aside the cauldron. "That's what the incense is for."

The breeze shifted and moved the smoke closer to him. Paul nimbly stepped aside. "To make them sneeze so hard that they can't see you because their eyes are watering?"

I chuckled and started moving around the circle, dipping my fingers in the blood/wolfsbane mixture and smearing it at the four points in the circle corresponding to north, south, east and west. "No. Here's where the magic gets a little abstract."

"Like it wasn't before?"

I shot him a look and continued speaking. "Rosemary and mint are good for attracting beneficial spirits and the faerie folk. The fey traditionally have the power to cast glamours. Well, I'm not sure if the spell actually summons a faerie to cast the glamour or if using the incense ingredients focuses the power to allow me to temporarily cast a fey–like glamour." I shrugged. "Dad and PopPop have debated that one endlessly. I actually don't care. It just works, which is good enough for me."

Paul frowned. "Isn't it dangerous to cast a spell without knowing exactly how it works and why?"

I looked at him. "It should be. But this particular one works anyway. Both of them have cast it any number of times without harm, and Dad would never teach me anything he thought would hurt me, so, I guess I've never worried about it."

I could see from his expression that he was still troubled, but he didn't pursue the topic.

"It's time for me to start casting. Now I need to concentrate."

He nodded. "I'll patrol the perimeter. Will we be able to see through the veil, or will you be invisible to us also?"

"None of you will be able to see me. I'm not good enough yet to exclude certain people from the effect."

"So if I can still see you in fifteen minutes or so, I probably should let you know?"

"Give me more like thirty, but yeah, if you can still see me after that, let me know. I'd hate to spring the trap too early."

He nodded. "Done. Good luck and be careful."

"I will."

He started to leave, but I thought of something and stopped him. "Hey, wait a sec?"

He turned and watched me while I rummaged again in my backpack. I took out all but one of the potion bottles and handed them to him. "Here. They won't do us any good in my backpack."

Paul nodded and took them. He examined the labels, and slipped one into a pocket. "I'll give the rest to Runner to distribute to his people when they arrive."

"That should work."

"You kept back one for you?"

I took out mine and put it into a pocket, along with the mace container. "I'm set."

"Good." And with that, he turned and left.

I went back to my preparations. Before I started, I glanced around for a place to hide my backpack. It wouldn't do us any good to have that sitting out in plain sight. I didn't see any good hiding places and sighed. I'd stash it in Paul's car.

Luckily he'd left it unlocked, and I tossed the backpack into the back seat, on top of his blanket. Then I went back to my circle.

I checked to be sure the chalk marks hadn't been scuffed. They were intact, shining a soft silver in the reflected security lighting. I nodded, satisfied with how everything looked and began casting.

Since this wasn't a true ritual magic, I didn't need all the chanting I'd done before. This was more visualization magic. First, I cast the circle by walking the perimeter, white-handled knife held in front of me. I visualized energy pouring from the tip of the knife to form the circle.

Lots of people think that real magic has pyrotechnics and something you (or the caster) can actually see, but it doesn't work that way. There's no real way to tell the difference between me casting an actual spell and a non–talented witch casting a ritual circle. All the difference is in how I can manipulate the unseen energies. So if you were expecting pretty light works, sorry to disappoint.

I knew the power was working, however. As I completed the circle, I could feel the power hanging around me, kind of like how you can almost feel the approach of a strong storm.

Once the circle was cast, I focused my attention on the smears of blood and wolfsbane. I visualized them as crosses of light, hanging in the air and extending their glow around the circle. Once they were in place, I softly spoke, "Activate!"

Power surged around me, and I felt the spell settle into the circle. Now I was protected against both infected and natural werewolves. I nodded. So far so good.

Now for the harder spell. I'd only cast a few glamours, but I felt confident it would work. The solid circle of protective power around me gave testament that I was in good form tonight.

I put down the knife and picked up the incense holder. One more time around the circle, this time channeling power through the gently wafting smoke. As clearly as I could, I visualized a veil settling on the circle, concealing not only the protective crosses, but also anything within the circle. As an added bonus, it would also conceal the chalk–drawn circle itself, leaving nothing to indicate anything unusual was present.

I heard faint tinkling laughter in the distance, and I felt the second spell settle on the circle. Power surged from me, and I had to sit down suddenly. I don't usually cast two powerful spells one right after each other.

Fortunately, I'd anticipated my weariness, and I took a bar of chocolate out of my pocket and slowly ate it. I felt new energy rush through me, and I knew I'd be okay for the fight to come.

I gathered up my materials and realized I'd forgotten something. Where to put all my stuff? I sighed, realizing I should have kept my backpack on me. Live and learn. This was the closest I'd ever come to combat magics, and I guess it's no surprise I'd made a mistake. I put everything except the knife into a small pile to one side of the circle. The knife I put in a pocket. If needed, I could leave everything else behind. I'd hate to lose the cauldron, but it was a small one, easily replaced. The knife, however? I'd invested a lot of energy attuning it to me and my aura, and I didn't want to lose that if it could be helped.

Everything as set and in place as it could be, I checked the time on my phone. 5:30. Right. I was ready in plenty of time. I settled down on the ground to wait for the wolves to arrive.

That was easily one of the longest half hours ever. I must have checked the time at least every five minutes. The damp pavement was uncomfortable under my butt. The heavy air threatened rain, and I didn't fancy sitting there in a downpour. Every sound made me jump. Moving shadows made me look again. Sweat rolled down my back, even though the morning temperature was cool for early September. Thank goodness for the veil. I didn't want Paul and the others to know how freaked out I was. I shifted position, trying to find a more comfortable spot on the blacktop, but no matter how I shifted, something poked at my ankles or thighs.

By the time the enemy wolves finally arrived, all I felt was relief. Now we could actually do something.

My first impression was that the wolves were over-confident. I guess I'd expected them to slink in furtively, glancing around to look for danger. Instead, six big wolves loped out of the woods. They moved as a unit, making no effort at concealment.

I took a long look at them. Although I'd seen them in the fight in the alley a few nights ago, I hadn't been able to really study them. I was surprised to see how big they were. I'd looked up wolves on Wikipedia when this all had started, and I'd seen that gray wolves are the biggest type. Males can reach as much as five feet in length and almost three feet high at the shoulder. These were at least six feet long and maybe three and a half feet tall. Their heads were big, eyes large and alert with pricked ears flicking back and forward as they moved. Their mouths were open, tongues lolling, and I could see long white teeth gleaming in the half–light of false dawn.

The wolves trotted across the parking lot, solid mus-cles rippling under thick fur. One paused, raising his head to test the air. The others paid him no attention, continuing to the buildings. The lone wolf gave another sniff and joined the rest.

I relaxed a tiny bit. My veil appeared to be working so far. I stood up, careful to make as little noise as possible. The veil worked by making them not want to notice me. Too much noise could overcome the glamour and blow it. I checked the mace canister in my pocket. It would take me only a moment to get to it. My potion bottle was in my right hand, and the sport top was popped, ready for me to swallow.

The plan had been for me to reveal myself when the lead wolf appeared, but so far there were only the six, and they were almost to the building. If this trap was going to have any hope of working, I was going to have to reveal myself in the next few moments.

Just as they reached the door and a moment before I'd decided to break the veil, another wolf appeared, loping around the building to my right. He was less than twenty feet from me and close enough to recognize as the wolf I'd seen in the videos Laura had found.

I suppressed a gasp. I'd realized he was big from the video, but there's a difference between seeing something on a screen and watching it approach in person.

This wolf wasn't that much bigger than the infected werewolves, but he had a presence about him that made him appear twice as large. His fur was definitely thicker than the others, and I suspected it would make good armor. A stab of fear shot through me at the thought of Paul fighting him. The vampire was strong and tough, but this thing looked like he could chew him up. I hoped the potion would shift the balance in my friend's favor.

The wolf paused and glanced around. Where the other werewolves had been casual in their approach, this one took the time to examine his surroundings. His nostrils flared, and his ears twitched, turning to listen in every direction.

After a moment, he stiffened, and I knew he'd sensed something. He opened his mouth, and I thought he was about to bark a warning.

I shifted my shoulders. It was time.

I concentrated for a moment and released the energy maintaining the veil. The lead wolf saw me immediately and snapped his mouth shut with a loud click.

His surprise didn't last long, and he barked, twice, short and loud.

The other wolves whirled and began coming my way.

I'd like to say I had complete confidence in my circle and felt no fear as seven wolves padded over to me, but I'd be lying. The six infected werewolves were snarling, and the one in the lead opened his muzzle in an unmistakable canine grin. You know how on your family dog it looks cute? Yeah, not on a six–foot long predator. On him it looked like the threat it probably was. I met his eyes and saw fierce joy. He was savoring the thought of tearing me to pieces.

I forced myself to remain outwardly calm. Undoubtedly they could hear the pounding of my heart, but I managed to keep my breathing steady and only a bit faster than normal.

The six wolves encircled me while the lead wolf slowly walked my circle. His green eyes gleamed in the half light. I wanted to turn to follow his progress, but I remained still. The longer I could keep their attention on me, the longer the others had to move into position, and

I suspected I'd hold their attention longer if I stayed calm.

It seemed to be working. One of the infected wolves sniffed the air and cocked his head. The gesture looked like confusion to me, and I allowed a small smile to curve my lips. He snarled, showing long, white, sharp teeth, but I didn't let my smile falter.

Finally, I guess one of the wolves couldn't stand the suspense any longer. I watched the muscles in his back legs bunch, and I braced myself, ready to gulp the potion and run like hell if the circle didn't hold.

The wolf leaped at me. I heard the leader bark what sounded like a command, but it was too late. The leaping wolf hit my invisible barrier and bounced back with a yip of surprise.

That's when my allies attacked.

Three huge wolves, about the same size as the lead wolf, charged from the cover of the parked trucks. At first I was mesmerized by their smooth motions, but I quickly came to my senses and whirled to my left at the sound of movement on pavement.

Two other wolves, even larger than the three I'd just seen, ran from around the farthest building. They were Runner and Mack, and I had no idea how they'd managed to get from their hiding place by the trucks to behind the building without being seen, but I was glad they were there.

My five allies surrounded the enemy, but the infected wolves didn't pay attention to the tactical situation. They just threw themselves into the fight.

The lead wolf, however, slipped back to evaluate the situation. He was probably wondering what I was going to do.

At that moment, Paul leaped out of the darkness and hit the lead wolf solidly, knocking him over before leaping back.

The wolf recovered quickly, skidding a few feet before getting his feet under him and turning back to leap on the vampire.

Paul easily dodged his charge, and I knew he'd already consumed the potion. I frowned, knowing that the extra speed and strength wouldn't last him long. I stayed behind my barrier, ready to act as the reserve if needed.

I glanced away from Paul to see how the rest of the wolves were faring.

Runner was whirling and slashing at two of the wolves. As I watched, he dodged behind one of his opponents, biting at a hind leg in an attempt to hamstring him. I saw streaks of red covering Runner's flanks, but the injuries didn't seem to be slowing him down. I figured he'd also consumed his potion, and I hoped the fight wouldn't last too long.

The other four natural wolves were fighting one on one with the rest of the pack, and they seemed to be holding their own. The one attacking the smallest werewolf seemed to be moving the slowest, and I assumed he was the one without a potion boosting him.

As I watched, the unboosted werewolf went down, his opponent slashing deep into his throat. The two of them wrestled for a moment, and then my ally slid out from under the wolf, and staggered back, bleeding profusely from throat and side. He held one of his front legs close to his body, and his tail was tucked between his legs. He still snarled, however, and showed his teeth.

I lifted my potion, prepared to enter the fight, but Paul shouted, "No, Dafydd!"

At that moment, Mack bowled over his opponent, teeth flashing to nip at side, throat and face. He grabbed the smaller wolf by the back of his neck and shook his head. Once. Twice. I heard the "snap" of bone, and the other wolf went still. Mack let him fall, and I watched in fascination as fur melted away into naked, bloody flesh.

Without hesitation, Mack left his fallen foe and raced to help his ally. I relaxed a bit. One down. Six to go. Runner was having some trouble with his two wolves, but a moment later one of the other natural werewolves sent his opponent yelping off into the woods, limping on two legs. That ally went to help Runner, and now we outnumbered them. I thought we had a good chance of winning.

I turned to see how Paul was doing. The vampire and the lead werewolf were circling. The wolf dripped blood from his side, and he was holding one foreleg carefully. But the fight hadn't been one–sided. Paul oozed blood from his chest, and he had one long slash down his face, dangerously close to his right eye.

The wolf gathered himself as if for a leap, and Paul glided to one side. At that moment, the vampire slipped, probably on a puddle left from the earlier rain. He didn't go all the way down, but for one crucial second, his balance was off, and the wolf leaped, overbalancing him and knocking him down.

White fangs flashed, aiming for my friend's throat.

As soon as I saw Paul slip, my hand moved, without conscious thought, and I swallowed my potion. Suddenly the world seemed to stop moving. Paul fell in slow motion, and the lead werewolf's leap seemed to take at least a full minute to complete.

Before his fangs reached Paul's throat, I raced from my protective circle. I covered the distance in a moment, my mace canister extended. It looked pitifully tiny compared to the bulk of the werewolf, but I felt like I had plenty of time to position and aim. I triggered the canister and sent a jet of pepper spray directly up the nose of the wolf.

Several things happened then.

The wolf howled and leaped back, shaking his head and sneezing.

Paul yelled, "No!"

And as I turned to follow the retreat of the lead werewolf, I saw the remaining three enemy wolves disengage from my allies and start to charge in our direction.

Oh shit!

My eyes darted to my protective circle, and the increased reaction potion rushing through me allowed me to see with alarming clarity that I had scuffed the chalk circle in my rush to save Paul. If I hadn't broken the circle, I could have simply stepped back into its protection. But now I was exposed, and I was the only one to come to this battle without super–human speed, strength or thick fur for armor.

I did the only thing that made sense. I ran for the building behind me. With it at my back, they'd only be able to come at me from the front and maybe I could hold them off for a few seconds with my pepper spray. Hopefully long enough for my allies to regroup and save my sorry warlock butt.

A fireball or lightning bolt would have come in so handy right then, but I didn't have anything like that in my arsenal, so I just put my back against the building and braced myself for werewolf onslaught. As fur and fangs charged my way, I sent up a silent apology to my dad for raising such a foolish son.

Only one of them made it to me. Three of my ally wolves were still standing and in fighting condition, and they intercepted two of the enemy wolves. The lead werewolf was still sneezing, and those few seconds gave Paul enough time to recover his footing. He moved like a striking rattlesnake, claws extended and fangs bared. I didn't have the best vantage point, and I was a bit distracted by several hundred pounds of wolf baring down on me, but I thought I saw the vampire hold the enemy werewolf with his claws while he tore open its throat with his fangs.

I had just enough time to wonder if werewolf tasted good to a vampire before I had my hands full with my own werewolf.

The magic of my potion was still racing through my blood, and I shot the wolf with my pepper spray. He was ready, however, and he dodged the blast, so I only hit him with a glancing shot. It was enough to slow him for a moment, but it wasn't nearly enough to send him running.

I wasn't quite sure what to do, but at that moment my body took over.

One of my brothers had gone through a karate craze when we were kids. I think he'd seen *The Karate Kid* on late-night TV, and he'd bugged my dad incessantly until he relented and let Todd take classes. As the youngest brother, I was the designated punching bag for him to practice on. At least until dad caught on and made him stop.

Apparently I'd learned something from the experience, and I watched in surprise as my body delivered two precise blows to the werewolf. My right hand, still holding the mace canister, slammed into his snout as my left hand, fingers stiff, delivered a direct blow to his right eye.

The werewolf skidded backwards in an almost comical slide. He recovered quickly, however, and came at me again. I was ready with another shot of pepper spray. His eye was still watering from my blow, and his aim was off. I dodged to one side and triggered another blast. This time he couldn't see well enough to dodge, and my spray hit him, right in the eye I'd already stabbed.

That was enough for him, and he tucked his tail between his legs and fled, yipping like a puppy whose tail had been stepped on.

It was a good thing he ran because at that moment

my potion ran out, and I was left with merely human reactions. I looked around wildly to see if there were any more werewolves coming my way.

Slam!

I fell back with several hundred pounds of fur, muscle and teeth on top of me. I managed to get my arms up to protect my throat, but that was it. My head hit the ground, and I saw stars for a moment, but I frantically shook my head to clear it, knowing that to pass out now meant death.

As my vision cleared, I realized it was the lead wolf who had attacked me. Paul had hurt him. One of his eyes was gone, and he dripped blood all over me, mostly from the long slash on his neck. His fangs sank into my arms, and I screamed. All my instincts told me to pull my arms back to break the grip of those fangs, but if I did that, I'd leave my throat open, so I just pushed back as hard as I could. My efforts were about as effective as a kitten trying to wriggle out of a neck scruff, but I did manage to hold off his teeth from my throat for a few more seconds.

My mace canister was still in my hand, but it was pointed toward me right now, and I couldn't turn it around.

My feet scrambled at the ground as I tried to slither out from under him, but he was too heavy and too strong.

I'd pretty much decided I was dead when his weight went away. I'd closed my eyes in my struggle, and I wasn't sure I really wanted to open them to see what was happening, but I scrambled backwards, in the blind hope to get out of danger, and opened my eyes.

Paul was standing over me. He was so covered in blood that I almost didn't recognize him for a moment, but his stance was steady. The werewolf was just getting back on his feet about ten feet away, and I guessed Paul had picked him up and thrown him off me.

Before the wolf had time to get up, Paul leaped on him. He grabbed the wolf by the neck with both hands and twisted. One direction and then the other.

The snap of bone sounded clearly in the early morning air, and the wolf went still.

I blinked and tried to get up. My arms hurt and didn't want to hold my weight so I fell back again.

The noises of fighting had stopped. All I could hear were some low–pitched whines. I shook blood out of my face and tried again to get up. This time I ignored the pain in my arms and pushed myself to my feet.

I looked around. The parking lot looked like a war zone with blood and fur everywhere. Three of the enemy werewolves lay nearby, shifted to their human form. A little farther away lay two more wolves. I tried to see if they were breathing, but in the dim light I couldn't tell.

Four other wolves stood nearby, panting. One of them, Runner, was licking a long wound on his leg, and he was holding one of his back paws off the ground. The other three looked similarly wounded.

Paul knelt nearby, his head down and hands on his knees. He was covered in blood, and his clothes were so ripped that he might as well have been wearing nothing.

I staggered over to him. "Looks like we got them all." Inane, I know, but it was all I could think to say. I suspected the two wolves on the ground were also dead, and I wasn't yet ready to face that.

Paul looked up at me, and I stepped back a pace. His eyes were still glowing yellow, and his fangs extended over his lower lip. I glanced down and noticed that his claws were still extended. I looked back at his face. He looked ... haggard, something I'd never seen on him. There was a disturbing glow in the back of his yellow eyes, and I thought maybe I was seeing him hungry for the first time. He hadn't looked like that before, even when burned after the fight with the shuggoleth.

Suddenly, his expression changed, his eyes returned to their normal gray, and his fangs and claws retreated. "Sorry about that." His voice was rough, but his tone was gentle.

I nodded. "Yeah. No problem. Guess I've never seen you like that before."

He shook his head. "No, I don't think so." He stood up, swaying slightly, and surveyed the battlefield. "That one was tough."

Runner limped up to us. One moment he was a wolf. The next he was a man, completely unselfconscious about his nudity. "We lost two of ours."

I winced and closed my eyes. For just a moment, I forgot about the pain in my arms.

A strong hand gripped my shoulder, and I opened my eyes again. It was Paul, his hand dripping more blood over my filthy shirt. "I know," was all he said.

I looked at Runner, searching his eyes for condemnation or blame. Neither were there. He only looked sad and tired.

"But we got four of them, including the leader," the werewolf said. Shrugging, he added, "And I guess that's not bad, considering."

Paul nodded. "It's not. The infected ones may have been young, but they were tougher than I expected."

"Side effect of the spell that changed them, perhaps?" Runner looked at me.

I couldn't answer. All I could think was that if I hadn't left the circle, hadn't left myself vulnerable, maybe we wouldn't have lost any.

Paul's hand squeezed my shoulder. "One of them was already down when you left the circle. And you did save me. He was fast. I think he would have torn my throat out before I could have recovered."

Runner nodded. "We needed you."

Mack limped up, also naked in human form. "Those potions were good, warlock. You can fight on my side any day."

I heard their words, but they didn't really mean anything. "But—"

Paul moved his hand from my shoulder to my waist and pulled me in tight against him. "No, Dafydd. No buts. You fought well." His tone lightened. "Although I'm not sure where you came up with that Three Stooges move."

I blinked, not sure what he meant. Then I remembered hitting the wolf in the eye. "Oh. That. My brother used me for a punching bag when I was little. I guess my body remembered some stuff."

He let me go with a final squeeze and said, "I think I might be able to teach you enough to get by if you'd like."

He didn't seem to need an answer right then, which was good. My brain was still working through cotton candy.

"We'd better go," Runner said. "The sun's coming up in just a couple of minutes. No place for a vampire to be."

Paul nodded and motioned to the bodies. "What are you going to do with them?"

Runner indicated the nearby trees. Several people had emerged from them and were walking our way. "Those are my people. I figured we'd need a clean-up crew. They'll take care of it."

Mack started to drop down to all fours but paused to say, "You'll still do the spell for Jimmy?"

I blinked. With everything that had happened in the past few minutes, I'd almost forgotten why we'd done this. The image of the kid flashed before my eyes, and I nodded. "Yeah, give me at least a day to sleep, and I'll be able to do it."

He grinned briefly. "Thank you." Then he dropped to the ground, a naked man one moment. A wolf the next.

Runner also changed form and limped off to join the rest of his people. Just like that. It was over. I knew it had changed me, but I wasn't quite sure how. Not yet.

I'd need to do some thinking.

"Can you drive?" Paul asked, his tone concerned as he glanced at the glowing horizon.

I shook myself and said, "Sure. I'll get you home. Let's go before the sun gets any higher."

On our way to the car, I checked the angle of the sun and my internal clock. Not quite sunrise but getting close. I thought we'd make it without needing to resort to the blanket in the back. Paul climbed into the front seat.

"We'll probably make it, but just in case."

I nodded. "No problem. I'll drive. In this town we could always run into an early morning rush hour accident."

But our luck held, and I got him home just as the sun peeked over the horizon. We made our trip in silence. I didn't know what Paul was thinking, but I was trying very hard to not think about what had happened. I was tired, and I needed sleep. If I thought too much right now, I'd never drift off, and I wanted to consider everything when I was reasonably well rested.

Paul got out of the car. Before he went into his house, he turned to look back in the window. "Call me this evening?"

"Sure," I said.

"I'm guessing you'll want to talk by then."

I nodded. "Probably. I'll call you at sundown."

He nodded and turned to go into his house while I pulled back onto the street and headed home for some much-needed sleep.

Chapter 12

Wednesday, September 9, 2009: early evening

I'D LIKE TO say that I slept dreamlessly, but I'd be lying. Blood and death followed me into slumber, and I couldn't escape them, no matter how I tossed and turned. By the time the phone rang, around 4:00, I'd tossed and turned myself into enough sleep that I was no longer tired enough to keep trying.

I fumbled for the phone, not bothering to even sit up. Laura.

"Hey," I said as I answered.

"Thank goodness you're all right!"

Oh, yeah. Probably I should have called or texted her before I'd crashed.

"Sorry. I was wiped after I took Paul home, and I just came back and crashed."

"I'd kind of figured it was something like that, so I waited as long as I could."

"Thanks." I sat up and leaned against the wall.

"How are you? Everyone else okay?"

I sighed. "I'm okay. Paul, Runner and Mack are okay. We got all the bad guys. But a couple of Runner's people died."

"I'm sorry." Her voice was warm and full of sympathy.

"Yeah, me too." I sat there, not sure what to say next.

"Want to talk about it?"

"Not really. Not yet. I kind of need to work some stuff out first."

"I have a bit of what might be good news."

Her voice was cautious, and I forced some animation into my voice. "I need some good news. What is it?"

"McDonald held a press conference today."

That made me sit up straighter. "He did? What'd he say?"

I heard the smile in her voice. "He announced he was postponing his development plans for the 14th Street area. No real reason given. Just some nonsense about controlling cost overruns and environmental impact."

I snorted. "Environmental impact? In that part of town? Ridiculous!"

"Exactly. The reporters tried to get more details, but he just made his statement and left with no further comments." She paused and added, "As he was leaving, one of the reporters did ask about his wolf."

"What'd he say?"

"Nothing. But you should have seen his expression. It stopped reporters from calling out any other questions. I don't think any of them wanted to draw his attention after that."

"I'll let Paul know. He'll want to warn the werewolves to be careful for a while. I'm thinking McDonald is the kind who might want revenge."

"I think you're right. They've lost enough of their pack already."

"Thanks for the news. It was good."

I suddenly became aware of my filthy clothes and all the blood caked on me. "Hey, thanks for calling, but I gotta go. I was so tired I just crashed, nasty clothes and all. I need a shower and some food before calling Paul to return his car."

"All right. Want to drop by later?"

"I'd like to, but I need to get everything ready to do the ritual for Jimmy. Sunrise would be best, and I've got a lot of setup to do. Plus a quick nap so I'm rested."

"Yeah, that takes priority."

"Tomorrow though, if you'll be around."

"I'll be here."

We hung up, and I smiled. It was good to have friends like Laura.

I showered, ate and played with the ferrets. I don't think I've ever worked so hard at not thinking about something, but, call me a coward if you will, I wasn't ready to process last night. Not just yet. I wanted a couple of hours to just live first.

Around eight, I picked up the phone to call Paul. He answered on the first ring.

"Hey." His voice was gentle and held a lot of questioning.

"Hey. I guess you're up."

"Yeah. A couple of hours ago, actually."

"Laura called. McDonald held a press conference."

"Really?"

I filled him in. When I finished, he said, "I'll call Runner and let him know to warn his people. He'll probably suggest the rural packs stay out of town for a while."

"Can you also tell him to ask Mack to bring Jimmy by just before sunrise."

"You're ready to do the spell?"

"I will be by then."

"Want me to come by and pick up my car? I'm guessing you'll need time to prepare."

"No, if it's okay, I want to come over. I think I need to talk."

His voice was gentle again. "I thought you might. I'll be here."

"Thanks. I'll be by in a bit."

We hung up, and I put the ferrets back in their cage. Gimble gave me the look, but she settled down without any more protest. I grabbed Paul's keys off the table and left. Now it was time to think, but I didn't want to do it alone.

I HIT SOME traffic. I think there was some accident on I–395, which always backs up the side streets, even at this time of day. I did my best not to think on the way over. Paul's car has an MP3 player jack, so I plugged in my iPod and focused on the music. *Shine On* by Wayne Jackson was the perfect soundtrack for my mood.

When I finally arrived at Paul's house, I got lucky

and found a spot out front that was big enough for my limited parallel parking skills. I climbed out of his car and walked up to his door, which opened just as I reached the top step.

"Hey," Paul said by way of greeting. His voice was soft.

"Hey," I said. Now that I was here, I wasn't sure how to start. I'd spent several hours not thinking about things. Now that I had someone to talk to, I wasn't sure I was ready.

I walked past him and headed for the living room. As always, I glanced up at the bayonet over his fireplace. One day I'd ask him about it. But not today.

"Want something to drink?" Paul asked. He was leaning on the doorway between the hall and the living room.

"Yeah, got anything with some kick to it?"

He quirked an eyebrow at that but said simply, "I've got some very good Scotch."

"Sounds good." Yeah, I knew it was the coward's way out, but right now I needed some liquid courage to help me face the thoughts that were starting to break through my self–inflicted numbness.

Paul nodded and moved gracefully to a large cabinet and took out a bottle. He poured some into two glasses and walked over to hand one to me. I took it and downed a gulp. It was strong and made me cough. Paul just swallowed his with no visible reaction and sat down in the chair opposite me.

I wasn't sure what was going to come out of my

mouth when I spoke, so what I said surprised me. "I know you usually fight alone, against the bastards you hunt, but have you ever fought with other people?"

"You mean have other people ever died for me in one of my fights?"

I slumped on the couch and tossed back another swallow of Scotch. This time it felt smooth going down. "Yeah, I guess that is what I'm asking."

He took another swallow before answering. Before speaking, he glanced at the bayonet on the wall. "Tomorrow is my birthday."

I blinked, surprised at first by the irrelevant disclosure, but then my brain started working as I realized, even in my fog of misery, that Paul was finally going to give me personal details.

"I was born in 1832, so I'll be 177 tomorrow."

I looked again at the bayonet. "That is yours. You fought in the Civil War."

He nodded. "I was an officer, so the short answer to your question is, yes, I have led people into battle, and they died for me."

"Do you ever get used to it?"

He shook his head and took another swallow of Scotch. "Not and remain human."

That word hung between us like the gulf that always separated us. Me a human. He a vampire.

"Is that why you became ... what you are?"

"No." His voice was firm. "That was done to me against my will. It had little to do with my service."

I wanted to know more. I always wanted to know

more, but for now, I let it go. "Then how do you deal with it? I tried to sleep, but every time I closed my eyes, I saw the bodies."

"Which ones?"

"Huh?"

"Which bodies did you see? Theirs or ours?"

"Oh." I thought for a moment. "Mostly ours. But yeah, I kept seeing theirs too. The way they were so still. The way the blood spread out from their bodies." I stopped, not sure talking about blood with a vampire was such a good idea.

Paul gave me a small smile, obviously reading my concern. "It's not a problem. It's what I am."

"Does it mean something? That I saw both sets of bodies?"

He finished his Scotch and put down his glass. His hand shook slightly, which I'd never seen before. "It means you still care. About all the ones you brought death to. It means you are still human. Not a monster."

Every muscle in my body relaxed. I hadn't been consciously aware of it, but that had been my fear. I'd led men to die. What did that make me? Ironic that it took a monster to reassure me that I wasn't one.

Paul was looking at me, and I suspected he knew exactly what I'd been thinking. A faint smile ghosted around his lips. "I'm willing to bet your father and grandfather have done battle before. And probably some of the people they led also died."

I guessed he was right. By the time I came along, as the youngest, both of them had retired from actually doing battle with demons and other evil. If they had led others, it was before my time and the people who died would have been strangers to me. Their strengths lay in teaching, not in fighting.

Which made me wonder. What were *my* strengths?

"Would you do it again?" Paul asked.

I finished my drink before answering. I put the glass down beside his, the last drops of amber liquid shining in the faint light from the street. That was a good question. It wasn't that I didn't know the answer. I did. And it scared the crap out of me.

"Yeah, I would. If it were the right thing to do."

Paul nodded. "Good."

"Good? How can you say that? People died today. Good people. I didn't know them, but they must have families. Others who love them and are now asking why they aren't ever coming home."

"You're right. But how many others would have died if we hadn't done what we did?"

I shook my head. "That's too easy. The old 'needs of the many outweighing the needs of the few' and all that. It's too pat. Too easy."

"No, Dafydd. It's never easy. It's always hard to do the right thing. If it were easy, then I guess evil wouldn't exist."

I sat back, knowing he was right but not quite ready to admit it.

He waited, saying nothing, his gray eyes calm.

"I can figure out who you are now, you know."

He didn't even blink at my non sequitur. "I know."

"And you don't mind?"

"I trust you. That's why I was there this morning."

I wasn't sure what to say to that. "Was that the only reason? You weren't there to do good? To do the hard thing?"

"Of course I was there for those reasons. But you don't think Runner and I could have kept you out of it, handled it ourselves?"

"You wouldn't have!"

"No, I wouldn't have. But there's a big difference between 'wouldn't have' and 'couldn't have.' You needed to be there with us. You needed to see what happens when you take a stand. It's not like in the books. People die. There's blood and pain, and it never leaves you. Not completely."

And that's what I was afraid of. That I'd never be able to sleep again. But I knew that fear was unfounded. Men went to war. And learned to live with it later.

I took a deep breath. "We did it for the right reasons."

He nodded. "Yes, we did."

"Then I can live with that."

"What's next?" he asked.

I sighed and stood up. "Home. I've got another ritual to get ready for."

He nodded. "Good. Want a ride?"

"Yeah, that would be good."

AND SO LIFE goes on. I did the ritual in the morning, and it worked. Jimmy is now a "normal" werewolf and changes just during the full moon. He's doing well with a pack that lives in the Shenandoah. I haven't seen him again, but Mack sends word through Runner sometimes.

In case you were wondering, I even found some time to get a birthday present for Paul. Actually, I got him two. The first he knew about that day, a DVD of *The Dresden Files*. He'd mentioned once that he hadn't seen it.

The other he didn't learn about until later. Yes, I could have figured out who he was. But I decided to wait until he was ready to tell me. Trust needs to go both ways.